# My
# GRANDMOTHER'S
# Inn

## BOOKS BY KRISTIN HARPER

*Summer at Hope Haven*

*Aunt Ivy's Cottage*

*A Letter from Nana Rose*

*Lily's Secret Inheritance*

# My
# GRANDMOTHER'S
# Inn

## KRISTIN HARPER

bookouture

Published by Bookouture in 2023

An imprint of Storyfire Ltd.
Carmelite House
50 Victoria Embankment
London EC4Y 0DZ

www.bookouture.com

ISBN: 978-1-83790-344-3
eBook ISBN: 978-1-83790-341-2

*To my kindred friends on The Cape and Islands,*
*with thanks for sharing your homes and lives (and the ocean)*
*with me.*

# PROLOGUE

## MAY 1943

A balmy spring breeze tousled the surface of the glimmery blue-green water, but the eight-year-old girl refused to even glance at it. Crying into the crook of her arm, she pleaded, "Please don't leave me here all alone, Papa."

"You won't be alone. Your aunt will be with you." Seated beside her on a large, flat rock near the end of the jetty, her father patted her back. "I know you're sad about leaving Anna behind, but soon you'll meet other children. You'll make so many friends and you'll have so much fun playing on the beach that when I return, you'll beg me to buy a house on Dune Island so we can live here forever."

"No, I won't. I'll never have a better friend than Anna and I'll never love any place as much as I loved our apartment in Queens." Sobbing harder, she repeated, "I don't want you to go."

"Hush now, child. Hush." He gave her a few moments to settle down before he gently moved her arm away from her face. Cupping her chin, he peered into her tear-filled eyes. "You know why I must leave. It's my duty to serve in the war. God willing, I'll be back to get you shortly. In the meantime, you need to be very brave because you have an important duty to fulfill, too."

Wrinkling her forehead, the girl sniffled. "What is my duty?"

"You must help your aunt and obey whatever she tells you. Mr. and Mrs. Frost are allowing you to stay in their home with her while I'm away because we've told them what a good helper you are. Promise me you'll do whatever is asked of you, without any complaining?"

She nodded. "Yes, Papa."

"That's my good girl. My precious, darling daughter." He smiled and let go of her chin. Lately, his smiles seemed almost as sad as his frowns and although she tried to contain her tears, a few dribbled from the corner of her eye.

"I'll be brave on the outside, but on the inside I'm going to miss you every day and every night," she said.

"I will miss you every day and every night, too," her father admitted. He was quiet a moment and when he spoke again his tone was lighter. "My chief petty officer will probably keep me too busy standing watch or scrubbing the ship's deck to write to you, but you could draw a picture or write a letter to tell me how you are and what you're doing."

"Pictures are for little children who don't know how to spell yet. I'll write a letter," she declared indignantly, smoothing her threadbare pinafore over her legs. "But how can I mail it to you if I haven't got any money for stamps?"

"Ah, well, that's one of the many wonderful things about staying in a home so close to the ocean. You don't need a stamp to send a letter. All you need is an empty glass bottle and a cork. You'll roll your letter up nice and tight and slip it inside. Then you can cast the bottle into the water, right over there from shore." He twisted around to point at the white sandy beach to the east of the jetty. "A week later, the bottle will reach me on the other side of the ocean."

"What if the waves carry it in the wrong direction?"

"Don't worry," he assured her. "A message sent with love always finds its way from one heart to another."

# ONE

Molly Anderson stood in the driveway admiring the riot of fat blue flowers spilling over the top of the white picket fence. The waterfront residence was named after the ample shrubbery, and a simple sign hanging from a wooden post in the front yard read: HYDRANGEA HOUSE.

*Savannah will probably change the name to Frost House after she shuts down the inn,* Molly speculated. *Or else she'll just rename it Savannah's.*

She heaved a sigh, trying hard not to feel resentful. For the past forty-seven years, Molly's grandmother, Beverly, had faithfully served as the innkeeper for Hydrangea House. Because she'd lived there for so long and she'd been so dedicated to caring for the property and accommodating the guests, people often assumed the residence belonged to her. However, even though she'd been close to the Frost family who owned the place, Beverly was technically their live-in employee, not a family member. And after she passed away in April, complete control of the estate was awarded to thirty-five-year-old Savannah Frost.

So Molly recognized that Savannah had every right to

rename the house whatever she wanted, just like she had every right to do whatever else she wished to do with it. Yet she couldn't help feeling disappointed that Savannah had decided to permanently close the inn so she could use it as her personal summer home. Her decision was especially frustrating because Savannah rarely took a full week off from work to visit Dune Island each year. Not to mention, her family already had two vacation homes—a chalet in Telluride, Colorado, and a villa in France—that she virtually never visited, either.

*It reminds me of when we were kids and she had so many toys she couldn't possibly play with them all—sometimes, she didn't even take them out of their packaging—but she wouldn't let anyone else play with them, either.*

Molly jiggled her head, as if trying to shake the memory from her mind. She didn't want to begin the summer at Hydrangea House on a sour note, so she reminded herself to look on the bright side of Savannah's decision. *At least she isn't selling the estate to a land developer, even though she could have made a fortune from it.*

With only seven guest rooms and one suite, Hydrangea House was small compared to most of the other inns and B and Bs in the five towns comprising Hope Haven. However, it was uniquely situated on the eastern point of the crescent-shaped road running alongside Dune Island's largest harbor. The house was angled so the front and western-side windows faced the port the town was named after—Port Newcomb. The windows in the back overlooked the private beach and the 900-foot jetty that seemed to cut a dividing line between the calmer waters of the harbor and the rollicking waves of Dune Island Sound, which could also be seen from the eastern side of the house.

Surrounded by a sprawling lawn, the inn provided a sense of solitude that was rarely found in Hope Haven's biggest and busiest town. Yet Hydrangea House's proximity to the port allowed convenient access to the main ferry dock and recreational boating, as well as to Main Street's shops, eateries and nightlife. Considering its prime location, Molly was thankful that at least the estate was staying in the Frost family; otherwise, the pristine beachfront property might have been exploited for commercial purposes.

*I'm also grateful that Savannah agreed to keep the inn open for one more summer, even if she initially resisted the idea*, Molly thought, her mind drifting to the day Savannah called and announced she intended to shut down Hydrangea House...

It had barely been three weeks since her grandmother Beverly died and when Molly first heard Savannah's news, she was utterly dismayed.

"But the inn has been such an important part of our families' lives," she protested. "Running Hydrangea House together was how our great-grandmothers supported themselves after the war. Being the innkeeper was how my grandma earned a living as a single mother when she was raising my father, too. If it weren't for—"

Savannah cut her off mid-sentence. "Spare me the history lesson, Molly. I already know what happened in the past." She softened her tone. "But the past is over. Our families aren't dependent on the inn any more, so there's no reason to keep it in business."

*She means now that Grandma is gone,* Molly thought, whisking a tear from her cheek with her fingers. Even though Beverly had been eighty years old and she'd begun to slow down a little, she'd always seemed to be the picture of good health. She'd claimed she planned to continue innkeeping for the next five years, at least. So Molly had been stunned when she'd unexpectedly passed away of "natural causes," while napping in her favorite chair.

As the finality of Beverly's death began sinking in, Molly

comforted herself with the knowledge that her grandmother's legacy as Hydrangea House's innkeeper would live on. She imagined the new innkeeper would try to uphold the same high standards Beverly had set for hospitality and service. And that the guests would continue to enjoy the beauty of the residence and the grounds that her grandmother had painstakingly maintained. But how could that happen if Savannah shut down the inn?

"Our families might not be financially dependent on Hydrangea House, but the guests depend on it for their summer vacations," she said, trying to build a case for family traditions and customer loyalty. "A lot of them have been returning to the inn for decades."

Savannah snickered. "No kidding. That's why I don't have any qualms about shutting it down. The public has had plenty of time to enjoy the estate. Now it's my turn."

"But you hardly ever take a vacation," Molly mumbled beneath her breath, but Savannah heard her anyway.

"Exactly. So when I *do* take one, I don't want to spend my very limited time off with a group of strangers."

"What if you reserved Hydrangea House for your exclusive use on whatever dates you wanted, and then rented the rooms out during the rest of the summer?" Molly proposed. "That way, you wouldn't have to sacrifice your privacy. You'd rake in a ton of passive income, plus you'd have the satisfaction of knowing you were still giving lots of people the opportunity to stay at one of the most gorgeous locations on Dune Island. I'm sure the guests would love you for it."

"That's a sweet sentiment and I can't deny that the extra revenue would be nice. But I'm a Senior VP, remember?" Savannah asked, as if Molly could have possibly forgotten that she held a high-power position in New York City. "I work from six in the morning until eight at night six days a week. When would I have time to oversee a side business?"

"Couldn't you hire someone to manage the daily operations and—"

"Nope, not interested." Savannah interrupted Molly a second time. "I've got too many employees to supervise and too much stress in my life as it is. I'm not taking on more. It was different when Grandma B. was the innkeeper because she could have run Hydrangea House blindfolded. But since no one will ever come close to filling her shoes, this seems like a natural time for the inn to revert to a family home—*my* family home."

Molly got the hint: the estate belonged to the Frosts, not the Andersons, and her suggestions about what to do with it were unwelcome. Her voice heavy with resignation, she asked, "I suppose this means you're closing the cottage to the public, too?"

Known as "Peace Place," and set back on the grounds, the estate's former carriage house had been converted into an upscale, three-bedroom cottage. For half the season, it was available for guests to rent. On alternating weeks, it was occupied by low-income families who applied for complimentary seven-day residencies. Savannah's grandmother Pearl and Beverly had established this practice decades ago, as a way of sharing Dune Island with people who were in desperate need of a vacation but who couldn't afford to take one.

Savannah huffed with exasperation. "Of *course* I'm closing Peace Place. Keeping it open would defeat the purpose of reclaiming the inn as my private home, because there'd still be outsiders on the property."

*Reclaiming the inn?* Molly rolled her eyes at her blatantly acquisitive attitude. *She obviously didn't inherit the generosity gene from her grandmother or great-grandmother. And* my *grandma would have been offended to hear her referring to the guests as "outsiders." Especially since those "outsiders" essentially funded Savannah's college tuition by patronizing Hydrangea House.*

Keeping her thoughts to herself, Molly asked, "When do you plan to close the inn and cottage?"

"I've already reached out to someone to handle the legal aspects of dissolving the business as soon as he has an opening in his schedule. In the meantime, I need to draft an email to inform the guests I'm canceling their reservations."

"You mean for *this* summer?" Molly was floored. She'd expected Savannah to say she was going to transition the inn into a home over the course of a couple of years. Or at the very minimum, that she'd wait until after Labor Day to shut down the business, since the inn was traditionally closed during the off-season anyway. She never dreamed that Savannah would pull the welcome mat out from under the guests' feet like that.

"Yes. I want to be able to remodel the inn at my leisure, but I can't get started if the guests are staying on site."

*What are the odds that she'll take any time off from work to go to Dune Island this summer?* Molly silently grumbled to herself. *Grandma would be absolutely crushed to know that Savannah's canceling the guests' reservations at Hydrangea House and Peace Place on such short notice. The guests are going to be devastated, too.*

Beverly had always treasured the relationships she'd built with the guests: she'd enjoyed welcoming newcomers to the inn, and she'd regarded the returning visitors to be almost like family members. And as someone who was raised by a poor, widowed mother, she'd felt a special connection with the low-income families who stayed at Peace Place.

The people she'd hosted were clearly as fond of Beverly as she'd been of them. Many of the long-time guests sent her cards during the winter holidays and when they returned in the summertime, they brought her small gifts from their home-towns. After learning of her death, they sent flowers to the church for the funeral, and they'd flooded the inn's mailbox with notes expressing how fond they were of Beverly and how much they appreciated her. Their outpouring of sympathy had been deeply consoling to Molly. Even if her suggestions were unwelcome, she felt she owed it to them and to Beverly to at least *ask* Savannah to keep the inn open for one more season.

"I get it that you're eager to remodel, but would you consider honoring the guests' reservations for one final summer, kind of as a tribute to my grandmother's memory?" she asked, hoping to appeal to Savannah's affection for Beverly. "The last time I spoke to her, she told me she could hardly wait for the guests to arrive. It always gave her so much satisfaction to help them enjoy their time on Dune Island. I think she would have felt terrible to know her death caused them to miss the vacations they've had scheduled for months."

"They don't have to miss their vacations. It's only April. There's still plenty of time for people to find other lodgings."

"Not in Hope Haven there isn't. Summer rentals anywhere on the island are usually booked in advance by the end of January. The only places that have openings at this point charge an arm and a leg," Molly countered. Not that she really expected Savannah to understand; money was no object to her —and she'd always held high-level positions, so she probably couldn't appreciate how difficult it often was for hourly employees to receive the time off they requested, either.

"That's too bad, but I'm sure the guests will understand and empathize. We didn't intend for this to happen, and it's not as if I can just hire a temporary innkeeper at the snap of my fingers. As I've already told you, I don't have time to go through the process of posting the position, and then vetting and inter-viewing candidates. It's not worth the effort—especially not for a single summer season."

Molly was struck by a solution that seemed so obvious she didn't even take a breath before volunteering, "You don't have to go through that process. I'll do it."

"*You'll* find an innkeeper? When? Grandma B. told me

you've been super busy." Ever since they were young girls, Savannah had referred to Beverly as Grandma B., even though they weren't related. "She said you've been tied up with some kind of writing project."

"I was working on a grant application earlier this spring, but I submitted it already." Molly's best friend, Jenny, was the director of a non-profit organization that provided professional clothing and coaching for women in need. Molly had volunteered to complete the funding application for her. "Besides, I didn't mean I'd find an innkeeper. I meant I'd *be* the innkeeper. Since I have the summer off, the timing is perfect."

"I thought you were working at a camp with Jordan?" Savannah seemed to know a lot about Molly's summer, which meant that Beverly must have told her about that, too; her grandmother spoke to Savannah a lot more often than Molly did. The two women had always been closer to Beverly than they were to each other.

"That, um, kind of fell through," Molly admitted reluctantly. "Jordan and I broke up, so I'm not going to help out at the camp after all."

"Oh, that's too bad." Savannah made a clucking noise. "But I've got to say, I'm surprised you'd let your personal feelings interfere with your volunteerism. That must have been one awful breakup."

It *was* awful. Molly had been thoroughly dejected and disillusioned when she'd found out that her boyfriend Jordan had been seeing another woman behind her back. However, she had no intention of telling Savannah about the whole humiliating situation, so she'd cheerfully replied, "It turns out for the best, because now I'm available to work at Hydrangea House."

Although Molly lived in Delaware, she'd visited her grandmother on Dune Island for at least two weeks—and often longer —every summer of her life. She'd always pitched in and helped

Beverly with whatever needed to be done, so she figured she was qualified to take her place.

"Thanks, but no thanks," Savannah said curtly. "I've already got a designer lined up to visit the inn with me so we can conceptualize the remodel."

Once the idea of serving as the innkeeper took root in Molly's mind, she couldn't give it up. Willing to do almost anything to make it happen, she suggested: "If you postpone your renovations until after Labor Day when the guests are gone, think of the accommodations revenue you'd accrue over the summer. You could use all that money to pay for your redecorating projects."

"*All* the money? Does that mean you wouldn't expect to receive a salary to keep the inn?"

"Nope, I wouldn't. I'd consider it a privilege to take my grandmother's place hosting the *last ever* public guests at Hydrangea House and Peace Place," Molly pointedly emphasized. "You'd only have to pay for the housekeeping services and any food I'd buy for the guests."

"You're not seriously suggesting that *you'd* prepare breakfast for them, are you?" Savannah tittered because at her very best, Molly was a mediocre cook. It wasn't that she was incapable of following a recipe, but since she didn't enjoy the process, she tended to rush through it as quickly as possible, forgetting ingredients and improvising shortcuts. The results were often... unpalatable.

"Hydrangea House only offers a continental breakfast, so I think I could handle making hard-boiled eggs and slicing fresh fruit. I'd buy pastries or bagels at the bakery."

"At five times the cost of the ingredients if you made them yourself?"

"It would hardly break the bank," Molly muttered, incredulous that Savannah was quibbling over such a small expense.

After a long pause, she conceded, "I suppose if I agreed to

let you be the innkeeper for the summer, we could work out a food budget. Who knows, maybe I could even drop in one weekend and whip up some of Grandma B.'s crepes with caramelized apples and crème fraiche for the guests."

Molly's happiness that Savannah seemed willing to keep Hydrangea House and Peace Place open for the summer was momentarily overshadowed by the prospect of her showing up at the inn. The two women had known each other virtually their entire lives. Molly was only six months older than Savannah and when they were in grade school, they couldn't wait to reunite at Hydrangea House in the summer. However, as teenagers, they developed very different interests, and their personalities frequently clashed. Even in adulthood, there was an undercurrent of tension between them. Molly suspected that if they hadn't both loved Beverly so much, they'd have nothing at all in common and their relationship with each other would have ended a long time ago.

But even if they'd been the best of friends, Molly couldn't imagine where Savannah would sleep if she came to the inn. All the rooms had already been booked for the duration of the summer. Molly supposed she could use the portable folding bed and give Savannah the queen-sized one, but she knew Savannah was too high maintenance to be willing to share Beverly's former room, where Molly planned to stay.

"You do make delicious crepes," she acknowledged. "But I'm sure I could provide a nice breakfast for the guests, one way or the other."

"Well, I still might visit. I've been telling Austin about Hydrangea House and he really wants to see it."

"Who's Austin?"

"My attorney."

"Your estate attorney?"

"No. He's *my* attorney," Savannah clarified with a throaty laugh. "Sorry, that's what I call him—private joke. What I meant is that he's the attorney I've been seeing for the past six months. Romantically."

"Oh. Grandma told me you've been seeing someone, but I didn't realize he was an attorney." Molly's apprehension skyrocketed. If Savannah's dating history was any indication of her current taste in men, her NYC lawyer-boyfriend would probably be arrogant, opinionated and demanding.

*Hopefully, he'll be just as busy as Savannah always is and he won't end up visiting Dune Island,* she thought. *But even if he does, then being friendly to him for a weekend is a small price to pay if it means the rest of the guests will be able to enjoy one final summer at Hydrangea House and Peace Place.*

"You don't have to look so glum about meeting him." For a moment, it seemed as if Savannah had read Molly's mind. "I know it's not easy being around people who are in love when you're nursing a heartache, but sooner or later, you'll meet someone else."

"Yeah, I guess," she answered, even though she wasn't exactly nursing a heartache over Jordan. It was more like she was nursing a grudge. Or maybe it was a little of both—a *lot* of both—but either way, meeting someone else was the last thing on her mind. Molly had barely begun to grieve the loss of her grandmother; she didn't have the emotional capacity to get involved with anyone romantically. "So, what do you think? Will you keep the inn open for the summer?"

"I'd really like to say yes," Savannah said. "But for some reason, I have a feeling it would be a bad idea."

"Oh. Well, I wouldn't want to push you to do something that makes you uncomfortable," bluffed Molly. She had done her best to focus on the benefits of keeping the inn open for the summer. But Savannah apparently didn't really care about the guests or share Molly's desire to honor Beverly's memory by hosting them for one final season. She wasn't motivated by money, either. Feeling desperate, Molly made a last-ditch attempt to change Savannah's mind. This time, she focused on the potential drawbacks of Savannah's decision, hinting, "I just hope the locals don't cold-shoulder you."

"Why would they do that?"

"Hope Haven's a tight-knit community and a lot of the residents depend on tourism for their livelihoods. Grandma told me they feel like if one hotel or inn receives bad publicity, it reflects poorly on the island's entire hospitality industry. Once the guests start complaining because you canceled their reservations at the last minute just so you could renovate, some of the locals are going to be pretty ticked off."

"Pfft." Savannah made a scornful sound, but Molly sensed she was wavering. Savannah cared too much about her reputation to risk annoying the permanent residents and business owners.

"Some of them might not be very accommodating when *you* need something, like a table next to the window in a restaurant or carpentry supplies and services for your renovations." Molly was ad-libbing; the residents would inevitably gossip about how Savannah handled the inn's closure, but she doubted they'd withhold services or goods from her. However, her comments did the trick and any guilt she felt about her little fib disappeared when Savannah immediately back-pedaled.

"I didn't say I *wouldn't* keep Hydrangea House open for the summer. I only said I'm nervous about you being the innkeeper. Do you really think you can manage it?"

"Absolutely."

"All right, then, the *volunteer* innkeeping position is yours."

"Really?" For the first time since she'd received word that her grandmother had died, Molly laughed aloud. She could picture Beverly beaming, too, elated that guests would be able to enjoy their much-anticipated vacations at the inn and cottage for another season. Despite her grief, the promise of being the innkeeper of Hydrangea House made Molly feel stronger and more purposeful. She hoped that following in Beverly's foot-steps would help her feel closer to her grandma, too. Her voice quavering with gratitude, she said, "Thanks, Savannah. I know this is what my grandmother would have wanted us to do."

A couple weeks after their phone conversation, Savannah enlisted Molly's help writing a human interest story about Beverly and Hydrangea House to submit to the local media. Molly carefully crafted what she thought was a relevant tribute to Beverly's service and the inn's history. However, Savannah was dissatisfied and she completely revised it. The new version shone a brighter spotlight on the Frost family than on Beverly. But knowing her grandmother as well as she did, Molly figured that's how she would have wanted it anyway.

When the article was published, along with the photo that Savannah had included of herself and Beverly, Molly shared a copy of it with her mother, Carol.

"Savannah sure knows how to make herself look good," Carol remarked in her usual straightforward manner. "The problem is, she's doing it at *your* expense. It seems like she's taking advantage of you, Molly."

"Yeah, she probably is," Molly acknowledged. "Or she thinks she is, anyway. But I don't care about getting paid. I was going to spend most of the summer volunteering at the camp anyway, and I really want to do this—for Grandma and the guests' sake."

"I know you do, and it's a very generous gesture. But this setup might be harder on you than you expect."

Sometimes it seemed that her mother still thought of Molly as an adolescent, instead of as a very capable, confident thirty-five-year-old woman. Suppressing her frustration, she replied, "Grandma managed to keep the inn operating smoothly, so I should be able to handle the workload, too. Especially since I won't have to bake anything and there will be housekeeping staff to help me with the cleaning."

"I didn't mean the workload—I'm sure you'll manage that just fine. What I meant was that after breaking up with Jordan and losing your grandmother, you're in a vulnerable position emotionally. Have you considered that returning to the inn might trigger a lot of memories of Beverly?"

"I hope it does. That's partly why I want to go there. Grandma died so suddenly and the funeral was such a blur I can hardly remember what happened that weekend. Being on Dune Island again will give me a second chance to... you know, to say goodbye to Grandma and the inn before Savannah closes it down." Molly paused to gather her composure, so she wouldn't prove her mother's point by breaking down in tears. "Besides, the change of scenery will be good for me. It'll help me get over what happened with Jordan faster than if I were hanging around town this summer."

"Mm. I suppose that's true," Carol agreed. "I just wouldn't want you to end up feeling even sadder than you've been feeling."

Suddenly Molly realized that her mother wasn't doubting her abilities; she was concerned about her happiness. *Have I really seemed that sad?* Molly knew how dismal she'd *felt* lately, but she'd been trying to put on a good face so her mother wouldn't worry about her. Molly's father had died when Molly was twenty-four and Carol remarried three years ago. Her husband, Ted, was recovering from a recent heart attack and Molly figured Carol had enough on her mind already, so she tried to minimize how distraught she was about Jordan and Beverly. Apparently, Carol had seen through her façade.

"Thanks for looking out for me, Mom. But it's like what Grandma always said... One of the best ways to feel better when you're sad is to do something meaningful for someone else."

"Another way to feel better is to call your mother," Carol reminded her.

"I'll call you whether I'm sad or not," Molly promised with a chuckle. "But please don't worry about me. I'll be fine."

A bumble bee buzzed near Molly's ear, startling her. She'd been so lost in thought that she hadn't moved beyond the fence gate. But now, she shook her long honey-brown hair over her shoulders, readjusted her grip on her suitcase and continued up the brick walkway toward the white, two-story gabled house. The portico over the dark green front door was modest compared to many of the columned porches on the island's other Greek-revival style homes, but Molly thought the entrance was the perfect balance of simplicity and classic embellishment.

She could picture her grandmother standing on the front steps, a welcoming smile on her lips and a twinkle in her green eyes. "I want every one of the guests to feel eager to come inside and sorry to leave," Beverly used to say.

Even as her eyes smarted with tears, Molly smiled at the memory. Pushing the door open, she silently promised, *I'll never be as gracious of a host as you were, Grandma, but I'm going to do my best to give the guests a lovely, memorable visit.*

And although she knew she shouldn't get her hopes up, Molly found herself thinking, *Who knows? Maybe before the summer ends, Savannah will decide she doesn't want to shut down Hydrangea House and Peace Place after all...*

# TWO

*Funny, but I don't remember ever feeling this frazzled when I used to help Grandma,* Molly thought, peeking into the hallway mirror. Although she had brushed her hair into a neat top knot earlier that morning, several wispy strands had come loose and they were frizzing near her ears. She could feel a trickle of perspiration running down the nape of her neck and there was a dusting of powdered sugar on her cheek. *Has that been there since I set out the pastries this morning?* She rolled her hazel eyes at her reflection and brushed the sugar from her pale skin.

When online bookings took off, Molly's grandmother had reluctantly switched to using apps and the inn's website for communicating with guests. The doors had also been outfitted with keypads so guests could use codes to enter the inn and their individual rooms. However, Beverly resisted the practice of "contactless check-in." She preferred to greet guests and to bid them good-bye in person, so for the past week, that's what Molly had been doing, too. As much as possible, she was trying to imitate her grandmother's practices, but it was more exhausting than she'd expected.

Usually by this point in the summer she would have picked

up a little color from the sun, but she'd been so busy she hadn't had time to go for a swim or even to walk to the end of the jetty. That was partly because she was still getting into the rhythm of checking the guests in and out, as well as tidying the common areas and the outdoor grounds on a near-hourly basis. It was also because Sydney, one of the housekeepers, had to undergo an emergency appendectomy, so Molly had been helping the other housekeeper, Lucy, clean the bedrooms, change the sheets, and do the laundry.

In a way, she was grateful that she didn't have much down-time; being so busy kept her from sinking into sadness because her grandmother wasn't there with her. However, after a week of nearly non-stop domestic chores and social interactions, Molly was eager to get away by herself for a while.

*Maybe when Sydney returns to work, I'll sneak off to go beachcombing,* she thought, heading outside to greet the single mother who'd just pulled into the driveway with her four children. As she was escorting them to Peace Place, she remembered how much her grandmother had always enjoyed showing "youngsters" the cottage.

"It tickles me to hear how expressive they are," Beverly had told Molly. "They notice the smallest details and they say exactly what they think."

Today's occupants were no exception. Their unbridled enthusiasm was so heartwarming that Molly wished Savannah could hear them; maybe it would make her have second thoughts about shutting down Peace Place.

"This living room is almost as big as our entire apartment," the oldest boy exclaimed.

"There's another bathroom up here," his sister shouted from the top of the stairs. "It's got two sinks and the tub and shower are in a separate room."

"Hey, Mom—look what I found on your bed!" A third child

announced loudly, emerging from the master bedroom holding the chocolate mints Lucy had left on the pillows.

"Indoor voices, please," her mother instructed them. She turned to Molly. "I'm sorry about the noise. It was a long trip, but they'll settle down, I promise."

"I'm happy they're so excited to be here," replied Molly with a reassuring smile. "One of the benefits of staying in the cottage is that families with young children don't have to worry at all about disturbing the other guests, and vice versa. So please make yourselves at home and let me know if there's anything else you need to enjoy your stay."

She had barely crossed the lawn on her way back to Hydrangea House when the cell phone for the inn rang. Because Molly had to carry it with her at all times in case a guest texted or called, she'd been using the inn's phone for her personal calls, too. She hoped it was her friend Jenny calling to say her nonprofit organization had been awarded the grant it needed. But the phone's display screen read: PRIVATE CALLER.

"Hello. You've reached Hydrangea House and Peace Place. This is Molly. How may I help you?"

"Hello, Molly. My name is Hazel Walsh. I'm calling to ask if you have a room available for two or three nights." Judging from the woman's quivery voice, Molly imagined her to be either ill or elderly. "The reservation would be for two people. We're flexible with dates, but the sooner we can schedule it, the better. I don't think I'm long for this world."

"Oh, no. I'm very sorry to hear that," uttered Molly, completely caught off-guard by the woman's statement. Was she using a general figure of speech or was she genuinely experiencing a health crisis? "Unfortunately, we're booked for the entire summer."

"The entire summer?" echoed the caller. "But the article in

the newspaper says there are still a few vacancies in early July and late August."

"Do you mean the article about Hydrangea House closing?"

"Yes, that's right. I'm looking at it right now and it specifically says there are still vacancies," the woman insisted.

"Mm, I think I see what the issue is. I'm afraid you must be reading an old article. There was one first published in April, shortly after my grandmother—the innkeeper—passed away. At that time, there *were* a handful of vacancies. But once word got out that this is the last summer Hydrangea House will be open to guests, the rooms filled up right away. However, there are several other B and Bs and inns on the island that I'm happy to recommend, if you're interested?"

"I'm sure they're lovely, but it's imperative that I return to the Frost home," she replied, which seemed like a peculiar way to refer to Hydrangea House. "Did you say your grandmother was the innkeeper?"

"Yes. Her name was Beverly Anderson." Molly heard the crunching of tires against the shell driveway behind her. She turned to see a silver car with Indiana license plates: more guests had arrived. Molly felt torn between speaking with Hazel and greeting the newcomers. *How did Grandma always seem to know just what to say and do in situations like these so that no one felt slighted?*

"Ah, that's who I thought you meant. Beverly had the sweetest dimple and such a lot of thick black hair," Hazel said. "I'm very sorry for your loss."

"Thank you," Molly responded automatically, but she was distracted by the woman's comment about Beverly's appearance. While it was true that her grandmother had had a dimple in her right cheek, her hair hadn't been thick or dark; it had been fine and sand-colored. Even toward the end of her life, it was naturally blonder than it was gray. However, Molly didn't want to embarrass Hazel by pointing out her error. "You said you want to *return* to the Frost home. Is that how you knew my grandmother—were you previously a guest at Hydrangea House?"

"A guest? No, I—I wasn't exactly a guest," she hedged.

The more evasive Hazel's answers sounded, the more curious Molly became about her connection to Beverly. "Were you a housekeeper?" she pressed.

For the past two decades, the inn had partnered with a local agency to provide vocational training and employment opportunities for women with intellectual or developmental disabilities. Lucy and Sydney had both been participating in the program for nearly five years. Molly didn't seem to recall that any of the other women who'd worked at the inn before them were named Hazel, but she might have been mistaken.

"I certainly did my share of housework, but I wasn't exactly a housekeeper, either. I knew Beverly when I was a young girl, and... well, I'd like to tell you more, but it's something that's better done in person. That's why I must return to the Frost home. You see, this newspaper article has gotten the story wrong. I need to set the record straight and—" Hazel was interrupted by someone calling for their mother in the background. Hazel abruptly whispered into the phone. "I've got to go, but I'll check back soon to see if a room becomes available."

Molly was about to ask for her number so she could call Hazel if there were any cancellations, instead of the other way around, but Hazel had already disconnected.

*That was a very strange conversation. What did she mean about the newspaper article getting the story wrong?* Molly wondered. *Did Hazel really know my grandmother when she was a girl? Or was she only making that claim because she thought she'd have a better chance of reserving a room if she pretended to have a connection to her?*

Maybe the entire call was a prank. For all Molly knew, the caller had been a bored teenager imitating an elderly lady to see if she would fall for it. Ever since she'd discovered that Jordan had deceived her, Molly had started second-guessing people's motives. She didn't like this new tendency in herself and since there was no way to confirm whether Hazel was being authentic or not, Molly dismissed her qualms and hurried to welcome the couple who was getting out of their car.

Because they were first-time guests, before showing them to their room, Molly gave them a tour of the common areas downstairs.

"I wish we had built-in window seats and bookshelves in our home," the woman remarked, her eyes darting around the living room. "And the molding and paneling is gorgeous."

"It's modeled after Greek architecture," her husband knowingly informed her, tapping a column on one side of the arched entryway. "That's why the trim and cornices are painted white —it's to imitate the appearance of marble."

"That's right," confirmed Molly, smiling at their appreciation. The Frosts had tried to stay true to the home's original Greek revival style design. The long windows, high ceilings and elegant paneling, trim, and ceiling plasterwork created a sense of grandeur that was complemented by dark, wide plank wood floors throughout the inn.

Each room contained period accent pieces, including mid nineteenth-century light fixtures and vases. However, the overall decor was contemporary, and the furniture tended to be more casual chic than formal or classic. Neutral coastal color schemes on the walls and upholstery enhanced the light and airy ambiance of the mostly open floorplan.

Yet, as impressive and inviting as the interior of Hydrangea House was, the views it offered of the *out*side were what Molly loved most about the old inn. From the parlor, kitchen and dining room on the western side of the house, she could watch the ferries and other vessels and boats coming in and out of the port. The parlor was also where she used to spend entire evenings curled up on a window seat in the dark, mesmerized by Port Newcomb Lighthouse blinking at her from across the harbor.

The living room on the opposite side of the house provided equally enthralling water views, although these were of Dune Island Sound. As Molly pointed out to the couple, "Guests whose rooms are on this side of the house can watch an ocean sunrise without getting out of bed—actually, without even lifting their heads from their pillows."

The crowning jewel of the house was the contemporary "sunroom" addition that stretched across the entire width of the back of the inn, with tall windows and French doors giving guests a panoramic view of the entire seascape, including both the lighthouse and the harbor, as well as the jetty and beyond that, the glistening expanse of Dune Island Sound.

"Wow. It's breathtaking." The woman pointed past the stone patio to the stretch of sand beyond the low seawall at the end of the back lawn. "Are we allowed to use that beach?"

"Absolutely. The land belongs to the owners of Hydrangea House, so guests have exclusive access. Feel free to enjoy the garden and back yard, too," Molly said. "There's a rack of beach chairs beside that shed and there are floats, water toys and lawn games inside it. We also have fishing rods, if you want to try your luck off the end of the jetty. One of our guests caught a couple of decent-sized stripers last week."

"Fishing?" The woman raised an eyebrow at her husband. "Didn't I tell you that you'd love it here?"

He gave her a sheepish shrug. "When you said you wanted to go to a historic harborside B and B in Massachusetts, all I could picture was a creaky, creepy old house with peeling wallpaper and doilies everywhere. But this is great."

"It's paradise," his wife agreed, which made Molly smile. She and her grandmother had always felt the same way, so it was fun to hear the newcomers' "love-at-first-sight" response to Hydrangea House and Dune Island.

After telling them about the continental breakfast, snacks and beverages that were available daily in the sunroom, Molly brought them to their gabled attic suite on the third floor. It included a balcony that was furnished with large, cushioned wicker chairs—the best spot on the property to watch the sun set.

"There's a welcome packet on the dresser that contains lots of helpful info. But if you have any questions or if there's anything else I can provide for you, please let me know."

"Thanks, but I think we have everything we could possibly need. It's so beautiful up here we might never leave our room," the woman remarked as she slipped her arm around her husband's waist. Even in broad daylight, the setting and scenery seemed to inspire romance.

*Grandma didn't call this the honeymoon suite for nothing,* Molly thought as she exited the room, closing the door behind her.

Unexpectedly, she felt a throb of longing for Jordan. For the way he used to murmur sweet nothings while he was kissing her. But now it was someone else's name on his lips. Someone else's *lips* on his lips...

For a moment, Molly was doubly lonely, both for her grandmother and for her former boyfriend. For the way things used to be. Her eyes filled, but she told herself, *Grandma wouldn't want me to be so sad that she's gone—and she definitely wouldn't want me to waste any tears over a cheat like Jordan.* Blinking, she lifted her chin a notch higher and hurried down the stairs.

Although a continental breakfast was the only meal served at Hydrangea House, in the afternoons Molly provided cold, thirst-quenching beverages for the guests to enjoy when they came in from the beach. Today, she'd made strawberry limeade and as she was retrieving the empty pitcher from the sunroom, she caught sight of the enlarged, framed article—written largely by Savannah—about the inn's closure.

Savannah had insisted that Molly display it in a prominent place in one of the common areas, so she'd hung it above the coffeemaker. Personally, she thought it seemed kind of self-promotional, but Savannah had claimed that the article would save Molly the trouble of explaining to guests why the inn was closing. So far, it was fostering more discussion about the topic than it prevented. Especially with the newcomers, who were dismayed to learn that their first visit to the inn would also be their last.

Most of the returning guests already knew about Beverly's death but after reading the article, they repeated their condolences to Molly. They also expressed how disappointed they were that the inn was closing. Although they were tactful about how they phrased their sentiments, it was clear that Savannah's decision was a bitter pill for them to swallow.

Molly completely understood why they felt let down and she didn't blame them for being irritated by the "tone-deaf publicity piece," as she'd overheard a guest referring to Savannah's newspaper feature. But she couldn't imagine why Hazel Walsh had complained that the story was inaccurate. Intrigued by what the elderly caller might have meant, Molly set the pitcher back down and leaned forward to peruse the framed copy.

Even though Savannah herself had written the article, she'd clearly tried to give the impression that a journalist had interviewed her for the piece. Titled, OWNER ANNOUNCES CLOSURE OF FAMILY INN, it read:

*Due to the recent death of long-time innkeeper, Beverly Anderson, the historic Port Newcomb inn known as*

*Hydrangea House will host its final guests this summer before permanently closing to the public.*

"I've known Beverly my entire life—she was like a grand-mother to me. So, on a personal level, I was heartbroken to lose her," said Savannah Frost, beneficiary of the waterfront estate on the eastern point of Main Street. "Her death is also a huge loss for Hydrangea House and its guests."

According to Ms. Frost, the residence's 73-year history as an inn is inextricably linked to her family's relationship with Beverly Anderson and Beverly's mother, Dora Grant.

Originally built in the mid-1860s by a prosperous whaling captain, Hydrangea House was purchased by the Frosts in 1902. When the family later moved to Boston, they retained ownership of the home, which sat unoccupied for many years. Eventually the estate was passed down to young newlyweds Jerome and Evelyn Frost—Savannah Frost's great-grand-parents.

In May of 1943, while Jerome was deployed abroad as a WWII combat engineer, Evelyn retreated to Hydrangea House for the summer. Suffering from a difficult pregnancy, she believed the fresh ocean air and tranquil setting would be beneficial for her and the baby's health. Evelyn was accompa-nied by her live-in maid, Opal, and her cook, Dora Grant.

Dora was also pregnant, and her husband was also serving in the Army overseas. Although Evelyn's baby was due in mid-September and Dora's wasn't expected until early October, both women experienced spontaneous labor during a violent storm on August 26. With no hospital on the island, it fell to Opal, the maid, to single-handedly deliver the babies at Hydrangea House. Evelyn gave birth to a son she named Harold; within hours, Dora's daughter, Beverly, was born.

The storm damaged the ferry dock, delaying the women's departure from the island until repairs could be completed. Meanwhile, Opal unexpectedly passed away, so Dora was

*tasked with caring for both of the babies: her own child and*
*that of her employer, as well as tending to Evelyn herself, who*
*was very weak.*

"That's an understatement," Molly uttered. According to the family stories she had heard, passed down to her grandmother Beverly from her own mother Dora, Evelyn had experienced postpartum hemorrhaging and nearly died. For two months afterward, she was so frail she could barely hold her son for more than a few minutes; Dora often had to rock both babies to sleep simultaneously.

But even if the phrase "very weak" was an inaccurate description of Evelyn's precarious health, Molly doubted that's what had troubled Hazel about the article. Granted, if she truly was friends with Beverly when they were young girls, someone would have told Hazel the story about the stormy night both Harold and Beverly were born. So she might have heard how sick Evelyn had been. But if Hazel had a quibble with the wording in the article, she could have just said that on the phone. No, there had to be a more compelling reason she was insistent on setting the record straight in person.

Molly continued reading:

*By the time the two women returned to Boston in late October,*
*they had developed a bond that was more like a close friend-*
*ship than an employer-employee relationship. The following*
*February, Dora's husband died in combat, leaving her a penni-*
*less widow at twenty-two years old. As a demonstration of*
*gratitude for Dora's devoted service, Evelyn promised to*
*always provide her and her daughter a place to live and work.*

*    In May of 1944, Evelyn was also widowed when Jerome*
*died of typhus in Italy. Drawing from the savings she and her*
*husband had accrued, Evelyn was able to keep her household*
*running for several years. However, by 1949, her funds were*

depleted. She sold her home in Boston and moved to Dune Island as a year-round resident. Dora relocated with her, and the pair resolved to earn an income by converting the house into a summer inn.

They opened Hydrangea House's doors to the public in 1950, with the mission of providing guests luxury accommodations at affordable prices. Evelyn acted as the inn's hostess and Dora was the housekeeper and cook, serving three full meals a day. Young Harold and Beverly played and attended school together like siblings.

In 1955, Evelyn married a former acquaintance, and she and Harold moved back to Boston with him. Because Evelyn's second husband refused to employ any domestic workers, Dora and Beverly remained at Hydrangea House. Dora earned a living by fulfilling her summer innkeeping responsibilities, and she also hosted off-season lodgers.

Beverly helped her mother run the inn she was born in until she turned twenty-one, and then she married a local baker named Joseph Anderson. She set up house in a nearby cottage and gave birth to a son a year later.

"That was my father, Gregory," Molly mumbled to herself. It may have been an oversight, but it bothered her that Savannah hadn't mentioned his name. Come to think of it, she hadn't mentioned Opal's last name—Brown—in the article, either. But she'd been sure to use the Frosts' surname plenty of times.

Shortly afterward, Beverly's husband died in a tragic fall, so she returned to Hydrangea House with her toddler in tow. The mother-and-daughter team shared innkeeping responsibilities until Dora died in 1976, at which time, Beverly became the sole innkeeper—a role she held for the next 47 years.

By the 1980s, Dune Island had developed into a vacation

hotspot and there was a significant shortage of affordable summer accommodations. Subsequently, in 1988, the Frosts converted the estate's carriage house into a three-bedroom cottage. For six weeks every summer, the cottage is rented to the public at modest rates. During alternating weeks, the Frosts make the dwelling available at no charge to low-income families headed by veterans or single mothers. The cottage is named Peace Place, in honor of Jerome Frost and all the US veterans who sacrificed their lives during WWII.

"I'm proud of my family's philanthropic history, including the establishment of Peace Place. I also admire my great-grandmother Evelyn's pledge to provide lifelong employment and a home for Dora and Beverly," remarked Ms. Frost. "Hydrangea House has served that purpose well. However, Beverly's death marks the end of an era."

Molly's eyes stung when she read the phrase, "Beverly's death marks the end of an era." It sounded so detached. So final. As if a page had been turned in her family's history and it was time to move on.

*It's not time yet*, she silently protested. *There's still at least one more season of guests to host.*

She reached for a napkin and blotted her eyes before continuing.

Evelyn Frost's will stipulated that after Dora and Beverly passed away, full control of the estate would revert to her eldest living descendant. Now, her great-granddaughter Savannah Frost has become the sole beneficiary of the property.

"Considering how many people have enjoyed vacationing on my family's estate during the past seventy-three years, I've found it agonizing to decide to close Hydrangea House and Peace Place to the public," said Ms. Frost. "However, after

*careful reflection, I realize my career as a senior VP in the
payments industry in NYC is too consuming to allow me to
run the inn and cottage in a manner that is worthy of our
guests' patronage."*

"Ha!" Molly guffawed. What had seemed to be agonizing
for Savannah was deciding to keep the inn *open* for the summer,
not deciding to permanently shut it down. *This must be what
Mom meant when she said that Savannah sure knew how to
make herself look good*, she thought.

Molly skimmed the rest of Savannah's lengthy quote, which
was technically a self-quote, since she was the one who'd
written the article:

*"While I'm personally eager to begin the exciting process of
converting Hydrangea House back into a family home, I
appreciate that this change will come as a disappointment to
the public. So, in appreciation for our guests' loyalty and in
honor of Beverly Anderson's memory, I have postponed the
closure and renovations until after Labor Day. In the meantime, it's my hope that everyone who visits Hydrangea House
and Peace Place this year will have a spectacular stay on Dune
Island."*

Following the story was an editor's note that stated:
*Although Peace Place is fully booked for the season, Hydrangea
House still has a handful of vacancies in early July and late
August. Beverly Anderson's granddaughter, Molly, will act as
the temporary innkeeper for the season.* The inn's contact infor-
mation was also listed.

Molly turned her attention to the photo accompanying the
article. It was a candid shot of Beverly and Savannah in the
kitchen at Hydrangea House, wooden spoons and mixing bowls
in hand and wide grins on their faces. They were wearing

matching aprons as they prepared breakfast for the guests, which Savannah used to love to help Beverly do. The photo made Molly smile, in spite of herself.

Blotting the sweat from her forehead, she scanned the article a second time, re-checking the names and dates. Despite Hazel's claim that something was amiss, all the details appeared correct. Was it possible that Hazel knew something about Hydrangea House and Beverly—or about the Frosts, for that matter—that Molly didn't know?

*Hopefully, next time she calls she'll share more information with me,* she thought as she carried the empty pitcher into the kitchen. *Better yet, maybe a room will open up and she'll be able to come here in person...*

# THREE

"Good morning, Molly. I know you're usually up with the birds, so I hope I'm not calling too early?"

"Hi, Mom. Your timing's perfect. I just got out of the water." Molly held the phone to her ear with one hand as she leaned sideways and squeezed the wet ends of her hair with the other. Fat droplets darkened the fine, bleached sand.

"You've already been swimming this morning? It's not even six-thirty," Carol exclaimed.

"Yeah, but we're going to have a lot of guest change-overs today and Sydney's still out, recovering from surgery, so I've got a full morning and afternoon ahead of me. This will probably be my only downtime all day."

During her first week at Hydrangea House, even when she wasn't cleaning or interacting with guests, Molly had remained inside the inn or in the yard. Erring on the side of caution, she'd tried to make herself available almost 24/7—except when she was running errands—just in case a guest needed her for something urgent.

However, by her second week, she'd loosened her self-imposed restrictions. Immediately following her morning trip to the bakery, while most of the guests were still asleep, she'd been stealing away for a walk. Or sometimes she'd go swimming farther down the beach, where she had more privacy.

Unfortunately, this morning she'd woken later than usual. She knew she wouldn't have time for a walk, but the air was so hot and humid that she'd been desperate to take a quick, invigorating dip in the Sound. So she'd worn her swimsuit beneath her clothes to the bakery. When she'd returned to the inn, she'd walked straight from the driveway to the private beach immediately behind Hydrangea House. She'd brought the boxes of goodies with her, so she could savor a scone in solitude on the beach after her swim, a guilty pleasure.

But right when her mother called, she realized she'd forgotten her towel in the car and she didn't want to walk all the way back to the driveway. So now she ambled over to the jetty and perched on a flat rock, stretching her legs out straight and facing east to dry her skin in the sun.

"Sounds like you've been really busy," Carol remarked.

"Yes, but not any busier than you've been. How's work?" As Carol shared an anecdote about training a group of new employees, Molly squinted at the silvery water. It's glittering, restless surface made her feel, quite literally, as if she were seeing stars so she swung her legs around and faced the west.

Across the harbor, a ferry was heading away from port and she could feel the jetty rocks vibrating from the thrum of its engine.

"Was that the ferry whistle I just heard?" her mother asked.

"Yes. I think it's signaling an incoming yacht." Port Newcomb Yacht Club was located on the western side of the harbor and most of its members were very respectful and responsible mariners. However, on occasion, a yacht would try to "play chicken" with one of the mighty ferries. Fortunately, that didn't appear to be what was happening now, because as soon as the ferry blasted its whistle, the yacht gave it a wider berth.

The sound and sight made Molly recall a funny memory. "Hey, Mom, remember that time a guest asked if Grandma could do something about the ferries blasting their horns because the noise was disrupting her afternoon naps?"

"Yes. Your dad and I thought it was hilarious that she seemed to believe your grandmother held that kind of influence over the ferry captains. But Beverly just empathized about the noise and gave the woman a pair of ear plugs." Carol chuckled. "The next morning, the guest complained that the light from the lighthouse had kept her awake all night and she wanted your grandmother to ask the lighthouse keeper if—"

"He could turn it down it a little!" Molly completed the sentence in unison with her mother. They both squealed with laughter at the memory.

"Even Beverly had difficulty keeping a straight face that time," Carol said. "But she apologized profusely to the woman because it hadn't occurred to her to provide sleep masks for the guests. Then she went straight to the store and bought one for everybody. Your grandmother was gracious to a fault."

Molly felt a twinge of guilt as she recalled how irritated she'd been when a guest had called her at 11:00 p.m. to ask if she had a bicycle pump he could use the next day. *No one would ever accuse* me *of being gracious to a fault,* she thought. "How has Ted been lately?"

"He seems to be doing all right. He's got an EKG and an appointment with his cardiologist coming up, so hopefully everything will check out okay. He said to say hello and to ask if there's been any whale activity in the Sound lately?"

"Not yet but tell him I'm keeping my eyes peeled."

On rare occasions, breaching whales could be spotted from

the property. Her stepfather Ted had only visited Hydrangea House twice, but both times, he'd been fishing on the jetty when a humpback happened to rear up from the depths in the distance. He'd been awestruck, which Molly considered to be a positive character trait in a man, since her father had always been fascinated with the mammoth creatures, too.

As a young girl, when she used to visit Beverly with her parents, Molly and her dad frequently ate their lunch on the end of the jetty, hoping to catch sight of the massive mammals. They especially wanted to see a right whale, which was the name given to the type of whales that used to be plentiful in Dune Island Sound before the commercial whaling industry endangered their species.

While they scanned the water, Molly's dad would teach her how to distinguish the different types of seagulls gliding by, or he'd tell her about growing up on Dune Island. He had such a knack for storytelling that Molly always felt like he was reading aloud from her favorite book, and she'd eat her sandwich as slowly as she could so he'd keep talking.

When they'd return to Hydrangea House, Beverly sometimes teased, "Ahoy, Captain Ahab! Ahoy, matey! Did you two spy any right whales?"

"Nope. We didn't spy any wrong ones, either," Greg would reply.

It was one of Molly's favorite "dad jokes," but instead of laughing at the memory, she suddenly felt like crying. *If I hadn't been sitting here just now, I might not have even remembered that Dad used to make that joke. I might not have remembered about Grandma giving the guest ear plugs, either*, she lamented silently. *What's going to trigger my memories once I stop coming to Dune Island?*

Shortly after announcing she was closing the inn, Savannah had told Molly in the future she could visit Hydrangea House "for a weekend sometime." While Molly appreciated the sentiment, she got the sense that Savannah had felt obligated to extend the lukewarm invitation. To be frank, Molly couldn't see herself returning to Hydrangea House just to visit Savannah, anyway. The only thing they had in common was Beverly, and now that she was gone...

"Molly, are you still there?" Carol prompted.

"Sorry. What did you say?"

"I asked if you heard anything from Jenny about the grant?"

"Not yet, but she thinks—"

Her sentence was interrupted by a cacophony of shrieking behind her. Molly twisted her neck to see what was causing the commotion. A great black-backed gull had opened the boxes of bakery treats that Molly had set on top of her shorts and T-shirt in the sand before she'd gone swimming. The bird was picking at a blueberry scone and intermittently raising its beak to screech warnings at the half-dozen smaller, squawking gulls that were threatening to swoop in and plunder its catch.

Leaping to her feet, Molly exclaimed, "The seagulls are eating the guests' breakfast!"

"You'd better go," urged her mother, laughing. "We'll talk again soon."

"Okay. Bye, Mom." Frantically waving her arms as she jumped off the rock into the sand, Molly shouted at the birds, "Get away from that! Get!"

They ignored her until she was within a few yards of them and then the smaller birds took flight. However, the black-backed gull used its beak to tug the entire box farther away from Molly.

"I said *get*," she yelled at him. Meanwhile, the smaller birds circled back to claim the treats in the other box. They were hovering so low and close that she could feel the air fluttering from their flapping wings. She grabbed her T-shirt from where she'd left it in the sand and twirled it over her head like a lasso, hollering.

It worked. The birds dispersed, including the biggest gull, but Molly's T-shirt slipped from her fingers. It sailed through the air and landed in the water. She gathered the boxes and the broken bits of pastries before fishing her shirt from the shallows. Even after wringing it out, it was too wet to wear, so she slid her shorts on over her suit, picked up the boxes and her phone and started walking toward the house.

*Hopefully, no one's awake yet,* she thought. Most of this week's guests hadn't been coming into the sunroom for breakfast until 8:00 or 8:30. She figured she could put on a dry shirt, make a dash to the bakery and return in time to slice the fruit she intended to serve in addition to yogurt and bakery treats. *I should leave a note near the coffeemaker to let guests know about the delay, just in case they come downstairs earlier than usual,* she decided.

When she reached the back patio, she was dismayed to hear voices coming from the sunroom. *I hope it's not departing guests who are in a hurry to get on the road,* she fretted. She didn't want to delay their trip, but she didn't want to send them off without breakfast, either.

Pulling open the door, it occurred to Molly that whoever was in the sunroom had probably witnessed her mishap with the birds and the scones on the beach. Oh, well. There was nothing she could do now except disguise her embarrassment by fixing a smile on her face and asking the guests if they had any special requests from the bakery. But when she stepped inside and saw Savannah standing at the coffeemaker, Molly was so surprised that her jaw dropped and she was momentarily speechless.

With her blonde hair falling around her shoulders in beachy waves, Savannah looked striking in a sleeveless, red and white floral-printed mini dress that showed off her long, lean legs. "Hey there," she said nonchalantly and took a sip from her cup.

"What are you doing here?" Molly blurted out.

"Umm... drinking coffee?" Savannah's upward inflection was rife with sarcasm.

"No, I know. I mean, it's nice to see you but I'm surprised you'd come to Hope Haven on a weekday."

She stepped forward and the two women gave each other a quick, perfunctory embrace. Only then did Molly notice the reddish-haired man standing on the other side of Savannah. He was about half a head shorter than she was, which was why Molly hadn't seen him at first.

"Hi. I'm Molly. You must be Austin?"

"Guilty as charged," he mumbled drolly, in an apparent reference to his occupation as a lawyer. The way he leered at her from beneath his eyelids made Molly wish she had put on her T-shirt, even if it was soggy. She shifted the boxes in her arms, trying to hide her swimsuit, as Savannah sidled closer to him and bumped his arm. Or was that a nudge?

"Now that you've met my attorney, say hello to Gina and Matt." She gestured toward the couple sitting in a loveseat in the corner of the sunroom. The man started to rise, as if he were about to come over and shake her hand, but Molly barely had time to glance in their direction before Savannah asked, "Aren't you supposed to serve breakfast by 7:00? It's almost 7:30. I'm famished."

Molly could feel the heat rising in her cheeks. In her ears and chest, too. "Yes, usually I have breakfast ready by 7:00. But as you probably saw, the birds helped themselves to the scones I bought at the bakery, so now I'll have to run out and get something else." She smiled sweetly but her remark was pointed when she added, "If I had known you and your friends were coming, I would have been here to greet you and to make sure I had breakfast prepared in time for your arrival."

"I didn't realize I needed to make a reservation to visit my own residence," Savannah retorted with a sniff.

"No, of course you don't need a reservation," Molly acknowledged quietly, trying to de-escalate the tension between them. Even though she resented Savannah's snitty attitude, Molly didn't want to get into an argument in front of her entourage. "There aren't any vacancies, though, so if you're planning to stay overnight—"

She was going to say that she'd give up her room and go to a hotel, but Savannah didn't let her finish. "Don't worry. We're only staying for the afternoon. That's why we came so early—I wanted to make sure Gina has enough time to get a good look around and take some photos. She's going to be my designer for the remodel."

"Oh. I see." Molly bit her lip, thinking about how Savannah had claimed she wasn't going to start the remodeling process until after Labor Day.

This past week, several more guests had been upset by her newspaper article. Yesterday she'd heard one of them remarking to another, "After seventeen years of patronizing Hydrangea House, it's difficult enough to know this will be our last summer here. I don't appreciate reading about how eager the owner is to remodel the place."

If that's how irked the guests felt after reading the newspaper article, how would they feel if they saw Gina snapping photos or making videos or whatever else she needed to do to start planning the remodel?

*Maybe after I get back from the bakery and set breakfast out for the guests, I can talk to Savannah in private and ask her to make sure Gina is discreet,* she thought. If the conversation went well, she might also hint that it would be a good idea to remove the framed article from the wall.

Hoping to buy time until she returned, Molly suggested, "Before you and Gina start conceptualizing, you might want to spend a few minutes enjoying the beach. It's humid up here at the house, but there's still a pleasant breeze down by the water. I'm happy to bring breakfast out to everyone on the patio when I get back from the bakery."

"Yeah, let's do that," Austin said to Savannah. "I want to check out the waterfront."

"Okay, fine." Savannah didn't sound too pleased about the idea, but she trailed after him. She stopped in the doorway and turned to face Molly. "I hope you're not going to take too long. I'm starving."

Molly forced a smile. "I'll be quick—I'm just headed to the other end of Main."

After Savannah left, Molly stole a glance at the loveseat, where Gina was dancing her fingers against Matt's bare knee. "I'm going to go down to the beach, too. You're coming with me, aren't you?"

He shifted his legs away from her. "Nah, I don't think so."

"C'mon. I don't want to be Savannah and Austin's third wheel." Gina stood up and tugged his hand. "Pretty please?"

Matt yanked his fingers free of her grasp and touched the corner of his dark-rimmed glasses, repositioning them on his nose. Then he crossed his arms against his chest, still not budging from his seat. "I'm going to hang out here and talk to Molly."

It seemed apparent that he was either upset or he was playing some kind of cat-and-mouse game with Gina, who puckered her lips into an exaggerated pout. Molly didn't know if he was trying to make his girlfriend jealous, but she didn't want him including *her* in their dysfunctional dynamic. More importantly, she was concerned that if Matt didn't go outside, Gina would stay inside, too—and then she might start taking photos just as the guests started coming into the sunroom in search of breakfast.

Molly kindly informed him, "Sorry, I don't have time to chat with you right now. As I said, I'm heading to the bakery. You're welcome to sit here for as long as you like, but I think you'd really love the beach—or the garden."

His mouth drooping with a defeated frown, Matt stood up. Until then, Molly hadn't realized how lanky he was—he must have been six-three or six-four, at least. Threaded with gray, his dark, curly hair probably added another inch and a half to his height. He mumbled, "All right. I guess I'll check in with you later, then?"

*Can't he take a hint?* Molly thought.

"No need to come looking for me," she replied brightly, hoping he'd finally get the message. "I'll bring a tray out to the patio for the four of you when breakfast is ready."


By 7:00 on any given morning during the summer, the line at Mainly Muffins snaked out of the store and halfway down the block. Tourists came from all over the island to purchase the shop's muffins—especially the legendary "dirt bomb," a kind of round muffin dipped in butter and rolled in cinnamon and sugar. Today the line seemed to be moving slower than usual, but Molly figured she'd spend less time waiting here than walking six blocks to the next bakery and waiting in another line that was probably equally long.

She'd finally crossed the threshold into the shop when her phone rang. She wondered if it was her mother again, or maybe it was Jenny phoning with news about the grant. Eager to hear a friendly voice, she slid the phone from her back pocket and glanced at the screen. *Private caller? I hope it's not a guest wondering where breakfast is,* she thought before giving her customary greeting.

"Hello. You've reached Hydrangea House and Peace Place. This is Molly. How may I help you?"

"Hello. This is..." The caller said her name, but the tiny,

bustling bakery was so noisy that Molly missed it. She covered her other ear and asked the caller to repeat herself. The woman enunciated: "This is HAZ-EL WALSH."

"Hazel—hello!" Molly was eager to speak with her but she could hardly hear over the din and it was almost her turn to place her order at the counter. "May I call you back in a moment?"

Now Hazel couldn't hear Molly. "What did you say?"

"CAN I CALL YOU BACK?" Molly repeated loudly just as someone tapped her shoulder.

"It's your turn," the man behind her said, pointing to an open space in front of the counter.

"I'll have to call *you* back," Hazel was saying meanwhile.

"No, wait!" Molly objected, not wanting to lose the opportunity to speak to her.

The customer behind her apparently thought Molly was speaking to him. "I've *been* waiting. Either take your turn or step aside."

"Sorry. Sorry," Molly said, both to him and to Hazel. She stepped out of line and got swept up in the tide of customers exiting the bakery from the side door. Before she knew it, she was out on the brick sidewalk again. She asked Hazel, "Are you still there?"

"Yes. I'm here. Where are *you*? Grand Central Station?

Molly had to chuckle. "It sounds that way, doesn't it? I was in the bakery on Main Street."

"Oh, yes, I know where that is. It's next to the five-and-dime. I can't recall the name of it though..."

There wasn't a "five-and-dime" anywhere on Dune Island; in fact, no one even used that term any more. But Molly knew which store Hazel meant because Beverly had frequently mentioned that's where her husband Joseph took her on their first date. Apparently, he'd bought her a "malted at the soda fountain," which was also an outdated expression. Molly figured if Hazel remembered the five-and-dime, then she must have visited the island a long time ago.

"Actually, the bakery I was in is called Mainly Muffins," Molly said as she traipsed down the sidewalk to take her place at the end of the line again.

"I don't remember that. It must be new."

"Kind of," agreed Molly, even though the bakery had been there for at least twenty years. She didn't want to get too far off the topic. "I'm really glad you called again—"

"Why?" interrupted Hazel excitedly. "Is there a vacancy?"

Molly felt awful for getting the elderly woman's hopes up. "Not yet, no. I'm sorry."

"Oh." She sighed, obviously disappointed. "Then why are you glad I called?"

This wasn't the right time for Molly to tell Hazel that she wanted to hear more about what was wrong with the story in the newspaper. So she told her the other reason she was glad Hazel called. "I wanted to get your number. That way, if a room does become available, I can call you right away."

There was a long pause before Hazel responded. "I'd really prefer to call you, instead. You see, I don't want my daughter to know I'm planning this trip. It's sort of a... a surprise. If she sees your number on our caller ID, it will ruin my secret."

"I understand," Molly said, even though there was a false note in Hazel's voice that made her think the elderly woman wasn't being completely honest. "My concern is that if there's a last-minute cancellation and I can't reach you, the opportunity might pass before you call me again."

"Good point," Hazel acknowledged. "I suppose I'll have to call more frequently, won't I?"

*Just what I need—more interruptions to my schedule,* Molly thought. But staying at Hydrangea House was obviously very important to Hazel. And learning more about the elderly woman's connection to Dune Island and possibly to her grandmother was important to Molly. So she agreed, "Yes, please feel free to call every day, if you like."

When Molly pulled into the driveway of Hydrangea House, she noticed the middle-aged couple who'd spent the last three evenings in Room 4 were loading their luggage into their trunk.

"Good morning," she said, striding toward them after she got out of her car. "I hope you're not leaving already? I'm sorry breakfast is late this morning, but I'll have it prepared in a snap."

"Thanks, but we've got to catch the ferry," the man answered.

"Oh, no! I feel awful that you haven't had any breakfast before your trip. Won't you at least take a couple muffins with you?"

"Is there a dirt bomb in there?"

"There's a *dozen* dirt bombs in here. Help yourself." Molly lifted the lid to the box. "I can run inside and get you coffee to go, too. It will only take a sec."

"We already filled our thermal cups and put them in the car," the woman assured her. "Please don't feel bad about anything. We couldn't have enjoyed our stay more than we did. You were a wonderful host, just like Beverly always was."

"Thank you." Molly was touched by the comparison to her grandmother. "It was a pleasure having you at Hydrangea House."

"We wish the inn weren't closing, but we feel fortunate that we've been able to come here for the past seven years." The woman began to duck into the passenger side of the car when she popped back up again and added, "By the way, I feel funny mentioning this, but the designer spilled coffee on the bedspread when she was making a video of the room. I'm sure she'll speak to you about it, but in case it slips her mind I didn't want you to think we'd deliberately neglected to tell you about damage to our room."

"Thank you for letting me know," Molly calmly replied, despite being appalled that Gina had entered the guests' room in the first place. "As my grandmother used to say, spills and stains are inevitable—it'll all come out in the wash. But I appreciate the heads-up so we can pre-soak it right away."

As she waved goodbye, Molly hoped her expression didn't register how ticked off she was. Even if Savannah had given Gina permission to video the departing guests' bedroom, she should have waited until they'd left the property. Checkout time wasn't until 10:00, so Molly hoped the couple hadn't felt as if they'd been pushed out of their room prematurely.

When she went inside, she was surprised to see Savannah standing at the kitchen island, slicing a pineapple. Without looking up, she growled, "You've been gone over an hour. What took you so long?"

"There was a line at the bakery." Gritting her teeth, Molly set the muffins on the counter and went to the sink to wash her hands. As insulting as it was that Savannah seemed to be tracking her time, she had to pick her battles. Right now, her main objective was limiting Gina's photography to the common areas of the inn. "I also spent a few minutes saying goodbye to guests in the driveway. They happened to mention Gina spilled coffee in their room."

"No kidding. Gina told me about it right away." Savannah scoffed, "I can't believe they *tattled* on her. How old are they anyway, seven?"

"They only told me so I could take care of the stain," Molly replied in a low voice. If anyone was in the sunroom, she didn't want them overhearing the conversation. They might think she was in the habit of gossiping about guests behind their backs.

"I already took care of it."

Molly couldn't imagine Savannah stripping the covering

from the bed and taking it to the laundry room. She wasn't even sure that Savannah had ever *been* in the laundry room. "You took care of the stain?" she repeated.

"Yes," Savannah confirmed. Molly felt bad for doubting her until she added, "It was the first thing I asked the housekeeper to do when she got here."

Because Lucy had been working at the inn for years and Savannah knew who she was, it bugged Molly when she referred to her as "the housekeeper." So she emphasized her name when she said, "Thank you for asking *Lucy* to rinse it before the stain set."

She slid a knife from the knife block and began slicing the kiwis. After a few moments she broached the subject of Gina's photography as tactfully as she could. "I know you want to get a jump start on remodeling and I realize Gina's only here for one day. But would you mind suggesting that she waits until the guests have left the property before she videos their rooms? I don't want them to feel rushed."

Savannah smacked the bowl she'd just filled with pineapple chucks down on the counter. "For your information, Gina asked those guests' permission before she went into their room, and they said it was fine. They were ready to go, they just needed to grab their luggage. If they felt like they were being pushed out, they could have told her to wait, instead of saying it was okay and then complaining to you about it."

"I can imagine why guests might be reluctant to tell the owner's designer not to enter their rooms, but they *didn't* complain to me about it. All I'm just saying is, in consideration of our guests—"

Savannah cut her off. "Don't act like *I'm* being inconsiderate to the guests. *You're* the one who couldn't be bothered to serve their breakfast on time because you wanted to go for a swim first. Grandma B. never would have done something like that."

Savannah's comment pricked Molly's conscience. It was true, her grandmother never would have gone down to the beach so close to the time she needed to serve breakfast. Molly also felt guilty because she knew the real reason it had taken her an hour to return from the bakery was because she'd lost her place in line answering Hazel's call.

"You're right. I thought I had time for a swim this morning, but I shouldn't have cut it so close. It won't happen again," she said, but it was more like she was talking to her grandmother than to Savannah.

Savannah looked startled, as if she hadn't expected Molly to be apologetic. "Okay, well, good." She picked up the knife again and conceded, "I suppose I can tell Gina to wait until after checkout time to video any of the departing guests' rooms."

"Thank you—and thanks for helping slice the fruit."

"No problem." She gestured toward Molly's cutting board. "By the way, you really should peel the kiwis with a spoon, not a knife. You're wasting too much of the fruit. Don't you remember Grandma B. teaching us that when we were teenagers?"

"No, I forgot," admitted Molly. "Either that, or I wasn't paying attention in the first place."

"Yeah, all you seemed to care about was getting down to the beach."

Molly gave her a smile and said, "I guess some things never change. Obviously, I *still* love going down to the beach in the morning."

"Yeah, and *I* still enjoy hanging out in the kitchen, although..." Savannah paused and when she spoke again, her bottom lip quivered. "It's not the same being here without Grandma B."

Touched by Savannah's rare display of vulnerability, Molly murmured, "No, it isn't. I miss her, too."

Their moment of shared melancholy was interrupted when

Austin burst into the kitchen. "What's the hold-up? I thought we were supposed to eat breakfast as soon as she got back."

Even though he was clearly addressing Savannah, Molly smiled and assured him, "It's almost ready."

He ignored her and beckoned Savannah with a jerk of his chin. "C'mon. Don't waste your day off playing waitress—that's what *she's* here for. Let her earn her keep."

Molly didn't know if Austin's comment was supposed to be a joke, but she didn't think it was funny. Even though it was none of his business, she snapped, "For your information, I'm not *earning* anything—I'm here as a volunteer."

He gave a dismissive, one-shouldered shrug. "Savannah might not be paying you, but you're still getting something out of the deal. Time will tell. Nobody works for nothing—not even a do-gooder like you."

Molly was so flabbergasted, all she could do was gape at him, but he wouldn't even look in her direction. Funny, since he couldn't seem to take his eyes off her when she'd been wearing her swimsuit.

Savannah seemed entirely unfazed by Austin's cynical pronouncement about Molly's motives. Was that because she agreed with him? "I've just got to finish hulling these strawberries," she said. "It'll only take a minute."

"I haven't *got* a minute," Austin barked. He must have recognized immediately how sharp his tone sounded because he softened his voice and explained, "Matt's delivering a lecture about how ocean waves form and Gina's pretending it's the most scintillating thing she's ever heard. I'm bored out of my skull. I need you out there with me."

Savannah giggled—a sound Molly seldom heard her make. "Ignore Matt and Gina. Try to relax and enjoy the beautiful view."

Austin inched closer and lifted her hair to kiss her neck. "*You're* the only beautiful view I want to enjoy."

She scrunched her shoulders. "That tickles—stop it."

"Not unless you come with me."

"Austin!" Savannah squealed when he continued to kiss her.

*Now I know what Gina meant about being a third wheel.* Molly focused on arranging the muffins on a platter as their flirting continued.

Finally, Savannah gave in. "Okay, okay. I'll go outside with you." She wiped her hands on her apron, hung it on the hook where Beverly used to keep it and then followed Austin from the room.

Still annoyed by his jibe that she needed to "earn her keep," Molly felt like telling him to keep on walking, right off the far end of the jetty. Of course, that wasn't a sentiment Beverly ever would have expressed—she probably wouldn't have even *thought* it—no matter how rude a guest was.

*But I'm not my grandmother and Austin's not a guest,* she silently argued with her conscience. It wasn't just that remark that irritated her; she was also peeved about his "do-gooder" comment. *What exactly does he think I'm "getting out of the deal" of volunteering here this summer, anyway?*

Admittedly, it was very rewarding for Molly to know she was enabling other people to enjoy their vacations. She also felt a special kind of satisfaction from trying to emulate her grandmother's example. Even if she wasn't actually on vacation, being surrounded by the seascape was revitalizing, and staying in the inn had sparked countless memories of the joyful times she'd spent on Dune Island with her family, especially her grandma.

So Molly certainly wouldn't deny that on an emotional level, she was benefitting from being the innkeeper for Hydrangea House. But the way Austin had said *time will tell* made it seem as if he were accusing her of harboring some kind of malevolent, ulterior motive for filling in for her grandmother for the summer. As hard as Molly tried, she couldn't fathom what he imagined her motive was.

*What do I care what he thinks? His statement is probably more of a reflection on* him *than on me, so there's no sense in trying to figure out what he meant,* she finally decided, as she deposited the fruit peelings into the composting bin and let the metal lid fall shut with a bang.

# FOUR

It was just before two o'clock when Molly and Lucy finished cleaning the final guest room. Usually on such a high turn-over day, they would have struggled to finish by 2:45, which would have meant they only had a few minutes to spare before check-in time began at 3:00. But after Molly got past her annoyance at Austin—and, to a lesser extent, at Savannah for showing up unannounced with her friends—her mind wandered to her morning phone call with Hazel. Molly was so preoccupied with wondering why the elderly woman was being so secretive that she was able to fly through her usual housekeeping tasks in a lot less time than it usually took her to complete them.

Fortunately, Savannah and her companions had left around noon to eat lunch at the yacht club. They said that when they were done, they were heading directly to the ferry dock. Knowing they wouldn't return to Hydrangea House filled Molly with relief. Since Lucy didn't drive and her home's manager, Delores, couldn't pick her up until her usual quitting time at 3:00, Molly suggested they take a break in the kitchen.

"This morning I set aside two dirt bombs for us," she told

Lucy. "I had a feeling we'd be hungry when we finished cleaning."

Molly had also set the muffins aside because she was aware that at least once or twice a week, her grandmother would have done the same thing. As hardworking as she was, Beverly appreciated the value of taking an extra break every now and then. She especially enjoyed sitting down to snack on a treat with the housekeeping team members.

Lucy, who rarely spoke directly to others, perched on a stool at the kitchen island and nodded when Molly asked if she wanted milk with her muffin. After filling a glass for each of them, Molly sat across from her and they ate in companionable silence. When Lucy finished her dirt bomb, she repeatedly dabbed the sugary leftover crumbs from her plate with her forefinger, which she then tapped against her tongue, obviously savoring the sweetness.

"Sydney comes back tomorrow," she mumbled, in between dabbing.

Even though Lucy may have been talking to herself, Molly replied, "Really? I didn't know that."

Sydney probably wouldn't be quite up to speed right away and Molly realized she'd need to continue helping with the housekeeping tasks for a while. But Lucy and Sydney made a formidable cleaning team and they were also best friends, so for Lucy's sake, Molly was very glad to hear Sydney was returning.

"Sydney comes back tomorrow," Lucy repeated, as she often did. Then she paused, her finger halfway to her mouth, and added, "Beverly's not coming back. Beverly died."

Molly understood that Lucy's repetition was her way of confirming information, as well as a way of consoling herself, and her heart ached for the young woman. She softly acknowledged, "That's right. Beverly died. She's not coming back."

Lucy furrowed her brows and Molly could tell she was mulling something over. She held her breath, hoping the young woman wouldn't ask her any questions about Hydrangea House. Both Lucy and Sydney had difficulty adjusting to new situations and they'd already experienced a lot of emotional distress because of Beverly's sudden death and Sydney's unexpected surgery. So Delores, their home's manager, thought it would be less upsetting and disruptive for everyone if she waited until the end of the season to tell them about the inn's closure.

Because they had difficulty reading, she wasn't too concerned that they'd find out about it from the article on the wall. And she figured that even if they overheard someone talking about Hydrangea House shutting down, they'd assume the guests meant it was closing at the end of the summer, like they were accustomed to it doing.

It pained Molly to imagine how upset Lucy and Sydney would be once they fully understood they wouldn't be working at the inn after this year. She'd promised Delores she wouldn't introduce the topic to them, but Molly had forgotten to warn Savannah not to say anything about it. Now, Lucy's troubled expression made her wonder if Savannah had spilled the beans.

However, all of a sudden, Lucy's face brightened. She licked her finger, clapped her hands together twice and announced, "There's work to do and people to serve." Then she hopped down from her stool to rinse her plate and glass at the sink.

Molly laughed, delighted that Lucy had quoted Beverly's motto and imitated Beverly's trademark hand-clapping gesture to end their break. She rose to her feet, too. "You're right, Lucy. There's work to be done and I think I just heard someone come in from the beach, so I'd better find out if they're thirsty."

She walked down the hall to ask how many guests wanted cranberry smoothies made with berries harvested from a local bog. But when she popped into the sunroom and saw Savannah's friend Matt peering at the framed newspaper article above the coffeemaker, the question that leaped from her lips was, "What are *you* doing here?"

He flinched and turned toward her, red-faced. "I-I was just reading about the history of Hydrangea House and Peace Place —it's fascinating."

"No, sorry. I meant what are you doing here at the inn?" Molly glanced toward the wall of windows, scanning the back yard and beach, but she didn't see anyone out there. Come to think of it, she hadn't heard any vehicles pulling into the driveway when she'd been taking a break in the kitchen, either. "Where's Savannah? Where are Austin and Gina?"

"Probably waiting in the vehicle lane at the dock—they were trying to catch the ferry to Hyannis right after lunch."

*Is he joking?* marveled Molly. It had seemed obvious this morning that Matt and Gina were having relationship issues. But she couldn't quite believe that Gina would ditch him in Port Newcomb or that he'd refuse to travel home with her, whichever the case was. "You're not going back to New York with them?"

"No way." His answer was swift and emphatic. Under his breath, he added, "No matter how many times Gina asks me to."

Although she recognized she shouldn't judge Matt without knowing all the facts, Molly couldn't help thinking that he was acting like a teenager. *Even if they had a huge argument and broke up some time between this morning and now, it seems immature of him not to ride home with her.*

Before she could think of a diplomatic response, he gave her a tentative smile and asked, "So, are you ready for me now?"

*Is this guy for real?* Molly paused, put a smile on her face, and tried to remember that her grandmother was kind and polite to each and every guest as she chose her next words carefully. "Listen, it seems like you've got a lot going on in your personal life. I can appreciate that you might need space from your girlfriend. But you're going to have to find it somewhere else on the island, because we don't have any vacancies."

"Whoa. Gina is *not* my girlfriend," Matt protested, waving his hands in front of him. "I hardly know her and to be honest, I don't like her very much."

Not knowing whether to be startled or amused by his candor, Molly's smile froze on her face as she tried to work out what Matt meant. "Oh... well, I'm sorry to hear you had to spend time with her. I'm afraid we have no vacancies, and I'm quite busy so I'm going to have to ask you to leave."

"But I have a reservation," he protested. "I'm a visiting faculty member at Dune Island Oceanographic Institute. I'm supposed to be staying here for the next ten weeks."

Ordinarily, guests weren't permitted to stay for longer than seven consecutive nights, because Beverly wanted to give a large variety of visitors the opportunity to vacation at the inn and cottage. But a few years ago Beverly had received permission from the Frosts to rent out Hydrangea House's smallest room, which was the only room that didn't have an en suite bathroom, for the duration of the summer to a faculty member or researcher visiting Dune Island Oceanographic Institute from its partner institute in California.

"But you can't be from the Institute," Molly objected feebly, her mind racing back to the names listed in the booking system. "The faculty member who's scheduled to stay at Hydrangea House is a woman named Karen."

"You mean Karen Hutchinson," Matt confirmed, and Molly nodded. "She had a family crisis that prevented her from coming, so I'm filling in for her. My full name's Matthew Driscoll. The Institute should have emailed you a couple weeks ago, but I have their number. You can call them to verify that I'm taking Karen's place."

"No, that's not necessary." Molly's face was flaming hot as she admitted, "The email was probably sent to my grandmother,

Beverly—she was the innkeeper. As you may have read in the article on the wall, she died last spring."

Molly only mentioned her grandmother's death by way of explaining how the message from the Institute might have been overlooked, but Matt cut in to say, "Yes, I did read that. I'm very sorry for your loss." His voice was soft and his big brown eyes were full of compassion, which made Molly feel even more mortified about how badly she'd misjudged him.

"Thank you." Despite her humiliation, she managed a small smile; he really did have kind eyes. Why hadn't she noticed that about him earlier? "Anyway, my grandmother's messages are forwarded to my account, but a lot of them wind up in my junk folder. That's probably why I didn't realize who you were or why you were here. I'm sorry for the oversight—and for not giving you a chance to explain."

"It's okay. I should have been clearer this morning, but you were in a rush and I figured my room wasn't ready anyway since I arrived way before check-in time. I actually hadn't intended to come straight here from the dock—I was going to spend the day acclimating myself to the OI campus. But then I met Gina and Savannah on the ferry, and they insisted on giving me a ride to the inn, which I really appreciated because otherwise I would have had to haul all my stuff around with me."

When he gestured toward the three dark pieces of luggage neatly stacked to the right of the love seat, Molly vaguely recalled seeing them there earlier that morning. But she'd been so flustered by everything else that was happening, she hadn't given a second thought to why there were suitcases in the sunroom.

It also dawned on her that when he said he'd check in with her later, he'd meant it literally. Molly was completely abashed that she had assumed he wanted to hang out and talk to her to make Gina jealous. *They weren't having an argument—they weren't even a couple. And Matt wasn't playing games. He was genuinely trying to make it clear to Gina that he wasn't interested in her.*

Realizing how mistaken she'd been, Molly felt compelled to repeat her apology. "I really am sorry for making assumptions and for trying to chase you out of here. I wouldn't blame you if you've decided you want to lodge somewhere else for the summer, in which case, I'll issue a full refund to the Institute. But I hope you'll stay because I think you'll really love it here—and I'm usually a much more welcoming host than what you've experienced today."

"Good, because for a minute there I thought you were going to call security on me." Matt grinned; apparently all was forgiven.

"I probably shouldn't say this, but we don't even have security." Molly returned his smile, delighted he was staying. She would have felt awful for his sake and for the inn's reputation if her behavior had caused him to cancel his reservation. Not to mention, if Savannah found out, she never would have let Molly hear the end of it. "Your room's ready now, so if you want to settle in, I can help carry your luggage upstairs."

"Thanks, but I've got it." As he looped one bag over his shoulder by its strap and then lifted the other two by their handles, Molly noticed that although Matt was lanky, he was *strong*. Jordan had possessed a kind of understated physical strength like that, too. Not that she was making comparisons; it was just an observation.

Before they left the sunroom, Molly recited her spiel about the continental breakfast and afternoon beverages, and she invited Matt to use the common areas downstairs for his leisure. As they walked into the living room, she remarked conversationally, "You know, I didn't even hear Savannah dropping you off after lunch."

"She didn't drop me off. They needed to get in line to catch the ferry, so I walked back."

"Savannah made you walk all the way back from the yacht club?" *That's rude,* Molly thought. Not that she was in any position to judge, but at least her own rudeness toward Matt had been unintentional.

"It's not that far. Besides, I enjoyed seeing the harbor."

"Yeah, but it's sweltering out there today. No wonder you're sunburned." Molly realized that's why he appeared so red-faced. Although the hair on his arms and legs had protected his limbs somewhat, they were pinkish, too.

"I am? I don't feel burned."

"Maybe not now, but you will in a few hours." Molly decided she'd bring him a chilled aloe vera leaf later. *It's the kind of thing Grandma would do,* she thought, as if she needed to justify the impulse to herself.

Matt had stopped in front of the ceiling-to-floor built-in bookcase in the corner of the room and set down his bags. Craning his neck, he studied the ship in a bottle that was displayed on the uppermost shelf. The clear, blown glass cylindrical bottle was about twelve inches long and five inches in diameter and the miniature wooden ship inside it had three masts with multiple paper sails.

"That bottle looks like the real deal," Matt said with admiration.

"Supposedly, it's from the late 1870s," Molly told him. "The man who built this house was a whaling captain. In between expeditions, his crew members used to lodge here. One of them must have left this behind because Savannah's grandfather found it in the attic when he was cleaning it out before the new insulation was installed."

"Is that the original ship?"

"Yes. As you can see, the paper sails and some of the rigging hasn't aged well, but otherwise, it's in great condition." Struck by a memory, Molly added, "When I was little, I asked my father how the ship got inside the bottle. He told me

Lilliputians built it in there with tiny hammers. I believed him for an embarrassingly long amount of time."

Matt chuckled. Then he adjusted his glasses and said, "Actually, building ships in bottles is a complex art form. It involves a lot of folding and threading and the masts have little hinges so they'll lie flat when—" He stopped mid-sentence. "You probably already know how they're constructed though, don't you?"

"Yes, I stopped believing the Lilliputians built them around the same time I stopped believing in Santa Claus," she answered, smiling.

"Sorry, I get carried away when it comes to discussing anything even vaguely related to the ocean."

Molly remembered Austin complaining about Matt's boring lecture on wave formation. But she found his enthusiasm about miniature ships to be kind of endearing, in a bookish sort of way. "No need to apologize—I love sharing what I know and learning new things about the ocean, too. What topic are you teaching for your course at the Institute?"

"It's a biological oceanography class that's part of a high school honors program."

"Is that your area of specialty at the OI in California, too?"

"Well, I am a marine biologist, but no, that's not what I usually teach. I mean, I *don't* usually teach. I haven't taught since I was a grad student." He frowned, which Molly took as a sign he wasn't happy about being on faculty.

"Were you told to come here when Karen had a change in plans?"

"Told? No way. I volunteered and I was thrilled they allowed me to fill in for her, even though I don't have recent teaching experience." His face darkened to a deeper shade of pink as he admitted, "I like a challenge, but I'm wondering if I've bitten off more than I can chew. The students are very bright, but it's a big class. I'm concerned I won't be able to hold their attention and, well, crowd control isn't my thing."

"I think I know what you mean. I'm a reading specialist for middle schoolers in Delaware. Fortunately, I get to work one-on-one with them or in small groups. I'd be overwhelmed if I had to teach a large class. But I'm sure you'll be a natural since you're so passionate about your subject matter."

"I appreciate the vote of confidence." Matt turned his attention toward the ship in a bottle again. "That could be in a maritime museum. It's probably very valuable."

"That's why my grandmother kept it on the top shelf. She wanted guests to enjoy looking at it, but she didn't want it getting broken."

Just then, Lucy quietly appeared in the threshold of the door. Without looking up or entering the room, she intoned, "It's three o'clock. Time to go."

"Oh, you're right, Lucy. Before you leave, I'd like you to meet Matt." Ordinarily Molly didn't introduce Lucy to the guests because the young woman was so shy it stressed her out to meet new people. However, since Matt was going to be at Hydrangea House for ten weeks, Molly thought it might help her feel more comfortable around him if she knew his name. "He's going to be staying with us for the whole summer, so you'll probably see him a lot in the mornings and on weekends."

"Hi, Lucy." Matt took a step forward and started to stretch out his arm to shake her hand, but Molly grabbed his fingers and pulled them down to her side.

Lucy didn't acknowledge either of them. "It's three o'clock. Delores is here. Time to go," she repeated.

"Okay, have a good afternoon." Molly released Matt's hand.

"Bye, Lucy," he chimed in.

She nodded but left without saying anything aloud.

After Molly heard the side door open and then shut, she explained to Matt, "Sorry to squeeze your fingers like that, but

Lucy would have gotten upset if you'd tried to shake her hand. It's nothing personal. She's just very sensitive about people she doesn't know well entering her personal space."

"Ack." Matt pushed his glasses up to rub his eyes. "I'm sorry."

"Don't feel bad about it. She didn't even notice, so there's no harm done. Besides, it's my fault for not giving you a heads-up before I introduced you to her."

"No, I should have read her cues. What a numbskull." He let his glasses drop back onto his nose. "And I thought Gina was being dense when she kept intruding on *my* personal space..."

Molly chuckled at his remark, but she knew full well that Gina wasn't being dense; she was being persistent. *In this instance, persistence* didn't *pay off,* she gloated, still a little annoyed at the designer for being so pushy with this morning's guests.

As she ushered Matt upstairs, Molly was worried that he'd feel like the room was too small, especially for someone his height. But when he ducked through the threshold, he immediately looked at the windows and exclaimed, "I've got western *and* northern views of the water? Awesome."

Considering how unwelcoming she'd been toward him today, Molly was especially relieved that he liked his accommodation. Although she'd extended the invitation to dozens of guests already this summer, she never meant it as sincerely as when she told Matt, "If there's anything else you need to enjoy your stay at Hydrangea House, please just let me know."


It was only ten-thirty when Molly collapsed into bed, exhausted. The heavy, muggy afternoon air had lifted earlier this evening and now a dry, stiff breeze created ideal sleeping conditions. Yet as tired as she was, she lay awake, replaying in her mind all the things that had gone wrong that day.

No matter how effortless Beverly had made innkeeping seem, Molly recognized that it couldn't have always been smooth sailing. But she doubted that her grandmother had ever experienced quite so many problems in a single day, especially not problems that she herself had created.

*Maybe trying to fill Grandma's shoes was a bad idea*, she thought. *I seem to be making a lot of blunders.*

Out of the blue, she recalled Beverly's words, "Spills and stains are inevitable." Molly suddenly realized her grandmother wasn't just talking about coffee and bedspreads; she was referring to other kinds of mishaps and missteps, too. And when Beverly said that everything would "come out in the wash," what she really meant was that things would be fine in the end.

Now that Molly thought about it, everything *had* turned out okay today. Admittedly, it hadn't been a stellar morning, but it hadn't been disastrous, either. *June isn't even over yet. I still have almost the entire season to give the guests, including Matt, a wonderful stay on Dune Island. And even though Savannah already started conceptualizing the remodel, she seemed pretty nostalgic in the kitchen this morning. Maybe she'll end up deciding that she doesn't want to hang around Hydrangea House without Grandma here and she'll change her mind about shutting down the inn...*

Hopeful about the possibility, Molly rolled over, closed her eyes, and allowed the fragrant music of the surf to lull her to sleep.

# FIVE

"Did you win the grant?" Molly asked as soon as she answered the phone.

Jenny Evans, her closest friend, chuckled at Molly's impatient greeting. "Sorry, I didn't mean to get your hopes up. I haven't heard anything about the grant yet. This is just a friendly check-in to see how things are going."

"So far, so good, although I've been super busy." Molly slipped into her bedroom to chat so the guests wouldn't overhear her. "I used to help my grandmother whenever I'd come here to visit her, so I thought I had a good sense of what was involved in innkeeping. But now that I'm managing Hydrangea House and Peace Place by myself, I realize there was so much more work she must have been doing behind the scenes. I would have helped her if I had known, but I think she spared me from it because in her usual gracious way, she wanted me to feel like a guest, too."

"Aww, you were so lucky to have a grandma like her."

"Yes, I was." Tears unexpectedly welled in her eyes. Because celebrating the Fourth of July was her grandmother's favorite summer tradition, for the past few days, Molly was more acutely aware of her absence than ever. She quickly covered the phone mic with her thumb, so Jenny wouldn't hear her sniffling.

"So, what's the gossip from the inn? Anything scandalous happening?"

It was on the tip of Molly's tongue to tell Jenny about Hazel's phone calls. But she decided against it for the same reason she hadn't told her mother yet: Molly didn't know for certain quite what to make of the enigmatic woman. She needed to get a better sense of Hazel and to hear more about her connection to the inn and to Beverly before deciding whether she was trustworthy. Meanwhile, Molly didn't want anyone else to influence her perception—after what happened with Jordan, she had to learn to trust herself again. So she shifted the focus to Jenny, asking about her recent camping trip with her fiancé and future in-laws.

"Let's put it this way. It rained for five of the seven days, but everyone was still on speaking terms when we parted, so I think that's a good sign for our future together," she said with a laugh. After telling Molly about her adventures, she asked, "Are you going to watch fireworks tomorrow night or do you have to stay at the inn so you're available for the guests?"

"I'm doing both, actually. There's an amazing display over the water in Beach Plum Cove, which is on the opposite side of the harbor. We can watch it right from the back yard."

"*We?* Who do you mean by *we?* Did you meet someone?"

"Ha, right," scoffed Molly. "Didn't you just hear me griping about how busy I am? When would I have time to meet someone?"

"I thought maybe an incredibly smart, good-hearted and good-looking guest realized how fabulous you are and asked you out."

"Nope—but even if there was a guest like that, I wouldn't go out with him. It's one of those things that's sort of frowned upon."

"*Frowned upon?*" Jenny tittered. "Is that what's written in 'ye olde innkeepers' manual'?"

"No. It's written in Beverly Anderson's Code of Conduct for Respectable Young Ladies Handbook," replied Molly, only half joking. She launched into a story about how when she and Savannah were children, they were allowed to play in the back yard or hang out at the beach with guests their age. But that changed the year Savannah was fourteen and she got caught kissing a boy in the back stairwell.

"The stairwell? Not very romantic."

"Well, it was a rainy day, so there was nowhere else for them to go, and besides, they were teenagers so they didn't care about ambiance," Molly said, laughing. "It was a winder stair-case and it was very narrow, so the guests rarely used it. Savannah and the boy were sitting on the steps near the bottom around the corner, where I couldn't see them. She asked me to stand guard at the top landing. On the off chance a guest came to use the stairs, I was supposed to warn Savannah and the boy —his name was Paul Davis—by coughing."

"You willingly agreed to this?"

"Yeah. Savannah and I were a lot closer back then and I looked up to her, even though she was six months younger than I was. Besides, I wanted to read—typical, right?—so I sat on the top step for about an hour, until I finished my book—"

"An *hour?*" Jenny snorted with laughter.

"Like I said, they were teenagers. Anyway, while I was getting a new book from my room, my grandmother happened to come to the bottom of the stairwell to go *up* it, which Savannah and Paul obviously never anticipated, and she caught them in the act." Molly shook her head and added indignantly, "To this day, Savannah blames me for not keeping my word to warn her if an adult was coming, even though I was stationed at the top of the stairs, not the bottom. Can you believe it?"

"Revisionist history. It happens all the time with me and my siblings, too," Jenny remarked, chuckling. "What did your grandmother do when she saw them?"

"The boy scrambled off like a scared rabbit before my grandmother could say anything to him. But she told Savannah and me to go get our jackets and umbrellas because we were going out. You have to understand how serious this was—except for grocery shopping or running essential errands, my grandma *never* left the inn unless there was a pressing emergency. All I could think was, 'She's going to yell at us and she doesn't want the guests to hear her.'"

"Did she?"

"No. She took us to Bleecker's Ice Cream Parlor, which makes the most delicious homemade ice cream I've ever tasted. Especially their cranberry flavors, choco-cran and van-cran. They use berries harvested from a local bog, and—"

"Molly!" Jenny broke in. "Stay on topic. What did your grandmother do when you got to the ice cream parlor?"

"Oh, right, sorry. She ordered three hot fudge sundaes and sat us down at a table in the corner. While we were waiting for the server to bring our ice cream, she very quietly and calmly lectured us about how we were to conduct ourselves, especially while we were at Hydrangea House. She told us that from that day on, we weren't allowed to kiss, touch or flirt with anyone who was a guest at the inn, ever. She said it wasn't respectable behavior and she wouldn't tolerate it."

Jenny chuckled. "That was pretty old-fashioned. Kind of sexist, too, isn't it?"

"Not really. She would have set the same rule for us if we'd been boys and I think she had good reason for it. My grandma and great-grandmother—and Savannah's great-grandmother, too—worked really hard to establish the business and develop the inn's reputation. Sometimes guests made unwelcome passes at them, so I understand why she had to set a strict boundary in both directions. I realized later that she was trying to protect *us*, even more than the inn's reputation. If you think about it, we were young, naive girls essentially sharing a house with complete strangers."

"How did Savannah react?"

Molly cringed, remembering Savannah's sassy reply. "She had the nerve to tell my grandmother that she didn't have to follow the same rules I did, because she wasn't related to us. She didn't say it outright, but the implication was that she was a Frost family member, not an employee."

"Oh, puh-lease. I hope your grandmother put her in her place?"

"Yes, in her own way. She very matter-of-factly told Savannah, 'Whether you abide by my rules or not is your decision. However, if you don't abide by them, you're not welcome to stay at Hydrangea House for as long as I'm the innkeeper here.'"

"Your grandmother had that kind of authority even though Savannah's family owned the inn?"

"Apparently, she did," Molly said. "The point is, that was the only time I ever heard her lay down the law like that, so I knew it must have been a pretty important rule. Obviously, Savannah chose to follow it."

"And you've followed it all these years, too, in deference to your grandmother's wishes?"

"Yes, but not just because my grandmother would disapprove if I didn't. It's also because getting involved with someone who's paying to stay at the inn seems kind of... unprofessional." Molly didn't know how else to explain it. "I just can't see myself ever going out with a guest."

"Even if he was irresistibly charming?"

Molly scoffed at the notion. "I thought Jordan was irresistibly charming at first but look how that turned out. Besides, as I keep saying, I don't have any time for romance, especially not with a guest." Switching the subject, she told her friend about Savannah's recent surprise visit.

"Sounds like she's really full of herself," Jenny commented. "Do you think that's because of Austin's influence on her or has she always been like that?"

"It's hard to say. She was super-spoiled when we were kids, but I think that's because her mother died when she was six years old and everybody understandably felt sorry for her," explained Molly. "When Savannah's father remarried, his second wife had three babies within five years—all boys. It seems like Savannah's spent most of her life trying to regain the spotlight or prove that she's as worthy as her brothers are. She also tends to get involved with men who are a lot like her father was and I think they bring out the worst in her. Don't get me wrong. Savannah's very bright and driven and successful, and I think she should be proud of what she's accomplished. It's just that I can't stand it when she acts so superior toward other people, including me."

"Yeah, it's too bad she treats you like that. Especially since you said you two used to be close."

"Well, we weren't close-close—I think she liked my grandmother more than she liked me—but we were a lot closer when we were kids than we are now."

"Did something happen to drive you apart?"

Molly was going to say they developed different interests, which was partly true. But because she was talking to her closest friend, she confided the other part of the truth. "We had a huge falling out the summer we were sixteen."

"About what?"

"A boy, what else?" Molly rolled her eyes at herself, because it seemed like such a cliché. "See, as a kind of sweet-sixteen birthday present, my grandma invited us to spend the entire season at Hydrangea House, which was a special privilege, since we usually only stayed two weeks. But it wasn't exactly a vacation. Not for me, anyway—I had to get a job to earn spending money and to buy my clothes and stuff, so I worked as a lifeguard. But Savannah's parents were loaded, so she could just hang out, doing whatever she wanted to do all day."

Jenny bluntly asked, "Were you envious?"

"Maybe a little at first," admitted Molly. "But once I started working, I didn't mind that much because there was this really cute guy, Adam Garfield, who taught swimming lessons at the beach where I guarded. During our lunch break, we'd talk and goof around together. I *really* liked him and I was ecstatic when we started going out. Unfortunately, he had a second job as a server at the yacht club in the evenings and on weekends. So by the time our shift ended, we'd only have enough time to go hang out at the boardwalk or grab fish'n'chips at The Clam Shack. Sometimes, we were so tired from being in the sun and water all day, we'd spread a blanket and lay in the dunes, talking."

Jenny was skeptical. "Just talking, huh?"

Molly distractedly licked her lips, recalling the saltiness of Adam's kisses and the topsy-turvy feeling of falling in love for the first time. "We also watched the clouds drift by."

"That's a new name for it."

"*Any*way..." Molly said loudly over Jenny's laughter. "We'd been going out for about six weeks and he finally got a Saturday evening off from the yacht club and he didn't have any family obligations, either. So, he asked me on a date. We were just going to listen to an outdoor concert at the pavilion, nothing fancy, but since it was the first time he was picking me up at the inn, instead of going out right after work, I wanted to get dressed up. I was taking a shower when he arrived and Savannah answered the door. Once he saw her, I didn't stand a chance. Even when she was sixteen, everyone used to tell her she could be a model—"

Jenny interrupted, "Says the woman with naturally high-lighted hair and a flawless complexion."

"Thanks, but what I meant was Savannah had that *look* that appealed to most teenaged boys and she had the flirty act to go with it. By the time I was ready to leave, Adam had invited her to come with us—and she'd said yes."

"She barged in on your date? Didn't she know how much you liked him?"

"Of course she knew—I talked about him nonstop." Molly scowled at the memory. "They spent the entire night flirting right in front of me. By the time he brought us home, I felt like I never wanted to see either of their faces again."

"Ug. I don't blame you. Did you break up with him?"

"Yep. And he only waited one day—*one* day—before he asked Savannah out." Molly could still recall how humiliated she'd felt that Adam hadn't even *pretended* to be upset she'd broken up with him.

"Please tell me Savannah didn't say yes?"

"Oh, she said yes all right. They went out twice but then she decided she wasn't interested in him after all." Savannah's nonchalant indifference toward Adam had added insult to injury for young Molly, who'd cherished her own relationship with him. But at least she'd felt a tiny bit of triumph to know that Savannah had shown Adam what it felt like to be dumped for no good reason.

"So do you think she stole your boyfriend just to prove she could? Or was it that she was jealous because you were so happy with him?"

"I have no idea. All I know was that I was heartbroken—and furious," said Molly. "It sounds petty now, but at the time, it felt like a huge betrayal."

"It *was* a betrayal. Did you tell her off?"

"No, I didn't want to give her the satisfaction. Besides, she would have claimed that she didn't do anything wrong because

I'd already broken up with Adam before she went out with him." Molly unabashedly admitted, "Instead, I did the one thing I knew would really get to her—I ignored her. I refused to speak to her or look at her. I pretended she simply didn't exist."

"How did she take it?"

"She played the role of a victim and went bawling to my grandmother, saying I was being mean to her. So, of course, I burst into tears and told her what Savannah had done." Even though Molly had felt her anger was justifiable at the time, in hindsight, she wished she'd been more considerate of how her and Savannah's behavior had affected Beverly. "My poor grandma. She wanted to give the three of us a special summer together. Instead, she wound up right in the middle of our melodramatic teenage angst."

"But she sided with you, didn't she?"

"Not really, no." Molly hesitated. That summer was perhaps the only time she'd ever felt let down by her grandmother. Even though she came to understand the wisdom of Beverly's response to the conflict, she was reluctant to admit how disappointed she'd felt at the time. "In her typical diplomatic style, that evening she called us into the parlor and served strawberry-rhubarb pie with fresh whipped cream on her best china."

"Uh-oh. Dessert again. That meant a lecture was coming, right?"

"Yup. She reminded us that the reason we were invited to spend the summer with her was because we weren't little kids any more—we were maturing into young women. And as such, we needed to work out our differences on our own."

"That's it?"

"She also said something to the effect of, 'Young men will come and go in your lives, but the friendships you make with other women have the potential to last a lifetime.' Then she told us the story again about how my great-grandmother and Savannah's great-grandmother had supported each other after their husbands died in World War Two. It wasn't very subtle, but she made her point."

"Did you and Savannah make up after that?"

"Not right away. I still gave her the silent treatment for a few more days—I just didn't do it in front of my grandmother." Molly laughed. "Anyway, the following weekend the inn was super busy and my grandmother came down with a terrible headache. So Savannah and I had to take over her responsibilities. Savannah was surprisingly very helpful, especially with the guests' breakfast. After that, we sort of tacitly agreed to put the Adam Garfield incident behind us."

"But you weren't ever as close as you were before she went out with him?"

"No, we weren't. I mean, I forgave her for coming on my date and for flirting with Adam—I think she did me a favor—so it's not as if I'm still nursing a grudge over some high school kid." Molly paused, struggling to put how she felt into words. "But after that, it became difficult for me to trust her. Maybe it's because she didn't apologize or acknowledge how hurtful what she did was, but I started to see her as being, well, self-serving. As someone who does whatever she wants, without caring about how it will affect other people. Unfortunately, over the years she's done a lot of stuff to reinforce that opinion of her."

"Like closing the inn, you mean?"

"Among other things, yes." Molly could hear someone padding up and down the hall. Was a guest looking for her? "Uh-oh, I've got to go, Jen. Thanks for listening to me reminisce but now please take my comments about Savannah with a grain of salt. Like I said, she's also got a lot of admirable qualities."

"So do you, my friend. That's why I wish you'd meet a man who appreciates how amazing you are." Jenny teased, "Just promise that if you *do* get involved with someone on Dune Island, he understands it's only a summer fling and you're coming back to Delaware at the end of the season. After we win the grant, I need you here to help me plan a grand-opening gala."

"*If* you win the grant," Molly corrected her, laughing. "But don't worry, I'll be back."


Molly scurried along the water's edge like a piping plover. It was 7:00 p.m. and she couldn't get away from the inn and the guests fast enough.

It seemed like from the moment she ended her phone call with Jenny until she'd sneaked out the side door a few minutes ago, she'd been bombarded with nonstop questions and requests. Molly had earnestly meant it when she'd invited the guests to let her know if they needed anything to make their stay more pleasant. It's just that she hadn't imagined that they'd need quite so *much*, or that they'd need it quite so often.

Granted, most of their requests were completely under-standable: extra towels, ice for their beach coolers, restaurant recommendations. Even when they made unusual appeals, Molly indulged them. Like playing badminton for an hour so they'd have an equal number of people on each team. Or loaning her sunglasses to the woman in Room 3 who'd forgotten hers at home and didn't want to waste "prime tanning time" going to the store to buy a new pair.

As much as she tried to go above and beyond to provide good service, some requests were non-negotiable. No, a guest couldn't *reserve* the grill for 5:00 the following afternoon; it was available for everyone to use on a first-come, first-serve basis. Sorry, Molly wouldn't babysit for the four-year-old twins and the baby staying at Peace Place, although she was happy to provide a list of local nanny agencies. The problem was that every request, whether reasonable or not, involved a disruption of her other duties and sometimes, a lengthy conversation, as well.

*How did Grandma ever do it—and do it with such a good attitude?* she grouched to herself. *I feel like if I have to engage with one more person who wants something from me today, my head's going to explode.*

As Molly headed around the curve of shoreline, heading east, it occurred to her that the only person who hadn't asked her for anything since he'd arrived was Matt. She had delivered aloe vera to his room the evening he checked in and they'd made small talk when he came downstairs for breakfast in the mornings. But otherwise, she hadn't heard a peep out of him. *If I could give out prizes, he'd win the best guest award,* she thought.

Confident she was no longer within view of the inn, Molly peeled off her cover-up and tucked it into her canvas tote, which she set in the sand above the high tide line. Then she waded into the chilly, choppy waves. When she was chest-deep, Molly paused to adjust her goggles. Turning sideways, she orientated herself parallel with the shoreline, took a deep breath and plunged forward.

She didn't consciously choose what stroke to swim; her mood chose it for her. The butterfly required so much strength and coordination that she completely forgot about the inn, the guests, and how cranky she'd been. The only things on her mind were the fluid, undulating motions of her body, the careful timing of her breaths, and the exhilaration of being alone at last in the vast blue sea.

Molly swam until she'd nearly exhausted herself and then she playfully dived into deeper water. Savoring the solitude as she propelled herself along the ocean floor, she mused, *Now I understand why whales are so elusive.*

Eventually, she surfaced and planted her feet in the sand. Catching her breath, Molly hugged her arms around herself and faced the western horizon: it was thick with clouds. *Aww, too bad the new guests won't get to watch the sun set tonight*, she thought.

Her renewed concern about them indicated she was ready to return to the inn. She sloshed out of the water and headed back to the spot where she'd left her bag. Molly had just put her cover-up on and began walking again when she heard the rhythmic footfall of a runner coming up beside her.

"Hi, Molly." He slowed down to match her pace.

Still too giddy from exercise endorphins to feel self-conscious that a guest was seeing her right after her swim, she exclaimed, "Oh, hi, Matt. I was just thinking about you."

"Uh-oh." He sounded genuinely apprehensive. "What were you thinking?"

Molly laughed. "I was wondering if you're comfortable in your room and how things are going at the Institute?"

"My room's terrific, thanks, and so is work." As he side-stepped a spiny, dark brown horseshoe crab shell, Molly noticed that Matt's calves and thighs were already more tanned than hers were. They were tighter, too; he had runner's legs. "Classes don't start until after the holiday, so I've been working on the syllabus and meeting my colleagues. They seem like a great group of people—not hyper-competitive like the team I work with in Cali."

"Is that another way of saying east coast oceanographers aren't as smart as west coasters?"

"No. What I meant is that there's more collaboration and information sharing here. The environment seems a lot more relaxed." Matt bent his arm upward to touch the corner of his glasses. He did that a lot. Was it a nervous tic or were his frames really that ill-fitting? "Although it's possible that it's not the environment. Maybe *I'm* the one who's more relaxed here because I don't have to work on the same team with my ex-fiancée any more."

"Oh! So *that's* why you applied for a faculty job even

though you don't have recent teaching experience. You came here to get over a breakup," Molly blurted out her epiphany before she realized she was thinking aloud. She quickly added, "I'm sorry to hear that."

"Thanks. But it's not exactly that I need to get over the breakup." His voice went low and rough. "I, uh... I was the one who called off our engagement. I'm not saying it wasn't difficult for me, because it was, but I think it was worse for my ex."

Molly didn't want to pry, but it seemed like Matt needed to talk about it. Stealing a sideways glance at him, she prompted, "It must have been uncomfortable to see each other every day at work."

His curly mane bounced when he nodded. "Yeah. I tried hard not to let our personal situation affect our professional relationship, but, well, like I said, she was pretty upset with me. And you know how it is when word gets around in a small office. Some of our coworkers chose sides and it affected our team morale. The tension was so bad that I started to hate going to work. I figured it would be best to leave for a while. To give everyone some breathing room." Matt swatted at the mosquito droning around Molly's head, his fingers nearly grazing her cheek. "It probably seems immature of me to take a job all the way across the country just to avoid a stressful interpersonal situation at work, doesn't it?"

"Not necessarily. In some cases, distancing is a very healthy thing to do." Because Matt had been so open with her, Molly felt comfortable confiding, "This summer I backed out of a commitment to volunteer at a camp with my former boyfriend."

"Because you would have felt too uncomfortable working with him?"

"That was part of the reason." Molly sucked in a lungful of air and let it out before admitting, "But it was more that I would have felt too uncomfortable working with the camp director— she's the 'other woman' he'd been seeing."

"Ug." Matt winced. "And I thought *my* situation was awkward."

"Yeah, but at least I found out before I started volunteering, so I guess I dodged a bullet in that regard." They'd reached the seawall stairs on the beach near Hydrangea House and Molly could see guests milling about on the back patio. Although she was glad that she and Matt had gotten to know each other a little better by exchanging breakup stories, she didn't want anyone else to overhear her talking about her personal life. It felt different telling Matt, somehow. Almost like she wasn't talking to a guest.

Switching subjects, she invited him to the Fourth of July gathering on the back lawn the following evening. "It's a tradition my grandma started and the guests love it because they don't have to deal with traffic jams or large crowds. We sit over there near the firepit and angle our chairs toward Beach Plum Cove—we've got a perfect view of the fireworks," she said, pointing to the west. "We're not licensed to serve alcohol at the inn, but sometimes people bring beverages outside to share and I'll supply the makings for s'mores, which the adults seem to like as much as the kids do."

"That sounds like fun," Matt said. "Except I already accepted a colleague's invitation to a cookout. Supposedly, she's got a great view of the Cove from her home, too."

Molly was surprised by how disappointed she felt, but she told him, "I hope you have a good time. If you get back early, feel free to join us."

"Will do, thanks."


Although Matt didn't show up for the Fourth of July gathering, everyone else from Hydrangea House did. The family staying in Peace Place dropped by for a while, too, and the four-year-old twins were the life of the party, turning somersaults across the lawn in their pajamas.

As the sun set, saturating the horizon with a glorious orange palette, the man from Room 1 treated everyone to a violin recital. Then he switched to singing and playing his guitar. Several guests got up and danced, while others sang along, but Molly just leaned back in her Adirondack chair, taking it all in. Although she was pleased that the occasion was so festive, it was bittersweet to celebrate without her grandmother.

Feeling near tears, she consoled herself, *Grandma would have been proud that I carried out one of her favorite traditions.* The very next moment, a glittery burst illuminated the sky in a brocade pattern; Beverly's favorite kind of firework. Molly laughed out loud and for the duration of the display, she couldn't stop smiling.

As always, the show was dazzling and the grand finale left everyone awestruck. But this year, instead of heading into the house even before the blue haze had dissipated over the Cove, they lingered outside almost till midnight.

When the gathering began to disperse, a senior-aged guest with elaborately braided hair nearly lost her balance as she rose from her chair. Molly reached out to steady her and the woman, whose name was Kaye, kept her arm linked through Molly's as they shuffled across the back lawn.

"Today marks my eleventh Fourth of July at Hydrangea House. Did Beverly ever mention why I started coming here in the first place?" Kaye asked softly. Molly shook her head. "Almost twelve years ago, on September second, I was diagnosed with stage-three ovarian cancer."

"Oh, Kaye," uttered Molly. "That must have been awful for you."

"It was *brutal*," she replied emphatically. "But one of my friends had just returned from vacationing on Dune Island and she raved about Hydrangea House—and about Beverly. She told me I'd love coming here once I was better. The very next day, I called to book the upstairs suite for the following Fourth of July weekend. As you're aware, your grandmother didn't usually accept reservations until January first for the following summer."

"Right, because she wanted everyone to have a fair chance to book a room."

"Yet when I told her my circumstances, she made an exception. Such a small act of kindness, but it made such a big difference to me. I honestly believe that the hope of coming here was what got me through the next six months of surgeries and chemo. I've been cancer-free ever since then. I've been coming back to the inn ever since then, too. This place has special meaning for me, and I thought the world of your grandmother. She was an extraordinary woman."

"Yes, she was," Molly murmured, a lump in her throat. "Thank you for sharing your story with me. I'm sorry you won't be able to return to Hydrangea House next summer."

They'd reached the door to the sunroom and Kaye paused. "I'm sorry, too. But one of the things that became painfully clear to me when I was ill is that we can't take anything or anyone for granted. We can't assume we'll still have them tomorrow because there are no guarantees. We can be bitter about that, or we can be grateful for what we have for as long as we have it. We can appreciate that each day—each *moment*—is a gift." She gave Molly's arm a gentle squeeze before letting go and wishing her a good night.

Molly admired Kaye's perspective and she knew she was right about having a spirit of gratitude. But as she tiptoed through the downstairs rooms making sure the doors were locked and the nightlights were on, she didn't feel very appreciative. After hearing Kaye's story and watching the guests enjoy themselves this evening, Molly felt more disappointed than ever that Savannah was shutting down Hydrangea House and Peace Place.

For the umpteenth time, she grumbled to herself, *What's the sense in owning a home you'll hardly ever use?* It seemed like such a waste, especially when so many people could benefit from staying at the inn and the cottage—and Savannah could benefit from sharing the residences, too.

*If I owned Hydrangea House, I'd spend all summer on Dune Island and I'd come here during my school breaks throughout the year*, Molly fantasized. *I'd also allow a few teachers or visiting medical professionals to live in Peace Place or the inn during the off-season.*

The cost of living year-round on the island was so exorbitant that Hope Haven had a difficult time attracting essential employees, such as utility workers, teachers, and medical professionals. About ten years ago, Beverly had managed to persuade Savannah's father to allow her to rent out a couple rooms to visiting workers from October through late May. However, the rate he set was unaffordable for the workers and he refused to negotiate. So Beverly had abandoned the idea, which was a shame, since she would have enjoyed having company at the inn during the long winter months.

*Now that Grandma's gone, Savannah will probably board up Hydrangea House for the off-season*, Molly speculated. *I bet she won't even come here for two full weeks next summer. Even though she seems eager to start remodeling now, I know what she's like. She's going to lose interest in the house—just like she lost interest in Adam Garfield when we were teenagers.*

It suddenly occurred to Molly that she may have stumbled upon a reason to be hopeful: if she waited until Savannah's enthusiasm about the renovations waned, Savannah might reconsider keeping the inn and cottage open—especially if she could reserve Hydrangea House for whatever dates she wanted.

*The only obstacle is finding someone she'd trust enough to run the business, since she's too busy to oversee it herself,* Molly thought. As she closed her bedroom door behind her, she was struck with another idea. *Savannah wouldn't necessarily need someone to live here year-round, so why couldn't I be her business manager? I've already stepped into Grandma's shoes as the innkeeper. I'm sure I can learn to take care of the licenses and accounting and whatever else is needed to keep Hydrangea House and Peace Place operating smoothly. I'd do most of the administrative work remotely and then in the summer, I'd come back here to host the guests. If I continue to work as an unsalaried volunteer, Savannah would be a fool to turn me down.*

In the back of her mind, Molly had a niggling doubt, but it wasn't about Savannah; it was about herself. Yesterday, she'd been so irritated at the guests that she'd felt like screaming. Was she sure innkeeping was something she wanted to do indefinitely?

She quickly dismissed the concern. *I only felt that way because it was a hectic day and I hadn't taken a break. I'll be fine once I figure out how to balance the guests' needs with my own,* she thought. *There's still plenty of time for that, especially since right now Savannah seems to be going full steam ahead with her plans.*

If Savannah started to waver, Molly intended to be prepared to demonstrate what a capable business manager she could be. But it was late and she needed to get up early to go to the bakery for breakfast treats. So Molly slipped into bed and drifted off thinking, *The only thing better than paying tribute to Grandma's memory for a summer would be permanently carrying out her legacy...*

# SIX

Molly had expected Hazel might call her every day, or at least every other day, but more than a week had passed since she'd last heard from her. At first, Molly chalked it up to the Fourth of July holiday.

*Maybe she had plans to visit her family, so she didn't bother to call because she knew she couldn't come to Dune Island, even if there was a vacancy,* she rationalized.

However, by July 6, when she still hadn't heard from the elderly woman, Molly began to wonder if she'd come down with the flu or a summer cold that prevented her from calling. By July 7, she feared that the elderly woman been hospitalized. And by July 8, Molly had convinced herself that Hazel had died. She knew she was letting her imagination run away with her, but she couldn't stop thinking, *Hazel Walsh had one final wish and I prevented her from fulfilling it.*

Not that it was Molly's fault; all the rooms were booked. Still, she felt guilty, especially after hearing Kaye's story about how the promise of visiting Dune Island had helped her through cancer treatment. Although her primary concern was for Hazel, Molly also felt disappointed that she might never learn more about the old woman's connection to Hydrangea House and to Beverly.

So, when Hazel called her on the morning of July 9, Molly was elated. "It's so wonderful to hear from you, Mrs. Walsh. I was worried something might have happened to you."

"Please, call me Hazel." She was speaking at a normal volume, which Molly assumed meant her daughter wasn't there to overhear her. "I'm sorry I haven't been in touch. The day I last spoke to you I was experiencing a bout of vertigo. I got up in the middle of the night to use the bathroom and I fell and hit the vanity. Rather amusing, isn't it, since they say that pride comes before a fall? Anyway, I broke one of my ribs and chipped another."

"That's terrible," cried Molly. "You must be in a lot of pain."

"Not as much now as the week after it happened. They've kept me doped up on medication. At first, I didn't want to take it because I don't like how addled it makes me feel. But eventually I gave in because acetaminophen wasn't providing enough relief. I could hardly take a breath without weeping. I'm such a baby."

"No, you aren't. I've heard that broken ribs are one of the worst kinds of pain a person can experience." Molly clucked in sympathy. "I'm so sorry you went through that."

"I'm not *through* it yet, but I'm making progress and my daughter takes good care of me." Without missing a beat, she added, "So if you have an opening at the inn, I feel strong enough to travel. We're only coming from Boston. It's a short trip."

Molly couldn't imagine anyone, especially an elderly person, traveling so soon after an injury like Hazel's. *She must be desperate to come here.*

Reluctantly, she said, "I'm afraid there still aren't any vacancies."

"None at all? What about the room in the north-west

corner? Surely you don't rent that one out—it's too small. But my daughter and I could fit in it. She wouldn't mind sleeping on a cot."

That was Matt's room. Molly explained that it was occupied by a visiting faculty member from the oceanographic institute. "Besides, with an injury like yours, isn't it difficult to walk up and down the stairs?"

"Yes, but I'd be willing to do it if it meant I could return to the Frost home. I'd really like to meet you and as I've said, there's something I need to straighten out in person."

"I understand and I admire your tenacity," replied Molly. "I know it's not the same as speaking face to face, but couldn't you tell me whatever it is you'd like to say over the phone?"

Hazel was resolute. "No. I need to be there. There must be some way you can fit us in. The newspaper article mentioned the carriage house has been converted into a three-bedroom cottage. Are those rooms occupied?"

"Unfortunately, they are."

Molly paused to weigh one last option: allowing Hazel and her daughter to stay in Beverly's old room. She'd already emptied it of her grandmother's personal possessions after the funeral, so in a way, it no longer seemed that much different from any of the other rooms in the inn. All Molly would need to do now would be to clean it and to remove her own belongings. She figured she could sleep on a portable bed in the adjoining sitting room, which was separated from the bedroom by a door.

*I know it's a little unusual to give up my bedroom for a stranger,* she acknowledged to herself. Then she rationalized, *But it's obviously vital to Hazel to visit Hydrangea House again, and unless she comes here in person, I'll never find out what she wants to set straight about the newspaper article. Besides, Grandma always said that "going above and beyond" is the hallmark of excellent service.*

Having justified her decision to herself, Molly cleared her

throat and offered, "I suppose, if you and your daughter wouldn't mind sharing a queen bed, then you could stay in my grandmother's old room. It has a lovely view of Dune Island Sound."

"We wouldn't mind sharing a bed at all," Hazel immediately asserted. "How soon will you be ready for us?"

Molly chuckled. "When would you like to arrive?"

"Let's see... I have a follow-up appointment with my doctor the day after tomorrow. When we come, we'd like to stay for three nights. Would next Friday through Monday be okay?"

"Yes, that would be fine."

"Perfect. What time is check-in?"

"Since the room isn't usually rented to guests, you're welcome to arrive anytime on Friday. However, just in case something changes between now and then—" she was going to suggest that Hazel provide Molly her phone number.

However, the older woman cut her off. "Wild horses couldn't stop me from coming," she declared, and promptly hung up.

A few minutes after Molly pocketed her phone, her text notification sounded. She hoped it was Hazel sending her number, but it was a message from Savannah:

> Austin and I are visiting Hydrangea House on Saturday. We're not staying overnight but we'll be hosting guests at the house for drinks and appetizers in the afternoon around 4:00. I'll take care of everything so don't worry about buying extra groceries on our account.

*I'm* not *worried about buying extra groceries*, Molly thought. However, she *was* concerned that Savannah wouldn't approve of her allowing Hazel and her daughter to stay in 'the innkeeper's chambers.' But without Hazel's phone number, Molly

couldn't reschedule the visit and she doubted Hazel would be
willing to postpone it until a later date anyway.

*Besides, it really shouldn't matter.* I'm *the one giving up my
room, not Savannah,* she told herself. *If she objects or gets angry,
I'll tell her it's what Grandma would have wanted me to do—
after all, she made an exception for Kaye, so I think she would
have made an exception for Hazel, too.*

Feeling calmer, Molly read the text again. She noticed
Savannah didn't mention Gina, so she hoped that meant the
designer wouldn't be accompanying her. It sounded more like
she was coming to Dune Island to socialize rather than to
continue conceptualizing the remodel. Molly assumed the
"guests" that Savannah and Austin intended to host were their
friends or colleagues from New York, or acquaintances from
Dune Island.

*I wonder how many people will be coming here.* Molly was
concerned that the paying guests might feel put out if the
common areas became too crowded. She wished she could find
a diplomatic way to ask, but Savannah would probably get
defensive and assert that Hydrangea House was her home, so
she could host as big of a party as she wanted to host in it—
which was technically true. *Oh, well. It's only for one afternoon.
If it starts to become a habit, I'll discuss it with her.*

She texted back:

> Thx for the heads up. See u then.

Savannah answered right away:

> YW. BTW, some yacht club ppl will be joining
> us, so you might want to make sure
> everything's in ship shape (see what I did
> there? ha ha).

Molly wasn't amused. *The inn and cottage are already*

*immaculate*, she thought. *Besides, we don't show preferential treatment for anyone—including "yacht club people."*

Although Beverly may have made rare exceptions to accommodate guests' extenuating circumstances, she never played favorites. To her, every single person she hosted—whether they rented the upper level suite or stayed in Peace Place free of charge—was special and every single person deserved the same amount of respect and the same quality of service.

Because that's how Molly felt, too, she sent a pointed reply:

> Hydrangea House is always sparkling and so is Peace Place—we don't do "VIP" cleaning.

A few seconds later, Savannah responded:

> Just warning you who's coming so you won't get caught putting on another show with the gulls or parading around inside the house in your swimsuit (which Grandma B. didn't allow us to do in front of guests once we became teenagers, remember?)

No one could push her buttons quite like Savannah and Molly swiftly dictated her reply, saying, *I wasn't "parading" around inside the house in my swimsuit. But if you're dishing out advice about what's considered appropriate behavior, you might want to tell Austin that most women don't appreciate being ogled.*

Fortunately, she thought twice and didn't send that reply. As miffed as Molly was about Savannah's remark, she supposed it may have been meant as a joke, not as a dig. Besides, if Molly hoped to persuade Savannah to reconsider shutting down the inn, she couldn't afford to squabble with her over something minor.

However, that didn't mean she'd let Savannah's remark slide completely. She replied:

I'd forgotten the bathing suit rule. I only remember the one about not making out with guests in the back stairwell.

Even though she didn't mean it, she added *LOL. Thanks for the reminder*.

Savannah texted back:

YW. Glad to help prevent you from embarrassing yourself in front of strangers! See u soon.

"Rarrrrr," Molly snarled and then she slid her phone back into her pocket. Sometimes, the best reply was no reply at all.

It was nearly 11:00 p.m. and Molly perched sideways in the parlor window seat, watching the lighthouse sweep its golden arm across the harbor waters and thinking about her conversation with Savannah.

Deep down, she recognized that Savannah's comment about Molly embarrassing herself was unmerited. After all, the incident with the gulls was unfortunate, but it was more comical than disgraceful and it was a one-off. Regardless, she found herself assessing her overall presence and performance at the inn.

*I seem to have a better handle on the daily routine, especially now that Sydney has returned to work*, she thought. *Almost all of the departing guests have mentioned how much they've enjoyed their stay and the Fourth of July celebration was a huge hit.*

If Molly had a significant shortcoming as a host, it would be that she hadn't done any baking. On occasion, guests remarked that they wished Molly served homemade goodies like Beverly used to make. But as Molly good-naturedly informed them, they'd change their tune if they ever actually tasted her baking.

Then she'd ask what their favorite breakfast treats were, so she could pick up exactly what they wanted on her next bakery run. They'd always seemed pleased by her offer.

*The only repeated complaints I ever hear are about the weather when it rains and how disappointed the guests are that the cottage and inn are shutting down, If Savannah thinks I'm embarrassing myself, she should hear what people think about her after they read her newspaper article,* Molly chafed inwardly.

Although she concluded that most of the guests would say she was doing a fine job of innkeeping, she realized that Savannah's opinion was the one that mattered the most. *If I want to persuade her to keep the inn open and let me manage it, I need to make a better impression than I did the last time she visited,* she acknowledged reluctantly. *I suppose I can be a little more pleasant to her guests, too, especially Austin—but I refuse to be ingratiating about it.*

As Molly was scheming, she heard the beep, beep, beep of the electronic keypad on the front door. Not wanting to startle the person if they came into the parlor, she called in a hushed voice, "Hello? It's me, Molly. Would you like me to turn on the lamp for you?"

A figure appeared in the doorway and although it was too dim to see his face, she could tell by his height it was Matt. "That's okay, I have good night vision. Besides, if you turn on a lamp, you won't be able to see the light from the lighthouse as clearly. I assume that's why you're sitting in the dark."

"Yes, how did you know?"

He pointed at the ceiling. "I have the same view from my room. It's hypnotic—I do my best thinking when I'm staring out the window, right before I fall asleep."

Molly liked it that he appreciated how appealing the water view was, even after dark. When she'd seen him in passing earlier that morning, Matt had mentioned that he and his fellow faculty members were going to Port Newcomb's most popular restaurant after work. So she asked, "Did you enjoy your meal?"

Matt patted his stomach before plunking himself down in an armchair. "The food was great."

"And the company?"

"Welllll," Matt drew out the word. "Let's just say that eating seafood with a group of oceanographers can lead to some rather peculiar conversations."

Molly laughed into her hand so she wouldn't wake the guests. "I can't say I've ever had that experience."

"Consider yourself lucky." He told her, "At Cali OI, we have a rule when we go out for seafood together. No talking about work and no talking about what anyone orders—otherwise, you have to pick up the tab for the entire group. It's a very effective deterrent."

"Maybe you should introduce that rule here."

"Nah, I'm still a newbie. For now, I think I'll just opt out of the group meals," he said. "How was your evening?"

"Good, thanks."

"I didn't get much of a chance to ask how the Fourth of July celebration went," Matt commented, which seemed odd, since Molly could have sworn that she'd already told him about it when she'd seen him in the sunroom the next morning. In fact, several other guests had been talking about it, too.

But she answered, "It was wonderful. As you saw, the fireworks were magnificent, and everyone here had a great time hanging out around the fire pit."

"You, uh, you mentioned that it was one of your grandmother's favorite traditions." He made a coughing sound. "So I guess what I'm asking is whether *you* enjoyed it, too, or if it was... difficult?"

Now Molly understood why he'd brought up the subject again and she was touched by his concern. "To be honest, it was a little lonely at first," she admitted. "But I tried to focus on the parts of the evening my grandmother would have enjoyed, and by the time the fireworks started, I almost felt as if she were there with me."

"That's good." His smile was barely visible in the near dark. "I'm glad."

"Thanks for asking." Molly smiled back, but it quickly faded when she said, "Oh—I almost forgot to tell you that Savannah and Austin are dropping in for a few hours on Saturday afternoon. She didn't say whether Gina is coming with them, but I figured I should warn you."

"In case I want to hide?" joked Matt. "I appreciate the heads-up."

When he rose from the chair, yawning and stretching his long arms, he reminded Molly of a sandhill crane lifting off from the marshland. "You sure you can see well enough to make it to the stairs?"

"Yep." He softly wished her a good night, adding, "Nice talking to you, Molly."

"You, too, Matt," she whispered back.


After Sydney and Lucy left on Thursday afternoon, Molly went into her room to begin preparing it for Hazel's arrival the following day. Transferring all her clothes, toiletries and other personal items into the sitting room was a more time-consuming process than she'd imagined it would be. Especially since the sitting room closet was a quarter of the size of the one in Beverly's room and Molly quickly ran out of space to stash her belongings.

*I should have thought twice before I offered to let Hazel stay in my room,* she said to herself as she crammed her rolled-up beach towel into an empty space on the top shelf. But she didn't really mean it; Molly was probably as eager to hear what Hazel had to say as Hazel was to say it. *I just hope that whatever it is she's going to tell me about the inn or the past isn't anything sinister.*

Almost immediately, Molly dismissed her qualm. There was something in Hazel's voice that made her seem like a decent person. Granted, Molly had been wrong about what kind of person Jordan was—and wrong about Matt in the opposite way—but usually she was better at assessing women's characters than men's. *Still, it's probably a good thing she's coming to Dune Island—it's easier to get a sense of how trustworthy someone is in person than it is over the phone.*

Once she'd finished emptying the closet and drawers and cleaning the room, Molly thought, *I might as well sleep in the sitting room tonight. That way, I can put fresh sheets on Hazel's bed now, and I won't have to scramble to do it in the morning.*

However, she realized the folded bed she needed for the sitting room was stored in the upstairs hall closet. Since Sydney and Lucy were already gone, Molly was left to her own efforts to deliver it to the sitting room. The frame had wheels on it, so she could push it across the hardwood floors. However, the bed was too heavy for her to carry down the stairs, so she had to remove the mattress and make two trips.

She figured that if she kept the mattress folded in half, she'd have enough room to carry it around the corner in the narrow back stairwell, which was closer to the sitting room than the main staircase. But the bedding was heavier than she expected and when she'd almost reached the turn, she needed to rest her arms. As she lowered the mattress to the step, it slipped from her grasp and sprang open, knocking Molly onto her rear and burying her legs beneath it.

Stunned and sore, she lay there for a moment, catching her breath. Then she tugged at the mattress, trying to lift it straight up off her lap. It didn't budge. She pushed down on the left half, hoping to tilt it sideways so she could wriggle free and crabwalk backwards up the stairs. But it was jammed between the narrow walls. *Now what?* she asked herself, with an audible groan.

"Molly! Are you hurt?"

She tilted her head way back to see Matt peering down from the top landing, a frown on his upside-down-face. "No, I'm fine," she assured him as he jogged down the stairs toward her. "Just stuck."

"Here, I'll get you out."

When he crouched down and leaned over her shoulder, reaching for the mattress, Molly smelled the faintly musky odor of perspiration. *He must have walked to the inn from the Institute, instead of taking the waterfront shuttle,* she thought, surprised by how heady their accidental closeness made her feel.

Matt gave the bed a firm tug, but it didn't move. He tried a few more times before telling her, "That's really wedged in there tight. I'm going to go around to the bottom of the stairwell —I can't get a good grasp on it from this angle."

Aware that their faces were nearly cheek-to-cheek, Molly nodded without speaking. He tromped away and within a minute, she could hear his footsteps on the stairs below her. He easily lifted the mattress and leaned it against the wall, allowing Molly enough space to use the railing to pull herself into an upright position.

"You sure you're okay?" His brows were furrowed and he looked peaked. Was moving the mattress more strenuous for him than it seemed?

"Yep. Just embarrassed—using the back stairs wasn't one of my best ideas."

"Why didn't you use the front? They're wider."

"I wanted to take a shortcut. Obviously, my plan backfired."

Finally, a smile played at Matt's lips. He tapped the mattress. "I'll carry this the rest of the way. You going upstairs or down?"

. . .

"This will be cozy," Matt remarked, after he'd positioned the mattress on the frame that Molly had opened in the middle of the sitting room. There were hardly eight inches of open space around the bed's perimeter.

"I think the word you're looking for is *cramped*, but it'll only be a couple of nights." She elaborated, "Usually, I wouldn't sleep in here, but I received a call from someone who's desperate to stay at Hydrangea House before it closes. Since we didn't have any vacancies, I agreed to let her and her daughter stay in my room."

"That's awfully nice of you."

Molly returned the compliment. "It was awfully nice of *you* to help me with the mattress. I'm glad you came along when you did. Usually I don't see you around here until early evening."

"Yeah. I have a migraine, so I decided to cut out of work early."

"Oh, Matt," she touched his elbow in sympathy. That explained why he looked so pale. "You walked all the way from the Institute with a migraine? You should have given me a call. I would have picked you up."

"Thanks, but the fresh air was helpful."

"Is there anything I can bring you now? Ginger ale? Acetaminophen? A doctor?"

Matt gave a weary chuckle. "Honestly, I feel a little better already. After a few hours of sleep, I'll be back to a hundred percent."

"Okay, but if you need anything at all, just let me know."

After he left to take a nap, Molly went to get a set of twin-sized sheets from the linen closet in the laundry room. *I can't imagine Jordan ever moving a mattress for me when he had a headache. At least, not without a lot of complaining,* she thought, as she lifted a pair of matching pillowcases from the neat stack on the top shelf. *It's a good thing that I don't get involved with guests and that Matt's just getting over a breakup, or I might be tempted to have a summer fling with him—and I'm way too busy for that.*

# SEVEN

Throughout the day, Molly kept peeking out the window, waiting for Hazel to arrive. She'd wanted to tell her and her daughter to feel free to use one of the accessible parking spaces on the side of the driveway closest to the house, regardless of whether Hazel had the required placard or not. Molly figured she'd have an easier time walking on the smooth, flat pavement than on the shell driveway; the last thing she wanted was for Hazel to fall and sustain another injury.

But that wasn't the only reason Molly was eager for her arrival: she also couldn't wait to find out what the mysterious older woman wanted to tell her. She'd bought and set aside extra sweets from the bakery so she could offer them with coffee or tea. Molly had no idea what kinds of treats Hazel might like or if she had any dietary restrictions. But as Beverly had taught her the day she'd taken Savannah and Molly to the ice cream parlor, challenging conversations were always easier when accompanied by a sweet. And Molly had the feeling that whatever Hazel wanted to discuss might be difficult for the elderly woman.

When a metallic-green sedan with Massachusetts plates rolled into the driveway at 3:30, Molly knew right away it was Hazel and her daughter. They'd already pulled into the accessible spot, so she didn't have to redirect them, but Molly hurried outside to greet them in person. By the time she got to the driveway, the daughter was leaning down by the open passenger-side door.

"It's okay, Mom. Take your time," she was saying, as Molly reached the car.

"Hello," Molly said softly, so she wouldn't startle Hazel's daughter when she came up behind her. "Welcome to Hydrangea House. I'm Molly Anderson."

Turning toward her, the heavy-set blonde woman smiled. "Hi. I'm Lauren Walsh and this is my mother, Hazel."

She stepped back, allowing Molly a view of a petite, fragile-looking woman with a mass of short-cropped silver curls. At first glance, she seemed much older than Molly's grandmother had been, but then, Beverly always looked young for her age. Sitting sideways in the seat, with her feet flat on the pavement, Hazel was hugging her torso. Although Molly couldn't see her eyes because she wore dark sunglasses, she appeared to either be upset or in pain. In a raspy voice, she said, "Hello, Molly. It's nice to meet you at last."

"Yes, it's nice to meet you, too. I'm very glad you're here. May I give you a hand? Or take your luggage?"

Hazel shook her head and at the same time, Lauren said, "Thanks, but we've got a system. I'll get our bags later. If we could have a few moments out here alone, that might be best."

"Absolutely. Take all the time you need." Molly directed them to the ramp entry on the side of the house. "It's longer than coming directly up the stairs, but it might not be as jarring."

As she returned to the house, she fretted, *What have I done?*

*I never should have encouraged Hazel to come here. She can hardly get out of the car! What if she slips and falls again and cracks another rib?*

Molly paced the hall until she heard the front door open; they must have decided to use the stairs. To her relief, Hazel's expression appeared brighter.

"I made it," she announced, sounding winded as she leaned on her daughter's arm.

"Would you like to enjoy the view in here before I show you your room? asked Molly, assuming that Hazel might need to catch her breath. "I can make tea. I picked up chocolate almond croissants from the bakery this morning. They should still be nice and fresh."

"That's very thoughtful, but once I sit down, it's hard for me to get up again, so I'd like to go straight to our room," Hazel said.

"Of course. It's in the back of the house, I'll show you."

Lauren and Hazel slowly followed Molly through the living room and down the hall to Beverly's old room. As Molly pushed open the door, Hazel told her daughter, "This was Dora's bedroom. She was the cook who was pregnant while I was staying here."

Surprised, Molly whirled around. "You were here the summer my grandmother was *born*? I thought you and Beverly were childhood friends."

"No, Beverly was just a baby when I stayed here. I thought I told you that." Hazel let go of Lauren's arm and hobbled past Molly toward the bed. "I distinctly recall mentioning what a shock of dark hair she had when she was a babe. A dimple, too."

*So* that's *what she meant about Grandma having dark hair!* Hazel was right; Beverly had said she'd been born with a mass of dark hair that fell out by the time she was six months old. Blonde, fine peach fuzz grew in its place. "Yes, you're right. I remember now. You did say something about her hair," said Molly.

She also recalled that Hazel had said that she'd been a young girl when she knew Beverly. Molly had assumed that Beverly must have been a young girl at the time, too, not a baby. She'd thought they'd been playmates, but clearly she was wrong. Then why was Hazel visiting Hydrangea House the summer Molly's grandmother was born? *Maybe she was one of Evelyn Frost's nieces and she'd come to Dune Island on vacation.* Molly had so many questions, but before she could ask any of them, Hazel piped up.

"I'm sure you're curious about what I've come to tell you, but I'm very tired and I need a nap," she said, sinking onto the bed with her daughter's help.

As Lauren bent to unbuckle her mother's shoes, Molly replied, "There's no hurry—we have plenty of time to talk. Have a good rest and if either of you needs anything, please let me know."

"Thank you," Lauren said, glancing up. If the dark circles beneath her eyes were any indication, she needed a nap, too.

As she wandered back down the hall, Molly felt a mix of concern and guilt about Hazel's presence in Hydrangea House. At the same time, she had to admit, she was more curious than ever to learn what the elderly woman came here to tell her. *I just hope the trip doesn't wind up being more trouble for Hazel than it's worth.*

For the next couple hours, Molly hung out in the sunroom and kitchen. Even though most of the guests had gone out for the evening and Molly would have liked to take a swim, she decided to stay inside Hydrangea House in case Lauren and Hazel needed anything.

At six o'clock, Molly unwrapped the pre-made chicken and vegetable kabobs she'd bought at the farmer's market that morning. If there was one drawback to staying at Hydrangea House, it was that full meals were no longer offered, like they had been in the past. The amount of work involved in serving lunch and dinner had become too difficult for Beverly to manage single-handedly.

However, Molly suspected that Hazel might be in too much discomfort to get into the car and go out to a restaurant. She supposed Lauren could go pick up takeout or they could have food delivered, but Molly decided it was just as easy to grill enough kabobs for three people as for one, so she added extra to the tray.

She'd almost finished grilling the food when the French doors swung open and Lauren stepped out onto the patio. Molly greeted her and asked how Hazel was doing.

"She's still sound asleep, which is what she needs. I wish she'd sleep right through the night. I know how much she wanted to make this trip, but I don't think she was prepared for the toll it would take on her."

"Aww, was she in a lot of pain this afternoon?" Molly sympathized.

"Physically? Probably, but mostly, I think she's over-whelmed emotionally. When she saw the house as we pulled into the driveway, it brought back a lot of memories for her and she became very weepy. That's why I asked you to give us time alone at the car. I hope you understood I wasn't being rude."

"Of course, I understood. You're both entitled to all the privacy you want. And although I'm very interested in what your mother came here to tell me, there's no pressure from me if she changes her mind and decides to keep it to herself." Even though she was burning with curiosity, Molly knew she had to respect whatever Hazel was ready to share.

"Believe me, she won't change her mind," Lauren declared. "Ever since her friend gave her a copy of a newspaper clipping about the history of Hydrangea House, it's become her mission to speak with you in person. The first time she asked me to book a room, I was relieved when I checked the app and saw that all the summer dates were blocked out. But apparently, she called you on the sly and finagled her way in."

"I think that's because she wanted to surprise you," suggested Molly.

"Oh, she surprised me all right," exclaimed Lauren with a rueful laugh. "She didn't tell me until yesterday morning that she'd made a reservation for tonight. I think she waited until the last minute so I wouldn't insist on canceling. My mother can be quite crafty when it comes to getting her way—but that's not to say she's dishonest. She's just very determined."

Noticing Lauren's cheeks flush, Molly assured her, "It's okay, I know what you meant."

Lauren chewed the corner of her lip, hesitating before she spoke again. "I promised my mother I'd let her tell you her story directly, so I can't say anything about it. But for what it's worth, I want you to know that as... as *unsettling* as what she has to say is, I believe it's true."

Molly struggled to keep her expression neutral. What information could Hazel possibly have to disclose that was so unsettling? *It must be an awfully unlikely story, if Lauren feels compelled to preface it by telling me she believes it's true.*

"Great. I'll look forward to hearing more from your mother when she feels up to it." Molly casually replied, even though her heart and mind were racing. Because Lauren had promised to let Hazel share her own story, Molly didn't want Lauren to feel pressured. So, she dropped the subject for now, asking, "Would you like to join me for supper? I've made extra kabobs and I still have croissants for dessert."

"That sounds wonderful, but I don't want to leave my mother alone too much longer, in case she wakes up. Because of her ribs, she has a hard time getting into a sitting position by herself."

"Then let me fix you a couple plates for you to take to your room—these are almost done."

As they waited for the kabobs to finish grilling, the two women made small talk about the weather and chatted about their jobs. Molly learned that Lauren had worked in human resources, but she'd been laid off nine months ago and she still hadn't found a new position.

"It's for the best, though, since my mother's health has been so poor and she's needed a lot more help than usual. So I came from Phoenix to Boston to stay in her assisted living apartment with her for a while."

"Your mother's fortunate to have a daughter like you."

"I've been even more fortunate to have a mother like her. To be completely candid, even though I'm upset that she's been ill, I'm glad I get to spend this time with her. And I'm glad I have an excuse not to return to work for a while. If I were still in Phoenix, I never could have accompanied my mother to Dune Island on such short notice. I would have missed seeing all of this. She made a sweeping motion with her arm toward the water. "It's gorgeous. If I lived here, I'd never go farther than the back yard."

"That's how I feel most of the time, too. But all five towns in Dune Island are beautiful for different reasons, so I hope you get a chance to explore them while you're here."

Lauren's eyebrows rose with excitement but then her features fell again. "Maybe, if my mother's up to it."

*As close as she and her mother seem to be, it must be challenging for Lauren to take care of Hazel 24/7,* Molly thought after Lauren had gone back to her room with a tray of food. *I wonder if she regularly takes time out just for herself?*

After eating supper alone on the patio, Molly decided to go for a swim before it got too dark. The surf was flat and the water was cold enough to be refreshing, but not so cold it took her breath away. She paddled about a quarter of a mile toward the east before turning and heading back toward the jetty.

Molly hadn't been aware she was holding so much tension in her body—it must have been from the suspense of anticipating Hazel's arrival—but with each kick and stroke, she felt a little more relaxed. When she was even with the private beach behind Hydrangea House, she slowed and treaded water, facing west.

Numerous people had clustered on the public jetty to watch the sun go down on the other side of the harbor. Molly was too low in the water to see over the rocks to the horizon, but the sky above them flamed with color. *Red sky at night, sailors' delight. Red sky in the morning, sailors' warning*, she said silently, repeating the adage her father had taught her when she was a young girl.

She recalled that was also when he'd told her that whales could be identified by the size and shape of their spout—the vapor cloud formed when they surfaced and expelled air through their blowholes, or nostrils. A right whale had a V-shaped spout, while a humpback whale's was balloon-shaped. A blue whale's column-shaped spout was the tallest and it could be seen from three to five miles away.

*You taught me so much about interpreting weather signs and identifying marine animals, Dad*, she thought wistfully. *But it's so much harder reading people. I sure didn't get Jordan's character right and I don't know what to think of Hazel yet, either...*

As Molly was contemplating what her father might have said in response, the people on the jetty broke out in applause. That meant the sun had entirely disappeared; clapping for a sunset was a Dune Island tradition. Eventually, the onlookers meandered off the rocks and returned to their cars in the nearby parking lot or else they walked along the harbor into town.

Molly waited until most of them were gone before swimming to shallower water and wading the rest of the way to shore.

As she briskly rubbed her towel up and down her arms and legs, she couldn't take her eyes off the western horizon. While she was admiring the view, a lone straggler on the rocks stood and turned in her direction. Although she could only see his dark silhouette against the rose-stained backdrop of the sky, Molly immediately recognized him.

*Matt and I seem to be on the same beach schedule lately*, she thought. She lifted her hand and he waved back before jumping off the rocks into the sand. While she watched him jogging toward her, a shiver raked down her spine. Molly pulled her black-and-white-striped sleeveless cover-up over her head and gave her hair a shake.

"Hi, Matt. Astonishing sunset, wasn't it?"

"Yeah, sure was."

"How's your head tonight?"

"All better, thanks." He glanced at her bare arms. "You have goosebumps. Cold swim?"

"It was a little chilly, but that's how I like it." They started ambling toward the house. "I just realized I haven't seen you go for a swim yet since you've been here."

"That's because I can't." He gave her a sheepish head tilt and Molly regretted embarrassing him.

"Sorry, my bad—I assumed everyone in California learns to swim and surf before they learn to walk," she joked.

"Oh, I know *how* to swim, but it has to be in a heated pool. I'm allergic to cold water—or to cold exposure, I should say."

"Meaning... what? That you don't like it?"

"Meaning it makes me break out in hives." Matt chuckled when Molly's jaw dropped.

"I've never heard of anyone being allergic to cold water. I didn't realize that was possible."

"I know, right? An oceanographer who can't go in the ocean. It seems like I'm working in the wrong profession. Or at least, that I'm working in the wrong ocean."

Molly laughed, but she was thinking, *Whether he's at the wrong ocean or not, I'm glad he's here.*

# EIGHT

Molly woke up at 5:30 and tiptoed from the room with her shampoo, towel, and a change of clothing. Last evening, she'd completely forgotten that she couldn't take a shower after her swim because the sitting room didn't have a bathroom in it. She'd briefly considered using the shower in the upstairs hall bathroom, but she didn't want to encroach on Matt's territory, since he didn't have private facilities in his room.

Throughout the night, her skin had felt itchy from the sand and salty water, so she couldn't wait to rinse off in the outdoor shower. She slowly pulled open the hall door, hoping she wouldn't disturb Hazel and Lauren in the next room. She'd heard their voices around 2:00 and then again at 3:30, and she was worried that Hazel hadn't gotten enough rest.

The large, enclosed outdoor shower with an attached dressing room had always been one of her favorite amenities of Hydrangea House. But like her grandmother before her, Molly never used the shower between the hours of 8:00 a.m. and 8:00 p.m., since she felt it was important for the guests to have priority access to it. On rare occasions when she did use the outdoor shower during tourist season, Molly was in and out of it in a flash.

However, because it was so early and no one was even up yet, this morning she lingered beneath the steamy spray for as long as she could before turning off the spigot. Once she'd changed into her clothes, she wrapped a towel around her head so her hair wouldn't leave wet marks down the back of her blouse.

As soon as she pulled open the French doors, she could smell the delicious aroma of freshly brewed coffee, even though no one was in the sunroom. *Someone must have made a cup and then taken it back to their room*, she guessed, as she padded across the floor.

She'd hardly completed the thought when she nearly collided with a man emerging from the kitchen. "Watch it," he snarled, stopping so quickly that coffee splashed from his cup and splattered across the tops of Molly's bare feet.

"Ow, ow, ow. That is *hot*." Dancing in place to flick the drops from her skin, Molly recognized that the man was Austin.

Savannah suddenly came up behind him. Peering over his shoulder, she conspicuously eyed the towel wrapped around Molly's head. "Hey, Molly. What are you doing up so early?"

*You mean besides being scalded by your boyfriend?* Molly thought as Austin elbowed past her to return to the coffee maker. "Hi, Savannah. I just came in from taking a shower."

"Outside? What's wrong with the shower in your room?" Savannah didn't give Molly a chance to answer before she cracked, "This is exactly why I warned you we were coming—so you wouldn't be caught looking like you just rolled out of bed."

"You didn't tell me you'd be coming at five-thirty, which *is* when I roll out of bed," Molly replied lightly, with the intention of starting Savannah's visit on a positive note. "What time did you have to catch a ferry to get here at this hour, anyway?"

"We came in yesterday evening on the nine-twenty. Austin's colleague invited us to stay in his summer home."

"Oh, I thought you said you weren't staying overnight." Molly was voicing her surprise more to herself than to Savannah. She didn't mean anything by it, but Savannah seemed to take offense.

"I told you we weren't staying *here* overnight as a courtesy, so you wouldn't worry that we were going to displace the guests," she snapped, her eyes flashing. "We're staying at Austin's colleague's house again tonight, if that's okay with you?"

Molly ignored the jab and replied as diplomatically as she could. "That's great. I'm glad you're taking a full weekend to enjoy the island. Obviously, I haven't been to the bakery yet so I've got to run out. I'm getting bagels, lox, cream cheese and smoked salmon. Do you have any other special requests?"

"No. We won't be here when you get back. I was just popping in to get a recipe from Grandma B.'s recipe box before we go grocery shopping so I can pick up everything we need."

"Hmm, sounds like you're making something complicated. Of course, any meal that uses more than five ingredients or takes more than three steps feels complicated to me." She was being self-deprecatory to lighten the mood, but Savannah turned and crossed the room without acknowledging her remark.

Molly retrieved a cloth and began to clean the spill from the floor near the doorway. She was crouched down, mopping it up when Austin returned with what was apparently a cup of fresh coffee.

"Can I get by?" he asked impatiently.

"Sure." Molly deliberately rose into a standing position as slowly as she could. Staring him in the eyes, she deadpanned, "My foot's fine now, by the way. I doubt it will even blister, and I cleaned up your spill to prevent anyone from slipping and getting hurt. But you really should be more careful with your beverages, or one of these days, someone's going to sue you."

Then she hurried down the hall, leaving him to guess whether she was serious or if that was her idea of a lawyer joke.


To Molly's dismay, it was 9:30 and Hazel and Lauren still hadn't come out of their room. She'd hoped to make sure the elderly guest was all right and to ask if there was anything she or Lauren needed. But Lucy had called in sick, so in addition to saying goodbye to departing guests, Molly had to help Sydney with the housekeeping.

The next time Molly came downstairs, it was almost 11:00. When she went into the sunroom to wipe off the tables and put away any uneaten food, she was startled by the scene outside the window. Lauren was supporting Hazel as she hobbled at a snail's pace across the back lawn toward the ocean. Matt was walking with them, carrying a beach chair.

Before Molly could make sense of what was happening, the trio stopped. Matt unfolded the chair and Lauren supported Hazel as she lowered herself onto it. She was so petite, Molly could hardly see her silver head above the back of the chair, but she could tell by Lauren and Matt's body language that they were concerned about her.

*Should I go see if they need a hand or would I be interfering?* Molly wondered.

She hesitated and after a few minutes, Lauren helped Hazel to her feet and then Matt folded the chair and picked it up. As Molly watched, she was struck by their devotion to Hazel's every comfort. In some regards, that was to be expected between a daughter and her ailing mother. But Matt's display of patience toward a relative stranger—especially in contrast to Austin's behavior earlier that morning—warmed Molly's heart.

When they finally reached the sandy stretch of waterfront,

Lauren settled Hazel into the chair, facing the ocean, a final time. Matt loped off toward the shed that contained beach games and outdoor furniture, but Lauren crouched down in front of her mother, and pointed back toward the house. Then she rose and walked toward Matt, leaving Hazel by herself.

It quickly became clear that Matt was retrieving extra chairs for himself and Lauren, but instead of setting them up near Hazel, they unfolded them on the lawn about twenty yards behind her, in the area Lauren had been pointing at. Molly's curiosity got the best of her and she flew outside to ask if everything was okay.

Just before she reached Lauren and Matt, he twisted in his seat and shielded his eyes. "Hi, Molly."

"Hi, Matt. Good morning, Lauren—although I guess it's almost afternoon. How are you?"

"Great, thanks." Before Molly could ask how Hazel was, her daughter explained, "My mother wanted to spend a few minutes on the beach by herself, so Matt was kind enough to help me get her there."

"Yeah, Matt's really nice like that." Molly grinned and caught his eye. "But now that I'm here, I'm happy to help Lauren and Hazel get back to the house when they're ready."

"You sure?"

"Yes. I'd love the excuse to sit here and chat with Lauren for a few minutes."

"All right. But if there's anything else you and your mom need me to lift while you're here, let me know," he told Lauren, relinquishing his chair to Molly.

After he strode away, Lauren commented, "If only I were fifteen years younger, he'd be just my type of man. My mom took a liking to him right away, too, and it's not easy getting her stamp of approval."

Molly smiled. "How's she feeling this morning?"

"She's okay, but for sentimental reasons, she wants some

solitude. She's going to signal me when she's ready for me to head back inside."

*Sentimental reasons?* Molly didn't know what Lauren meant by that, but she figured the little stretch of beach must have held a lot of personal significance for Hazel if she wouldn't even allow her daughter to join her there. Molly felt torn between wanting to find out why Hazel considered the spot to be so special, and knowing she needed to give her as much time alone as she needed.

After a pause, she asked, "Did you and your mother get enough sleep last night? I thought I may have heard you up."

"We woke you? I'm so sorry."

"No, I was already awake. I only mentioned I heard you because I was concerned about your mother's comfort."

"To be honest, she was in quite a bit of pain from sitting in the car for two hours yesterday. Unfortunately, she says her meds make her loopy, so she waits as long as she can bear it before she takes them, which is counterproductive because then she has to take twice as much in order to get any relief." Lauren heaved a sigh. "I contacted her doctor and he placed an order for a different medication at the pharmacy down the road. We're going to pick it up later."

Molly had an idea. "I'm happy to keep your mother company if you want to go into town by yourself and do a little sightseeing."

Lauren's face lit up. "I'd *love* that, as long as my mother agrees."


Thirty minutes later, Hazel was seated in a cushioned wicker chair in the sunroom. "I'm glad Lauren's getting some time alone. She takes such good care of me that I'm afraid sometimes she doesn't take good care of herself. Now you and I can talk and she won't have to listen to me rehash my story again."

"I'm glad we get the chance to chat, too. I think we'll have enough privacy in here, since there aren't any guests around, but if they come in, we can move our conversation somewhere else." Molly would have preferred to hold their discussion in the private sitting room, where they could close the door but the portable bed took up too much space. She supposed she could have folded it up and wheeled it down the hall, but she didn't want to wrestle with the mattress again.

"I'd prefer to be here anyway, where I can see the ocean." Hazel gazed toward the startling blue expanse beyond the window. Her expression was contemplative and somber, but at least her face wasn't tear-streaked, as it had been when Molly and Lauren walked her back from the beach. It was possible that her eyes had been watering from the breeze, but Molly suspected she'd been weeping.

As eager as Molly was to hear Hazel's story, she wanted to be sure the elderly woman was comfortable. "Can I bring you anything to eat or drink?"

"I'd like a glass of water, please. The pain medication I've been taking makes my mouth so dry."

Molly had just returned with the water, when Sydney came into the room and claimed that the bottom sheet kept "popping off" the bed in the suite upstairs. It took Molly a moment to figure out what she meant. "I think you might be putting a queen-sized sheet on the king-sized bed," she guessed. "That's probably my fault for placing the linens on the wrong shelf in the closet. C'mon, I'll find the right set."

She excused herself and went upstairs to help Sydney. Molly could hardly wait to return to the sunroom to find out what Hazel had to say, but as she came down the stairs, she heard Savannah calling her name. *When did she get back?* Molly hurried down the hall to find her standing in the threshold of the sitting room with her hands on her hips.

"Why is the portable bed in there?" she demanded to know.

Molly had been expecting to have this conversation eventually, but she wished she didn't have to have it now. Because Hazel was waiting to speak to her, Molly didn't mince words. "I'm sleeping in the sitting room for the weekend. A special guest—I mean, a guest with special circumstances—is visiting, so I let her have my room."

Savannah's perfectly arched eyebrows shot up in surprise. "By a *special guest*, I hope you're not referring to one of your friends or colleagues. Because if I had known you were allowing acquaintances to bunk in your room, *I* would have stayed in it."

"No. The guest isn't anyone I've ever met before now," Molly asserted, which made matters worse.

"You've never met her?" Savannah repeated incredulously. "Then why does she qualify as a special guest?"

In a quiet voice so Hazel wouldn't hear, Molly explained, "Apparently, she stayed here the summer my grandmother was born—which means she was here when your grandfather was born, as well. She has something very important to share about the inn and she wanted to tell me in person. She's in poor health so it seemed urgent for her to come here and since it doesn't look like we're going to have any vacancies this summer, I decided to give her my room while she was still strong enough to make the trip." She was about to justify the unusual arrangement by sharing that Beverly had made exceptions for guests with medical issues in the past, but Savannah cut in.

"You *gave* her your room? But you're still charging her for it, aren't you?"

"Well, I…" Molly let her sentence hang in the air, unfinished. She was sure that Hazel would pay for the accommodations, but they hadn't discussed a room rate yet. Primarily because Molly wasn't sure what to charge her, since Beverly's room hadn't ever been occupied by a guest before now.

A smirk writhed on Savannah's lips. "Wow. You have always been *so* gullible. I've got to meet this woman." She stepped down the hall to knock on the door to Beverly's old room.

"She's not there," Molly told her. "She's in the sunroom. We were going to chat while her daughter's in town picking up pain medication for her." In a round-about way, Molly was trying to hint that Savannah shouldn't be too aggressive, since Hazel wasn't feeling her best. But Savannah entirely missed her point.

"You're *babysitting* an adult guest instead of working?"

"Shh!" Molly hissed, losing patience. "I'm *visiting* with her. As my grandmother always used to say, making a guest feel welcome is one of the most vital aspects of innkeeping." She wanted to add, *So you'd better not offend Hazel.*

"There's a fine line between being hospitable and allowing someone to take advantage of you," Savannah retorted, flouncing past her.

*You should know—you try to take advantage of me all the time,* Molly thought, as she quickly followed her.

In the sunroom Savannah planted herself in front of Hazel's chair and leaned down, a big phony smile on her face. She spoke loudly and slowly, as if she assumed Hazel wouldn't be able to hear her, just because of her advanced age. "Hello. I'm Savannah Frost, owner of Hydrangea House. What is your name, sweetie?"

Hazel seemed almost amused. "It's not *sweetie*, that's for sure. Only my husband was permitted to use that term of endearment." She cocked her head at Savannah, who drew back in surprise, as if she wasn't sure whether to laugh or not. "I can't understand why so many young women who consider them-selves to be feminists have taken to calling older women 'dear' and 'sweetie' and 'honey.' You wouldn't tolerate a man you'd never met addressing you like that, would you?"

Savannah didn't answer but Molly confirmed, "No, I wouldn't like that at all. It's disrespectful and condescending."

"Exactly. That's why I don't like it, either, even if that's not how you intended it." Hazel looked directly at Savannah. "So please, call me by my name—Hazel. I'm Hazel Walsh."

Savannah dropped her saccharine pretense and cut to the chase. "Molly seems to believe you have a story to tell about supposedly visiting the inn the summer our respective grandparents were both born?"

Molly winced, hoping Hazel wasn't offended by the skepticism in Savannah's tone. She also hoped Hazel wasn't upset that Molly had told Savannah why Hazel had come to the inn.

But Hazel smiled. "Yes. I was just going to tell Molly about that summer now, so I'm glad you arrived when you did. Since it involves your ancestors, it's something you should hear, too."

Once again, the elderly woman had caught Savannah by surprise. Had she expected Hazel to be intimidated because she'd tried to cast doubt on her story? "As much as I'd love to sit down and chat in the middle of the day, I need to prepare for guests. Molly can fill me in on your story after she hears it." As Savannah was leaving the room, she added, "It was nice to meet you, *Hazel*."

Molly waited until Savannah was in the kitchen to say, "I'm so sorry for..." she hesitated. As embarrassing as Savannah's behavior was, Molly wouldn't badmouth her in front of any guest, and especially not in front of Hazel. She concluded, "For the *interruption*, but I'm all ears and I can't wait to hear what you have to tell me."

Hazel slowly nodded, gazing out the window. "Now that I'm actually speaking to you, I don't know where to start."

"Why don't you tell me what brought you to Dune Island as a girl, and how old you were when you visited?" prompted Molly.

Hazel began. "I was eight years old when I came here to stay with my aunt Opal..."

# NINE

Molly gasped. Hazel hadn't even started her story but Molly already interrupted to utter in amazement, "Opal Brown was your *aunt?*" She didn't pause for an answer before blurting out, "Evelyn Frost's maid? My great-grandmother told my grandma that Opal's niece stayed here for the summer, but I remember her name was Daisy, not Hazel."

"Hazel is my given name. Daisy was my father's nickname for me when I was young, but I stopped using it when I turned eighteen," she explained. "Did your grandmother or great-grandmother tell you anything else about me?"

"Only that Opal's niece—*you*, I mean—had to come here because your father was drafted. And that you loved to hold the babies, especially my grandmother, Beverly." Molly marveled, "I can't believe that was *you!*"

"Yes, it was me all right, although what you heard about my father isn't quite accurate. He wasn't drafted. He could have received an exemption because he was my only parent, but he voluntarily enlisted to go overseas." She took a sip from the glass she clutched on her lap. "I'm getting ahead of myself. I need to explain a bit of my family's background before I tell you about the summer of 1943."

"Please take your time," Molly encouraged her. "I promise to try not to interrupt."

"I guess the best place to begin is at my birth, which was on February 3, 1935, in Queens, New York. My mother and father had married against their parents' wishes. My father's parents didn't want him to marry my mother because she was Jewish. And my mother's parents didn't want her to marry my father because he was poor. Both sets of parents threatened to disown their children if they followed through with their plan to wed. It wasn't an exaggeration—after my mother and father eloped, their parents never saw or spoke to them again, even though they only lived ten miles apart."

Hazel's hand trembled as she lifted the glass to her lips for another sip of water. She continued, "My mother died in childbirth when I was four. The baby, my brother, died, too."

"Aww," murmured Molly, shaking her head.

"Yes, it was very sad," Hazel acknowledged. "I have no memory of my mother, but my father was devastated, of course. A family friend named Edna took care of me during the day. She had a daughter my age named Anna and we were inseparable. Everyone called us 'the twins,' even though I had a wild thatch of brown curls and Anna had silky smooth blonde braids —or 'gold angel hair,' as I thought of it."

Molly let out a little chuckle, glad to see Hazel's eyes sparkling as she recalled her childhood friend.

"Anna and I began attending school together in the fall of 1941, when we were six. In December, the US declared war on Japan and a few days after that, Italy and German declared war on the US—but you know that already." Hazel traced a finger around the rim of her glass, clearly lost in thought, before she looked up again.

She continued, "My father became more and more aggrieved about the atrocities being committed by the Nazis. Considering the kind of man he was, I believe he would have felt impassioned about defeating Hitler, regardless of whether my mother and I were Jewish. But because we were—and maybe because he'd experienced anti-Semitism within his own family—I think it deepened his sense of personal duty to enlist. I was later told that he was so torn between serving and staying in Queens with me that he paced a groove in the floor as he was mulling it over."

In the long pause that followed, Molly reflected on how agonizing such a decision must have been for Hazel's father, and for so many other men and women in similar positions. "But eventually, he chose to serve in the military?" she prompted softly.

"Yes, in the Navy. Even though he was anguished about the possibility of leaving me orphaned, he ultimately believed the only way to provide a hopeful future for me was to join the fight against Hitler." Hazel's eyes teared up. "As an eight-year-old girl, I didn't comprehend how he could leave me behind like that, especially since I knew how much he loved me. But when I matured, I understood the depth of his sacrifice and the greater love he demonstrated by making it."

Molly leaned forward to retrieve a box of tissues from the coffee table and offered them to Hazel. She dried the corners of her eyes and then pointed to the window. "See that jetty out there? The rocks may have been replaced and it extends a lot farther into the water now, but that's where my father said goodbye to me."

*Oh! That's why she was overcome when she drove into the driveway and that's why she wanted to sit alone on the beach today.* Tears abruptly stung Molly's eyes, too, and she pulled a tissue from the box for herself. "That was the summer of 1943?"

"It was late spring, 1943. My father arranged for me to stay with my great-aunt Opal. She was already estranged from our extended family, so she wasn't worried about being alienated if she associated with my father and me." Hazel gave a rueful laugh. "Not that she agreed to care for me because of the goodness of her heart—my father paid her almost all his life's savings. It wasn't very much, but it was more than she deserved."

Molly pressed her lips together, holding her tongue. She didn't want to pry by asking, but it was obvious that Hazel didn't care much for Opal.

"I really wanted to live with my friend Anna and her family, but the previous winter, her mother Edna had become very ill with influenza and her parents came to take care of her and the children. There wasn't enough room for me in their tiny apartment, so after a lot of pleading, my father finally secured a place for me with Opal."

"She was that reluctant to care for you even though your father was paying her?"

"No, I meant my father had to plead with Mr. Frost, Opal's employer, who was also about to embark for Europe. As you must know, his wife Evelyn was going through a difficult pregnancy and he was very concerned that someone like me might expose her to germs and her health would suffer."

"You mean he was concerned about you carrying germs because you were a child?" Molly's voice suddenly seemed unusually loud. Or else the house seemed unusually quiet. *I don't hear Savannah moving around in the kitchen any more. Did she leave?* Molly had been so absorbed by Hazel's story that she hadn't been aware of what was happening around them.

"I think he may have been concerned because I was a *poor* child." Hazel shook her head but then she broke into a mischievous grin. "He should have been more concerned about his own niece, Ramona Frost, who came to visit for two weeks in early August. She was literally the *snottiest* little girl I'd ever met. The entire time she was here she had conjunctivitis and when she left, she took my doll with her—my aunt said it was a mistake but I believe she took the doll on purpose—and I remember worrying that my baby doll would get pink eye, too!"

Hazel chuckled at her own anecdote and so did Molly. As their laughter faded, she could hear Savannah banging cupboards in the kitchen; apparently, she hadn't left the house after all.

"Even though I'm poking fun at Ramona, I'm very grateful Mr. and Mrs. Frost allowed me to stay here that summer with my aunt while she worked for them. Otherwise, I don't know what would have become of me." Emotion shadowed Hazel's features as she gazed toward the ocean, clutching a tissue in one hand, her half-empty glass of water in the other. Molly waited patiently for her to speak.

"Saying goodbye to my father was the most painful thing I'd ever experienced. Later, when I became a parent, I realized it was even more excruciating for him, although he didn't let it show. Before we parted, he tried to keep the mood light and hopeful by suggesting I should write him letters. He told me I could put the messages in bottles and cast them into the water, right over there." Hazel pointed a bony finger toward the stretch of beach. "He said the bottles would reach him on the other side of the ocean. I really wanted to believe him, but I was skeptical that the tide would carry them in the right direction. Do you know what he said?"

"No, what?"

Hazel lifted her hand with the tissue in it to her chest. "He said that a message sent with love always finds its way from one heart to another."

Molly was deeply moved by the father's tenderness toward his daughter. *He knew how important it was for Hazel to feel connected to him, even though they were separated by an ocean—and a war.*

"Did you ever send him any messages in a bottle?" she

asked, but before Hazel could answer, Lauren stepped into the sunroom carrying an armful of bags. Setting them on the table, she plopped herself into a chair beside them. Her cheeks were ruddy and her hair was flat and damp against her forehead, but she was grinning.

"Hi, Mom. Hi, Molly. I hope I wasn't gone too long?"

"Not at all," her mother answered. "Did you enjoy yourself? I see you've been shopping."

"Yes. The boutiques on the other end of Main Street are absolutely darling. I can't wait to show you what I bought." She picked up a brown paper bag. "This one is lunch from Captain Clark's restaurant. I thought we'd eat on the patio, if you two don't mind the interruption."

"Of course not." Although Molly had been on the edge of her seat listening to Hazel, she knew that any second now Sydney would come downstairs and they'd need to go clean Peace Place together. After helping Lauren assist her mother to the patio, Molly thanked Hazel for sharing her story.

"Thank you for listening," replied Hazel. "There's still a lot more to tell you. Perhaps after I have a rest this afternoon?"

"Yes. Whenever you're ready, just let me know."

As Molly was helping Sydney clean Peace Place, she marveled about how sad, yet fascinating Hazel's life was. *I wish Grandma could have met her as an adult. It's amazing to think that Hazel knew her when she was a baby.*

Molly pondered why her great-grandmother Dora hadn't ever told Beverly more about Opal's young niece. All she could figure was that Dora had her hands full cooking meals—and then taking care of the babies, as well as taking care of Evelyn. She probably was too busy to pay much attention to Hazel. Dora had apparently never said much about little Ramona Frost visiting Dune Island, either.

*I wonder if Hazel was still staying at Hydrangea House when her aunt Opal suddenly passed away. It seems like that would have been such a traumatic experience for a little girl, after everything she'd already been through...* Molly speculated as she vacuumed one of the upstairs bedrooms in Peace Place. *But maybe Hazel's father been discharged from the military by then, so she was already back in Queens with him?*

Not only was she intrigued to hear more about Hazel's life, but Molly was dying to find out what part of Savannah's newspaper article she thought was mistaken, and why. *I hope Hazel's awake by the time I'm done here,* she thought. *But I'll have to suggest we chat in Grandma's room. Otherwise, we might not have enough privacy, especially with Savannah's guests arriving soon.*

Eager to return to Hydrangea House as soon as possible, Molly funneled her excited energy into cleaning, but she and Sydney still barely managed to finish by 2:50, ten minutes before check-in time.

"Phew. We just made it," she announced. "The guests will be showing up on our doorstep any second now."

"I hope they wipe their feet on the welcome mat." It was difficult to tell if Sydney was being wry or if she'd taken Molly's remark literally. Either way, her reply made Molly recall that Beverly had often remarked what delightful young women Sydney and Lucy were.

*If Savannah does wind up carrying through with her plan to shut down the inn, I hope their next summer employer appreciates their personalities as much as Grandma did,* she thought.

The two women stepped outside and while Sydney waited in the parking lot for Delores to pick her up, Molly continued toward Hydrangea House, carrying a basket of linens. As soon as she opened the door to the side entrance, she noticed the strong aroma of garlic and... was that fish? *It's whatever Savannah's cooking,* she realized.

Ever since the inn stopped providing full meals for guests, Beverly had established a practice of cooking very bland foods for herself during tourist season. She'd claimed that she could get her fill of her favorite dishes—such as seafood or curry or almost anything with sauteed onions in it—during the winter months. But during tourist season, she avoided making spicy or strong-smelling foods, in deference to the guests' food and odor preferences and sensitivities.

*Savannah knows full well that Grandma never would have cooked garlic and fish when there are guests in Hydrangea House*, Molly thought. *Especially not with all the windows closed.*

As she strode into the kitchen, which was cluttered with dirty pots and pans, Molly reminded herself of what was at stake. If she hoped to have any chance of managing the inn in the future, she couldn't risk getting into a heated exchange with Savannah now. Shifting the laundry basket to her other hip, she took a deep breath and casually remarked, "Wow, you've been busy. Is that fish you're making?"

"No." Savannah didn't turn or look up from the pot she was stirring on the stove. "It's Oysters Rockefeller."

"Right. Well, anyway, it smells delicious." Molly paused, letting her compliment sink in before saying, "At least, *I* think it smells delicious. But other people might think the odor is a little pungent. Do you mind if I open a few windows?"

"Yes, I *do* mind—it's too humid to turn off the A/C. I don't want my guests to melt."

"They're not coming until four o'clock, though, right?" Molly suggested a compromise. "Maybe we can air out the downstairs for a while and turn the A/C on again right before they arrive?"

"No, because then *I'll* get too hot while I cook. Besides, I have the vent hood running."

"I'm sure that's helping, but the odor's still pretty strong."

Savannah's eyes flashed when she finally turned toward Molly. "Of *course* food smells when it's cooking—but what did you expect? I told you ahead of time I'd be preparing appetizers."

"I guess I thought you'd be putting together a charcuterie board or something."

"A *charcuterie board* for a business meeting with a dozen people from the yacht club?" ridiculed Savannah. "As *if.*"

"You're hosting a *business* meeting?" Molly was shocked by this piece of information; she'd assumed Savannah's yacht club acquaintances were coming to the inn to socialize, not for business purposes. *Is she hosting them because she wants to become a member?* Molly hoped not; it didn't bode well for her theory that Savannah would quickly lose interest in using Hydrangea House as her summer home. Trying to sound off-handed, she asked, "Does that mean you're joining the yacht club?"

"I didn't say that." Savannah pressed her lips together and turned her back on Molly again. Lifting a lid from one of the pots, she peeked inside and then replaced it. Obviously, she didn't want to discuss the purpose of her meeting and Molly respected that. But she felt obligated to pose another question on behalf of the overnight guests.

"Are your guests going to be carpooling or walking here, by any chance?" she tentatively asked.

"A few of them are couples, so they'll be arriving in the same car but no one will be walking. Why?"

"Because space is limited in the driveway, so I want to be sure the overnight guests all have room for their vehicles."

Savannah shrugged. "If the driveway fills up, there's plenty of parallel parking in the street. First come, first served."

Now it just seemed like she was being obtuse on purpose and Molly could hardly temper her response. "The new guests arriving today will have luggage to carry. Why should they have to cart it down the street?" Realizing she was practically screeching, Molly lowered her voice and started again. "Listen, Savannah, I appreciate that you've gone all out to host a business meeting and I hope it goes well for you. But I think our first obligation should be to the overnight guests' comfort and convenience. So I really wish you'd ask your guests not to park in the driveway—and I wish you'd open the windows, too."

Molly hadn't heard Austin come in but suddenly, he was standing behind her and he jeered, "That's priceless—kind of like a case of the scullery maid telling the lady of the manor what she should do in her own house."

"Ex*cuse* me?" Molly snapped and even Savannah twirled around in surprise at Austin's remark.

"Austin!" she barked.

He crossed the room and set two bright lemons on the chopping board. Speaking to Savannah as if Molly wasn't there, he said, "I was *kidding*. It's a joke because this is an historic home and she's got a basket of laundry beneath her arm. But really, if she's going to be so worried that we'll disturb the guests every time we come here, then maybe it would be better to close down the inn now. It's not like you're going to need the money."

Molly was livid that Austin seemed to think he had the right to interfere in an arrangement between Savannah and her. Now she took a turn addressing Savannah as if Austin weren't there, referring to him with a pronoun. "You know, *he's* right. We agreed to keep the inn open for this summer only, as a tribute to my grandmother's memory. If we can't provide a high-quality experience for our guests like she used to do, then maybe you should shut down the inn now. But if that's what you choose to do, you'll be on your own for informing the guests and processing their refunds."

Molly wasn't sure why she'd said that, since it was the exact opposite of what she wanted to happen, but she couldn't seem to stop talking now. "However, if you decide *not* to shut down the inn prematurely, I'd like us to come to a better understanding of our expectations of each other, since it sounds as if you plan to visit Hydrangea House throughout the summer. I think it's important that we both feel comfortable with how everyone at the inn is treated. We can talk about it one-on-one, whenever it's convenient for you." She hoisted the basket farther up on her hip and exited the kitchen, leaving both Savannah and Austin with their mouths hanging open.

In the laundry room, Molly's hands were shaking as she filled the detergent compartment of the washing machine. Although she'd felt it was necessary to draw the line with Austin, she wished she hadn't suggested to Savannah that it might be for the best if she shut the inn down now.

*It might be best for me, because then I wouldn't have to put up with Savannah and Austin's attitudes, but it wouldn't necessarily be best for the guests and it definitely wouldn't be best for Sydney and Lucy,* she fretted, fighting tears. *I shouldn't have let Austin goad me on. This is probably exactly what he wanted—for me to volunteer to give up my role as the innkeeper and allow Savannah to cancel her end of the bargain, too.*

Molly couldn't understand why Austin would care one way or the other what Savannah and she did with the inn. Was it that he wanted Savannah and *him* to have it all to themselves for the summer? That would have been unusual, at least for Savannah, although the fact that she'd already been here twice in less than a month was unusual, too.

And what did he mean when he told Savannah it wouldn't matter if she closed the inn because she wasn't going to need the money anyway? *Maybe she's getting another promotion,* Molly surmised. *Maybe that's why she's considering joining the yacht club or buying a yacht or whatever else she's discussing at her business meeting today.*

She knew it was useless to speculate about Savannah's intentions. And even though Molly wished she'd stopped short of suggesting that Savannah close the inn early, she didn't regret insisting that they discuss what their expectations of each other were in the future. For the sake of the guests, it had to be said. Now, she'd just have to wait to find out what Savannah decided.

All three of the new couples scheduled to arrive at Hydrangea House, as well as the family staying in Peace Place, texted Molly shortly after six o'clock to tell her they'd been held up at the dock due to a mechanical issue with the ferry's engine. She was admittedly relieved. Not only did the delay inadvertently resolve the parking issue, but it also allowed more time for the smell inside the inn to subside. It gave Molly the chance to get a little fresh air, too.

In a way, she was also relieved that Hazel and Lauren hadn't come out of their room for the rest of the day. Given the mood she was in, Molly wasn't sure she'd be able to keep from bursting into tears if Hazel told her anything as sad as what she'd shared this morning.

Ironically, after all of Savannah's complaining about how humid the weather was, her guests apparently requested that they meet on the patio instead of in the formal dining room. So Molly put on her best face to greet them as she stepped outside, and then she meandered east, along the deserted shoreline.

Although the day had begun with crisp blue skies and sea, now a bank of clouds tarnished the water, turning it a dull pewter color. Likewise, Molly's interaction with Savannah had cast a pall over her hopeful mood and no matter how hard she tried to put it out of her mind, she couldn't.

She was so lost in thought that she didn't register that the man headed toward her was Matt. Or else she didn't recognize him because instead of his usual running clothes, he was wearing khaki shorts, a short sleeve shirt, and an outback shade hat. A pair of binoculars hung around his neck.

"Hi, Matt." They both stopped walking. "Were you bird watching?"

"No. I was whale watching—or trying to. I didn't see any." He lowered his voice, "Word at the Institute is that a right whale has been spotted in the Sound recently."

"A right whale sighting! It's very rare to see them here. They're endangered—" Molly stopped speaking and made a chagrinned expression. "I guess I don't have to tell *you* that. Duh."

Matt shrugged off her obvious remark. "Their endangered status is why we try not to let too many people find out about a sighting until after the whales have left. Otherwise, everyone with a speedboat, sailboat, dinghy or yacht will be circling the area," he whispered, even though they weren't in sight of any other people and they were a quarter of a mile from the nearest public beach.

"It'll be our little secret," Molly promised. Figuring the new guests might be arriving soon, she changed direction and walked back toward the inn with him. On the way, she told him about how she and her father used to eat their lunch on the jetty, in hope of seeing a right whale. Matt, in turn, said he'd once had a close encounter with a pod of orcas when he was a teenager kayaking in Puget Sound.

"It was one of the most amazing and terrifying experiences I ever had," he said.

"Terrifying? I thought it was a myth that 'killer whales' attack and eat people."

"It *is* a myth—although they do occasionally mistake humans for prey they do eat, like seals," Matt confirmed. "The reason I was terrified is that they were breaching so close to us, I was sure I was going to get dunked... Cold water allergy, remember?"

"Oh, that's right!" Molly questioned, "Even if you hadn't crossed paths with the whales, wasn't it kind of risky to go kayaking in Puget Sound? I mean, because you would have had an allergic reaction if you capsized for some other reason?"

He touched the corner of his glasses, looking abashed. "Yeah, it was risky—and stupid. I was supposed to be wearing a wetsuit. But even when I was that age, I was already over six feet tall and I was super skinny. Someone joked that the wetsuit made me look like a string of licorice wearing glasses, so..."

"Aha." Molly nodded knowingly. "There were girls you were trying to impress on this kayaking trip, weren't there?"

"Yeah. It was summer camp for science nerds." He grinned. "Anyway, when I saw the orcas, what ran through my mind was, 'This is awesome.' But also, 'If I get tipped over, I'm gonna have a reaction and die and if anaphylaxis doesn't kill me, *Mom* will when she finds out I wasn't wearing my wetsuit!'"

Molly giggled. "I'm very glad you didn't keel over—in either sense of the expression."

As they sauntered along, Matt told her about his family and his non-work hobbies—biking and rock climbing—and what it was like to grow up in California. She mentioned the grant application she'd completed for the women's clothing and coaching center. Molly was so distracted by their conversation that by the time they neared Hydrangea House, she'd almost forgotten about Austin and Savannah, and even the smell of garlic in the air seemed a little less acrid.

Savannah and her guests apparently had left, because only Lauren was lounging on the patio, reading. Matt greeted her and he continued into the house, but Molly paused to chat.

"It wasn't very polite of me to say I'd be available whenever your mother was ready to resume her story, and then to take off down the beach," she apologized. "I hope I haven't kept her waiting?"

"No, you didn't. She's actually still resting. She feels a little nauseated so she said to tell you she'll chat tomorrow, if that's okay?"

"Absolutely. I'm sorry to hear that she's nauseated though. Does she need ginger ale or is there something else I can offer her?"

"No, I'm sure she'll be fine in the morning. It's probably a side effect of her new medication."

*I just hope the smell of Savannah's appetizers didn't make Hazel feel even queasier,* Molly worried as she headed inside for a glass of water. But she immediately discovered she couldn't even turn on the faucet because the sink was stacked high with pots and pans. *Is this for real? Savannah left her dirty dishes for me to do?*

A note on the counter provided the answer to Molly's silent question. It read:

*Dishwasher is full. The pots and pans need to soak overnight anyway. I'll be back in the morning to chat and I'll take care of them then.*

Molly crumpled the note into a ball and chucked it into the bin. *Seriously? She knows I can't leave these greasy, crusty pots and pans in the kitchen overnight, in case a guest wanders in here and sees this mess. Or takes photos of it and posts them with an online review,* she silently griped. *By 'I'll take care of them,' what Savannah really means is that she plans to ask Sydney or Lucy to wash the pots and pans tomorrow, which isn't fair to them—besides, they don't even work on Sundays!*

As ticked off as she was, Molly realized it was a waste of energy for her to sit here stewing while Savannah was out enjoying herself. She also recognized that the more upset she became tonight, the more likely she'd be to say something she'd regret tomorrow. So, in her best impersonation of Beverly—which wasn't nearly as accurate as Lucy's—Molly clapped her hands and told herself, "There's work to do and people to serve."

Then she took out a fresh scrubbing pad and began vigorously scouring the pots and pans, like any good scullery maid would do.

# TEN

Molly wasn't surprised that Savannah didn't show up the following morning. Instead, she sent a text:

> Sorry I can't make it to Hydrangea House today after all, because Austin needs to get back to the city ASAP. I'll call after I get home to discuss your concerns but you won't have anything to worry about going forward.

"Humph." Molly was puzzled by what seemed like Savannah's conciliatory tone. It wasn't like her to back down. What could have happened to cause her sudden change of heart?

Was it possible that she'd broken up with Austin, so they wouldn't be coming back; hence, Molly wouldn't have anything to worry about going forward? *Nah, that would be too good to be true*, she thought facetiously.

She typed her reply, keeping it short and sweet:

> Sounds good. Talk to you later.

Almost as soon as she sent the text, she received a phone

call from Delores, the manager of the home where Lucy and Sydney lived. She said she was sorry to call so early, but she wanted Molly to know that Sydney had been very upset after work yesterday. Apparently, while she'd been waiting outside for Delores to pick her up, she noticed a wrapper in the driveway. As she was bending to pick it up, a guest drove into the parking space beside her very quickly and nearly hit her.

"I didn't see it happen, but I believe her," Delores said. "She was quite shaken up—not because she was almost hit but because when the driver got out of the car, apparently he called her an idiot."

"That's terrible! I'm so sorry that happened." Molly believed Sydney, too, but she couldn't imagine any of the current guests behaving so rudely. "Did you ask her who the driver was?"

"She didn't want to tell me at first, but eventually she described him as having mean eyebrows and a lip that sticks up on one side. I don't know what that means."

"I think I do," Molly muttered. Sydney must have been referring to Austin. He wore a perpetual sneer and he had arrived at around the same time Sydney left yesterday. "I'll speak to the person and make sure it doesn't happen again— neither the reckless driving, nor the name calling. I'm very glad you told me about it."

"I thought it was necessary, since we don't tolerate any type of workplace mistreatment of the women from our house."

"Neither do I," Molly assured her.

After ending the call, she felt even more strongly than before about setting expectations and drawing boundaries for Austin's behavior at Hydrangea House. It took all her willpower not to call Savannah right then, but Molly had spoken rashly to her once already. If she reacted now while she was angry, she'd undoubtedly make things worse, instead of better.

Besides, she had to make sure the current guests had everything they needed, including breakfast. *I'm glad I didn't take Savannah at her word about doing dishes. Otherwise, I'd have to navigate around her mess this morning,* she thought as she arranged an assortment of pastries on a platter.

To Molly's delight, Hazel and Lauren were the first guests to show up in the sunroom. Although Hazel had dark circles under her eyes, when she remarked how delicious everything looked, Molly took it as a sign she was no longer queasy. She asked her how she felt.

"Much better, thank you," she replied. "The only thing wrong with my stomach now is that it's empty. But once I have a bite to eat—and when you have the time, too—I really do need to finish our discussion."

"I'd like that very much. I have a few things to do this morning, but I should be available after ten o'clock. Where would you like to chat today?"

"Somewhere private. I don't want anyone else to hear—except Savannah. I don't suppose she's available to be included in our conversation today, is she?"

Molly's curiosity was piqued; Hazel wanted privacy, yet once again she wanted Savannah to join them? She answered, "Unfortunately, Savannah already left Dune Island for New York City, but I'll be sure to share whatever you'd like me to tell her. As for privacy, would it be okay to meet in the room you're staying in, so we can close the door? The guests rarely ever use that hall, so there's not much of a chance they'll pass by and overhear us."

Hazel agreed and they met shortly after 11:00. Once again, Lauren took the opportunity to explore the area; this time, she went for a walk on a bayside beach in Lucinda's Hamlet.

"Where did I leave off yesterday?" asked Hazel. She was seated in the oversized armchair Beverly used to favor for reading. Molly was using the desk chair, which she positioned adjacent to Hazel.

"You were telling me about you and your father saying goodbye to each other. He'd suggested that you could send him a letter in a bottle... I was curious to find out if you ever did that or not."

"Not at first, no. Even supplies like paper and glass were scarce during that time. Besides, my aunt kept me too busy for letter writing. I helped her wash the windows, mop the floors and change the beds. I was also responsible for gathering all the dirty clothes and linens. Monday was laundry day, which was my aunt's most dreaded chore."

"Why was that?"

"Back then, we didn't have the kind of washers and dryers or even detergents like we have now. So washing clothes was an all-day process—it actually began on Sunday night, when she filled the copper tubs and sorted and soaked the clothing. Then the next day was the scrubbing and agitating and running the items through the wringer by hand, before finally hanging them on the line to dry." Hazel shook her head, apparently reimagining the steps.

"No wonder she disliked the process so much," said Molly.

"Yes, it was grueling, but most women of that era—especially those who were maids—were used to it. Mrs. Frost *did* have an electric iron for Opal to use, which was considered quite the luxury. But my aunt absolutely hated doing the laundry and I'm sorry to say that she bore quite a grudge against your great-grandmother, because Dora wasn't expected to help with it."

"That's a shame. From what I heard from my grandmother I thought Dora would pitch in with everything, even though she was hired as the cook." Molly thought back to Beverly's stories of her mother.

"Oh, yes, she did help with things like sweeping and

dusting and occasionally making the beds. But because Dora was 'with child,' Mrs. Frost insisted she shouldn't do any of the more strenuous housework, especially laundry. She wouldn't permit me to help Opal with it, either, since I was only a child and she didn't want me to get my fingers crushed in the wringer."

Molly commented, "That seems fair. You were too young to operate the machinery."

"Yes, but my aunt wasn't a very reasonable person. According to what I later learned, she'd been mistreated by her family when she was a girl. I believed it influenced her perspective. In any case, she was very resentful of any kind of perceived favoritism toward your great-grandmother," explained Hazel. "For instance, I loved spending time with Dora. I always wanted to help her measure ingredients or set the table and dry the dishes. But when my aunt found out what I was doing, she forbade me to go into the kitchen. She said if I didn't want to play on the beach during my spare time, she'd give me more chores to do. And she threatened that if she ever caught me helping Dora again, I'd have to sleep in the basement with the rats."

Molly gasped. "That's so cruel!"

"As I said, I think she was imitating how her parents treated her. I don't know whether the basement even did have rats or if she only said that to frighten me into obedience, but after that, I stayed as far away from the kitchen as I could."

*Is that why my great-grandmother didn't have much to say about Hazel? Was it because she rarely saw her?* Molly wondered. "Which room was your bedroom?"

"The littlest one in the back of the house upstairs. Opal slept in the room next to mine, which was unusually large for a domestic servant, especially because she had it all to herself. But rather than appreciate the fact Mrs. Frost gave us each a separate bedroom, Opal was bitter because Dora had *two* rooms

—this bedroom and the sitting room next door. She griped about it all the time under her breath. That was how I learned about everything that was going on in the house—I listened to Opal muttering. Even though she complained to herself or occasionally to me, she never would have voiced her discontentment to Mrs. Frost, not even when there was a legitimate reason. Like when the Frosts' niece Ramona took my doll home with her, I wanted to write and ask her to send it back, but Opal told me I couldn't."

"Why not?"

"She was concerned that if Mrs. Frost found out I'd asked for my doll back, she'd be offended that we'd implied her niece had done something wrong. Opal was very afraid of getting fired, so she was extremely deferential to the 'master and mistress' of the house, as she sometimes referred to Mr. and Mrs. Frost."

Inwardly, Molly winced, thinking of Austin's comment about Savannah being "the lady of the manor," and Molly being the scullery maid. Whether he was joking or not, there was a time not so long ago when the inequality between those positions was very distinct within Hydrangea House. At least, that's how Opal apparently saw it.

"My aunt may have wanted more space, but I loved my comfy little cabin," Hazel recalled. "At night, I'd listen to the waves and pretend I was on a ship, just like my papa was."

Molly was struck by how lonely Hazel's experience on the island must have been. "Did you make any friends your age while you were here?"

"No. The island wasn't very populated then. The few families who came to Port Newcomb with children were usually quite wealthy and they mostly resided on the other end of Main Street. But I had my imagination and my doll to keep me company—until Ramona Frost took her."

Hazel stopped speaking to rub her lips together, a twinkle in her eye. "I remember when Ramona, her three older brothers and her mother came to visit, Dora made lemon meringue pie. It was only supposed to be served to the Frost family, but your great-grandmother set a sliver of it aside for me. To this day, it was the best lemon meringue pie I've ever eaten in my life. I don't know if it tasted so delicious because Dora was such a talented baker or because her kindness toward me made it seem that much sweeter."

Molly smiled, thinking how similar her grandmother and great-grandmother were, in that they especially enjoyed sharing treats with people they liked. "Probably a little bit of both."

"Yes. Probably." Hazel wrung her hands, a far-away look in her eyes as she gazed toward the window. "I suppose I've dilly-dallied in setting the stage long enough. It's time to tell you about the mistake I came here to correct."

"It doesn't seem like you've been dilly-dallying," Molly assured her. "I could listen to you tell stories about the past all day."

"You might not feel that way after what I tell you about the night of your grandmother's birth." Hazel restlessly shifted in her chair, and Molly wasn't sure whether she was physically or emotionally in pain.

Although she could hardly bear the suspense of waiting to hear what the elderly woman meant by her warning, she interrupted her to ask, "Would you like a small pillow to put behind your back? You seem uncomfortable."

After Molly helped her into a more supportive sitting position, Hazel continued. "The newspaper account was correct in stating that there was a violent storm that evening. It was one of the fiercest, longest-lasting electrical storms I've ever witnessed. Even though it knocked out our power, the lightning was so constant it lit up the rooms. I wasn't a child who was normally afraid of thunder, but this was deafening and the wind and waves were roaring, too."

Molly empathized, "Even ordinary summer thunderstorms always sound much louder here than they do off-island."

"Yes, but as booming as this one was, I could still hear Mrs. Frost when she began screaming. At first, I thought she was as terrified of the storm as I was, but her cries didn't correspond to the timing of the thunder and lightning... Instinctively, I realized she was in pain, but I couldn't understand why, and I was too scared to go find out."

Molly could imagine how confusing this situation must have been for Hazel as a little girl. "You were in bed when she went into labor?"

"Actually, I was crouched in my closet, with a pillow over my head. The closet was my hiding place..." Hazel shivered, and rubbed her upper arms. "Shortly after Evelyn started screaming, my aunt shouted my name. She sounded so stern that I was more afraid of disobeying her than I was of the storm, so I ran down the hall to Evelyn's room. Opal told me to go tell Dora to bring her more water and towels. I bolted downstairs and I found Dora moaning in bed." Hazel paused and her lips twitched with amusement. "Can you believe I thought, 'Oh, no. Poor Dora has a bad stomachache, too, just like Mrs. Frost'?"

Molly exhaled as the moment of levity broke the tension. "In a way, you were right."

"Yes, but I thought they were sick because of something Dora had served for supper and I was worried that she was going to be fired," Hazel said. "Anyway, Dora wanted to sit up straight, so I arranged pillows behind her back, but she kept moaning. Then I helped her roll onto her hands and knees, but that didn't help either. No matter what we did, she couldn't find a comfortable position. I was there for quite a while and I was afraid Opal was going to be angry at me for taking so long to return, but Dora was in terrific pain. I couldn't just leave her there alone."

*That's because, even though you were only a little child, you understood how it felt not to have anyone around to comfort you,* Molly thought, swallowing hard. *Thank you. Thank you for staying with my great-grandmother.*

"Eventually her contractions subsided enough that I told her what Opal had said. Dora directed me to get the towels and water by myself and I ran upstairs with it. By then, Evelyn had stopped screaming. She was so silent and still, I thought she had died, but as the lightning flashed, I noticed her nightgown fluttering with the slight rise and fall of her chest."

"Was your aunt still in the room?" asked Molly.

"Oh, yes. Opal was bending over the wash basin on the dresser. Her back was turned toward me and suddenly, in between thunder peals, I heard the faintest whimper. It finally dawned on me that Evelyn had given birth. Opal had already cleaned the baby and I gave her the towels so she could swaddle it. When she asked where Dora was, I told her that she was in too much pain to get out of bed. Opal ordered me to sit in the rocking chair. She gave me the baby to hold while Mrs. Frost was sleeping and then she flew downstairs."

Although Molly already knew that her great-grandmother and grandmother both survived childbirth, she was on pins and needles waiting to hear what happened to Dora, but she refrained from prompting Hazel, who'd gone quiet again. Her arms were bent at the elbows and she clasped them together, as if she were cradling a newborn.

"I'll never forget how tiny Mrs. Frost's baby was, or the way its lips pursed as it made little kissing movements. It was the tiniest, sweetest little thing I ever saw. I remember thinking, 'I don't care if Ramona stole my doll any more—I have a real, live baby to hold.'"

Molly giggled; even as a child, Hazel's sense of humor was apparent.

"A few minutes later, Opal came back. She said Dora was doing fine on her own and nature would take its course. My aunt had absolutely no compassion for her." Hazel clicked her tongue against her teeth in disgust. "Her only loyalty was to Mrs. Frost. Opal tried to rouse her so she could nurse the baby, but she wouldn't open her eyes. After examining her, my aunt ordered me to go tell the neighbor we needed a doctor because Mrs. Frost was hemorrhaging. I didn't know what that word meant, but I understood it was very serious."

"She sent *you* out in the storm?" Molly exclaimed. "I understand why she couldn't call the doctor if the phone lines were down, but why didn't *she* go to the neighbor's house?"

"At that time, the nearest neighbor's house was almost half a mile down the road. She didn't know how to drive and she was probably in her late fifties by then, so I could run much faster than she could have run."

"But you were so young and it was the middle of the night. You must have been scared to death."

"I was. But before my father left, he told me my duty was to obey whatever my aunt asked of me, without complaining. So I tried to be brave. I had to go to three houses before I found someone who hadn't left the island for the season yet. I recall that Mr. and Mrs. Burke were in their bath robes when they opened their door. They quickly changed and then Mr. Burke dropped me and his wife off here, at the house, before he went to fetch the nearest GP. The doctor was able to stop the bleeding, but Mrs. Frost was weak for a long time after that."

Molly was quiet for a moment as she absorbed what Hazel had just told her about Opal. Until now, she'd always considered the Frost family's maid to be something of an unsung hero for single-handedly delivering two babies in the middle of a storm. But it turned out that she'd only delivered Evelyn's son, Harold, not Dora's daughter, Beverly. Assuming what Hazel said was true and she was the one who'd run through the rain and lightning to get help, then it was *Hazel*, not Opal, who had essentially saved Evelyn's life. And it was Hazel who had been more helpful to Dora during labor than Opal had been. *No wonder she said the newspaper account got the story wrong.*

"I'm so sorry that our families never gave you credit for doing what you did," Molly apologized. "I'm sure my great-grandmother didn't know, because—"

"She *definitely* didn't know," Hazel cut in. "The next day my aunt made me promise never to mention to anyone—especially not to Mrs. Frost—that she'd sent me out in the rain. I think she was afraid she'd get in trouble, even though it was an emergency and she had no other choice. Either that, or she didn't want *me* to get any accolades that she felt *she* deserved. Of course, the Burkes knew I was the one who'd knocked on their door, but everything was so chaotic that night, that by the time the doctor arrived, it hardly mattered how he got there."

"But it *did* matter. If it weren't for you being so brave—"

Again, Hazel interrupted. "I'm not telling you this because I want your acknowledgment. I'm telling you because I need your forgiveness."

"Forgiveness? For what? You were a *hero!*"

"No. I wasn't. I was a coward." Hazel's voice dropped. It seemed as if she were speaking to herself, not to Molly. "Even if it was understandable when I was a child, once I became an adult, there was no excuse. Especially after I had children of my own. I always second-guessed myself, because of the fever. Or maybe it was denial—I wanted to believe I'd imagined it. Now that I'm here again, I know for certain that what I thought happened really did."

Her rambling didn't make any sense to Molly, but from the way her voice was quaking, it was clear she was on the verge of tears. "Would you like to take a break for a few minutes?"

"No. It's better for me to press on, although I'm afraid what I have to say will be as shocking to you as it was to me... Maybe *you'd* like to take a break to prepare yourself? Perhaps get a glass of water?"

After a lead-in like that, Molly could hardly bear the suspense another second. "That's okay. Please continue."

Hazel licked her lips. "The morning after the storm, while the doctor and nurse were tending to Mrs. Frost in her room, I went downstairs and saw Opal in the parlor. She was cooing and smiling at the baby in one arm and gently stroking its cheek with the other—I'd never heard her sound so affectionate. She said, 'Come, see Mrs. Frost's darling bundle of joy.' So I skipped over to take a peek." Hazel's eyes went wide as if she were picturing the newborn in her memory. "As soon as I saw its face —I didn't even know the child's name or gender—I exclaimed, 'What happened to Mrs. Frost's baby?'"

"What do you mean?" Molly blurted out. "What was wrong?"

"The baby looked so different. It was as if it had gained three pounds overnight. Instead of having a mass of dark hair, its hair was reddish." Hazel met Molly's eyes and nodded gravely, as if to communicate some horrible truth.

Molly cocked her head. "I don't understand."

"It wasn't the same baby I'd held the night before. It was *Dora's* child, not Mrs. Frost's." Hazel tapped a finger against her palm emphatically as she said the women's names.

"Opal made a mistake?" Molly could understand how that had happened since Hazel's great-aunt undoubtedly had been awake all night. In her exhaustion, she must have gotten confused over whose baby was whose.

"No, there was no mistake. It was deliberate. She *switched* Evelyn and Dora's babies on purpose," Hazel cried, her voice cracking with emotion.

"What? No way!" Molly couldn't censor her knee-jerk reaction. She didn't mean to imply Hazel was lying, but she couldn't fathom someone doing something so preposterous, except maybe on a TV soap opera. "There hadn't been any lights on the night before when you were holding the baby. Maybe you didn't get a good look at him?"

"That's what I tried to tell myself repeatedly in the years that followed. But the night of the storm I hadn't been able to take my eyes off Mrs. Frost's baby." Hazel's tone was resolute. "The baby Opal was holding the next morning had a much rounder face. His cry was more robust, too. He even smelled different than Mrs. Frost's baby."

Molly could hardly speak. "But-but my great-grandmother and Evelyn would have noticed the differences, too—especially since the babies were different genders. It would have been obvious if Opal had switched their babies."

"Not if she switched them before either woman got her first glimpse of her own child," Hazel argued. "Consider this. Evelyn was barely conscious following the delivery. She couldn't even open her eyes, so she wasn't cognizant enough to know whether she gave birth to a boy or a girl, or even if the baby survived. It was almost three days before she was able to hold her child—rather, to hold the little boy she *thought* was her child."

Although the scenario Hazel described was possible, it didn't seem plausible to Molly. "What about Dora? She was conscious after she'd given birth, wasn't she?"

"Yes, as far as I know. But I'm sure that as soon as her son was born—it must have happened when I was running to the neighbor's house—Opal whisked him into another room before Dora could see him. She probably made an excuse, saying she needed to go clean and swaddle the baby. When she returned, she must have given Mrs. Frost's baby to Dora."

Molly wasn't convinced. "I've never given birth, but I can't imagine a mother not knowing which baby is hers... it just seems like it would be instinctual."

"My aunt knew what she was doing. When she gave Beverly to Dora, that tiny babe was desperate to suckle. I don't have to explain to you about hormones and how quickly a mother bonds with a child... By the time Dora and Mrs. Frost saw each other's babies, both women were already blinded by love for who they thought was their own son or daughter."

Molly had no doubt that as a little girl, Hazel had earnestly believed her aunt had switched the babies, but that didn't necessarily mean it had happened. After all, hadn't Hazel said she'd had a good imagination? What better person to create a fairy tale about than a sinister great-aunt. "How did Opal respond when you asked her what happened to Evelyn's baby?"

"She said, 'What do you mean? This little boy is perfect.' I said, 'But it's not Mrs. Frost's baby. Hers was littler, with black hair.' Opal reached out with one hand and slapped me across the face." Hazel touched her cheek, as if it still stung, decades later. "Her response proved to me that I was right. She told me to shut my mouth and said that if I ever told a lie like that again and it got back to Mrs. Frost, she'd kick us both out of the house. We'd be homeless and then when my father returned from the war and tried to find me, he'd think I died and he'd start a new life with a new wife and daughter."

"What a terrible thing to tell a child!" cried Molly.

"Yes. But for once, I was defiant. I felt so bad that Mrs. Frost and Dora had been given the wrong babies that I stuck my chin in the air—the tears were streaming down my face—and I said, 'I'll wait until my papa gets back and then I'll tell *him*.'"

Molly cringed. "Please don't tell me she struck you again?"

"No, although it might have been better if she had. Instead, she leaned forward and hissed, 'You stupid little girl. If you do that and the authorities believe you, they'll ship you off to prison for not telling anyone sooner. Either way, you'll never see your precious papa again.'" Hazel slowly leaned back in her chair, with a defeated sigh. "To guarantee my silence, she threatened the loss of what was most important to me—and it worked."

"But why would Opal switch the babies in the first place?

Even if she was envious of Dora, it doesn't seem like enough motivation for doing something so serious and deceptive."

"From what I could glean, she'd been almost certain that neither Mrs. Frost nor baby Beverly would survive. In the days following the birth, I'd hear her muttering things like, 'At least Mr. Frost will have a male heir to comfort him in his grief.' Or, 'Mr. Frost will be so pleased I helped deliver his healthy baby boy.' Once I even heard her say, 'If Dora knew, she'd thank me that her son won't grow up poor.'" Hazel sighed. "I think my aunt wanted to gain special favor from her employer. She rationalized her actions by telling herself that she was sparing Dora's son a life of poverty, and sparing Mr. Frost the devastation of losing both his wife and baby."

Molly was shocked. "She thought the girl baby would die—so she gave Evelyn the little boy? And she believed she was doing it for their own good?"

"I wouldn't go that far. Above anything, she was motivated by her desire for recognition, which she thought she'd receive from Mr. Frost. Her logic was twisted and what she did was unforgivable, but I don't think she was utterly without conscience. In fact, when she died suddenly, I believe it was guilt, not pericarditis, that killed her."

"Our emotions can definitely take a toll on our physical health," acknowledged Molly.

"Yes. Especially when someone's hiding a terrible secret, like Opal and I were," Hazel said. "My health was affected, too. After I discovered what she had done, I was sick to my stomach. For the next month, I could hardly eat a bite or sleep a wink. Dora was caring for both Evelyn and for Opal, who by then had taken ill. So I was allowed to hold Beverly for as long as I wanted, which made me feel so conflicted. On one hand, I loved this tiny little girl and I could see how much Dora loved her, too. Yet all I could think about was how wrong it was that Evelyn and Dora had each other's babies and they weren't aware of it. I finally decided that I was going to tell my papa what happened, because he'd advise me what to do. So that evening, I wrote him a note and rolled it up and put it in a bottle, just like he'd said I should. Then I hid it beneath a loose floorboard in my closet, planning to cast it into Dune Island Sound the next morning."

"But you didn't?" Molly asked, because she could tell from Hazel's dejected expression that something had prevented her from "sending" the message to her father.

"No, I didn't. A little before sunrise, a car pulled up to the house. Dora had called the doctor because Opal was barely breathing, but by the time he arrived, she had passed away." Hazel's lower lip trembled. "I felt like it was my fault that she'd died. I kept thinking that I shouldn't have threatened that I was going to expose her secret—and I definitely shouldn't have written about it to my father."

"It wasn't your fault at all," murmured Molly, even though she could understand why, from a child's perspective, it had felt that way to Hazel.

"I can't recall much of what happened over the course of the next several days. I must have been in shock. At around that same time, I came down with a virus—the guilt flu, I guess you'd call it, kind of like what happened to Opal." Hazel tried to joke, but her eyes were brimming with tears and she was shaking her head. "It seemed like the next thing I remembered, I was back in Queens with Anna and her family. Apparently, once my health improved and I was no longer contagious, Dora arranged for our old family friends to come and get me."

Molly let out an empathetic sigh. "You must have been so relieved to be with them again?"

"Yes. I was especially glad to see my special friend Anna." Hazel nodded for emphasis. "But things weren't quite the same. For one thing, I was weak from being so ill. For another, I'd been traumatized. The way I coped was to tell myself that what happened that summer was all part of a bad dream. Or that my mind had played tricks on me because I'd had such a high fever. I figured that once my papa came back from the war, he'd help me make sense of things again. So I put everything that happened on Dune Island out of my mind. I focused on my schoolwork and playing hopscotch with Anna or kick-the-can with her brothers and other kids from the neighborhood... and I tried to be a normal child."

"Did your father return soon after that?" asked Molly.

"No. The following February, his ship was destroyed. Everyone aboard died."

"Oh, Hazel." Molly gently touched the elderly woman's arm. *After making it through so many hardships, the poor little girl lost her father—it doesn't seem fair.* "How painful that must have been for you."

"Yes, it was." The long pause that followed was more telling than any other words Hazel could have added. Eventually, she spoke again, changing her focus. "I was fortunate that Edna and her husband Louis loved me and raised me as their own child. However, once again, I felt misplaced guilt. I thought I was being punished because I *hadn't* confessed what Opal had done. It was as if my father's death was my just dessert."

Molly didn't understand what she meant; to her, Hazel's circumstances seemed nothing but tragic. "Your just dessert?"

"Yes, I was getting what I deserved in the sense that Louis and Edna weren't my biological parents, just like Evelyn wasn't Harold's mother and Dora wasn't Beverly's mother either," explained Hazel. "You'd think the guilt would have caused me to break down and tell the truth. Instead, it made me bury the secret further in the recesses of my mind."

Although Molly was curious about what had compelled Hazel to share her story now, she didn't want to ask her directly —especially since she suspected it was a sort of end-of-life confession. She waited a moment and Hazel offered an unprompted explanation.

"When I saw the newspaper clipping, all the memories came flooding back and I told my daughter everything. I thought it would be cathartic to finally admit to another person what I'd done. But I quickly realized it wasn't enough to clear my conscience for my own sake. I had to come and tell you, too, and offer my sincerest apologies. Lauren didn't want me to—she said it would be too disruptive. But I believe you and your family deserve to know your true identity. I can't change what I did in the past, but by telling you, maybe I can change the future."

"The future?" Molly repeated numbly.

"Yes, the future. Or, more accurately, the present. In the paper it said that after Beverly died, control of the house would revert to Evelyn Frost's eldest descendant. From what I read in the article, your grandmother had at least one child, a son."

"Th-that was my father, but he died over a decade ago," stammered Molly. "My grandmother didn't have any other children. So if what you're telling me is true, then *I'm* Evelyn Frost's eldest living descendant."

"In that case, the Frost estate belongs to *you*."

# ELEVEN

Molly couldn't let her mind go there yet. She could barely figure out whether Hazel's story could be true, much less wrap her brain around the inconceivable possibility that she might be the beneficiary of Hydrangea House and Peace Place.

"Hazel, I'm sorry but I have to ask this. Do you think it's possible that you're mistaken, and that things didn't happen quite as you recollect?"

"Oh, I freely admit, I had my doubts before I came back here. But now I'm certain," Hazel confirmed. "There are several ways for you to be certain, too. The easiest and fastest is to look under the floorboard in the closet in my old bedroom. If you find the bottle with the note to my papa in it, you'll know I'm telling the truth."

Molly was quick to clarify, "It's not that I think you're *lying*—"

"I know you're not accusing me of that. But you're probably thinking whatever happened when I was a girl was so long ago and now that I'm an old lady, I must be confused, right?" Hazel chortled. Even as Molly tried to deny it, she spoke over her. "Listen, I'd think the same thing. Anybody would—and they *should.* It's an incredible story. But it wouldn't take very much to prove it's true. Just a quick peek beneath the floorboards."

Molly's thoughts were spinning, and she had to take a moment to slow down their conversation so she wouldn't impulsively agree to do something she'd regret later. "I realize pulling up the boards might seem like the easiest solution. However, the floors in all the upstairs rooms were ripped up about ten years ago, when the contractors needed access to install new lighting in the rooms beneath them."

She specifically recalled when the lighting was installed, because Savannah's father, Richard, had overseen the renovations, which also included putting in new windows and updating the tiling in the bathrooms. Beverly had been upset because Richard employed off-island contractors instead of the local carpenters whose services she knew and trusted.

Although it turned out their craftsmanship was exemplary, Beverly was distraught at how they'd mishandled the furniture they'd moved out of their way. In the process, a period piece mirror frame had been cracked and they'd stored several antique wooden tables in the basement, where they could have mildewed. Beverly had to hire some local high schoolers to move the items back upstairs—and the teenagers were far more careful than the professionals had been.

Molly was relatively certain if that's how reckless the contractors had been with antiques, they would have discarded an old glass bottle if they'd found it while they were tearing up the floor in the back room.

Not to mention that just because young Hazel had written a letter to her father describing what she believed had happened, that didn't mean the babies truly had been swapped.

She said, "If anyone discovered the bottle beneath the closet floor, it's long gone by now. So even if we lifted the boards again —which Savannah probably won't let me do, especially if she knew what I was searching for and why—we probably wouldn't find it. That doesn't necessarily prove your story *isn't* true, so why bother?"

"Because it's a good starting place. If you don't find anything there, you could move on to plan B—take a DNA test," Hazel readily suggested. "I assume you haven't taken one already, otherwise you probably would have discovered your ancestry isn't what you've always believed it was."

"No, I've never taken a DNA test—and neither has my grandma, as far as I know."

Hazel had obviously given this obstacle some thought already. "Would you happen to have one of her old brushes? You could test a strand of her hair."

As a matter of fact, Molly had found one of Beverly's brushes in the bathroom cabinet when she was clearing out the vanity on Thursday. But she didn't see what the results of testing her grandmother's hair would prove. "What good would it do to test her DNA—or mine, for that matter? We'd need to compare our results to my great-grandmother Dora's DNA, and we definitely don't have any trace of that."

"Lauren can explain it better than I can, but apparently the technology allows a person to trace their ancestry back as far as five or even seven generations. The results show what relatives you have in common with other people who are in the database." Despite claiming that her daughter could explain it better, Hazel seemed quite well-versed in the subject. "Do you know if any of Savannah's relatives on Mrs. Frost's side have ever tested their DNA?"

Molly vaguely recalled that someone in the Frost family had been working on building a family tree, but she couldn't remember who it was, or when, or even if they'd used DNA tests instead of historical records and archives. "I don't know. Possibly."

"Splendid!" exclaimed Hazel. "It's not absolutely necessary, but the more Frost relatives who are in the database, the better.

The results might not conclusively *prove* that you're related to Mrs. Frost. But Lauren says that you should be able to glean enough information to indicate that you share common ancestry with her. Of course, for the opposite reason, it would be helpful if Savannah were willing to take a test, too."

"I-I-I'm sorry," Molly stammered. "I'm not even sure *I'm* willing to take a test. I have to give this more thought, first,"

Someone tapped on the door, to her relief. Lauren poked her head in. "May I join you?"

"Sure," her mother told her. "I was just telling Molly that the quickest way to confirm my story is true is to look under the floorboards in my old room."

"Mom—you promised you wouldn't pressure her." Lauren sounded as dismayed as Molly felt.

"I wasn't *pressuring* her. I was making a suggestion," said Hazel.

Lauren turned to Molly and spoke in an exaggeratedly grave tone. "As someone who's been on the receiving end of a lifetime of my mother's 'suggestions,' I'm very sorry."

Molly couldn't help smiling at the remark, but Hazel scolded her daughter, "Don't act like I'm being bossy. I'm trying to look out for Molly's best interests. This house belongs to *her*, so she should do whatever it takes to claim it."

"Like I told you, Mom, maybe that's *not* what's in her best interest. If she really is the eldest descendant of Evelyn Frost, she wouldn't only be claiming a house—she'd also be claiming a new identity. What she does with the information you gave her doesn't just affect her. It affects other people, too. You need to back off and give her time to decide what she wants to do next."

Although Molly was a little surprised by how firmly Lauren had stated her case to her mother, she'd perfectly expressed Molly's own concerns and Molly was grateful for her support. "I appreciate it that you're both looking out for me," she said. "Lauren's right. I've got a lot of thinking to do. If I decide to lift the floorboards, I'd have to tell Savannah, first, since as far as she's concerned, this *is* her house. Not to mention, she has a vested interest in knowing her family's lineage, too. She's calling me later this afternoon. No promises, but maybe I can broach the subject then and talk to you later about what I decide?"

Hazel looked crestfallen but Lauren nodded. "That sounds like a good plan, especially since it's lunch time and I'm hungry. Do you feel up to going for a ride, Mom? I read about a café on the waterfront in Benjamin's Manor that I think you'd really like."

Before Molly left the room, she crouched in front of Hazel so they were eye level with each other. "Thank you so much for sharing your memories with me. I can imagine how difficult it was for you to relive that period of your life. You have my deepest admiration for being so tenacious and making it through so many hardships."

Hazel's features sagged with dejection. "I appreciate that, Molly, but as I've said, it's your forgiveness that I want. I should have told your family about what Opal did much, much sooner."

Whether Hazel was recalling the past correctly or not, Molly understood why she hadn't shared her version of events until now. She said, "I can't emphasize enough that there's no need for forgiveness—I promise, I'm not holding anything against you."

"But if I had told you earlier, your grandmother and father could have lived very different lives."

"It's a good thing they didn't, because then my father might not have met my mother at the low-cost college he attended and I wouldn't have ever been born," Molly joked, but her remark failed to elicit a smile from Hazel.

"Beverly could have been a lot wealthier. She could have had her own home, instead of taking care of someone else's."

"My grandmother *loved* being an innkeeper. She considered it her calling," insisted Molly.

Once, when Savannah was younger, she'd asked if Beverly ever wished she'd had the kind of rewarding career opportunities that were available to women in the twenty-first century. Molly had thought it was a bold question, but her grandmother hadn't seemed at all offended.

"No," she'd replied after a thoughtful pause. "I can't imagine a more rewarding vocation than helping others to enjoy the beauty of Dune Island and create happy memories with their loved ones. What's more, I get to meet people from all over the world and from all walks of life. It's a privilege to become acquainted with them and to hear their stories—I wouldn't trade it for anything."

Instead of sharing that memory with Hazel, Molly said, "Losing her husband at such a young age and later watching her son—my father—die of cancer were terrible griefs for my grandmother to endure. But otherwise, she led a very full and happy life and she wouldn't have changed her profession or where she lived for all the money in the world."

Finally, Hazel smiled. "I'm very glad to hear Beverly was content with her circumstances." Holding one finger up, she quipped, "Now, it's up to you to decide if you want to change *yours*. But as my daughter has not so subtly informed me, that's your choice to make, not mine."


Throughout the afternoon, Molly kept replaying Hazel's story in her mind. Certain elements had the ring of truth to them. *How would Hazel have known that Grandma's hair had been black when she was a newborn, if she hadn't been here?* she thought. *My great-grandmother couldn't have afforded to have a photograph taken back then, so it's not as if Hazel could have seen the photo later. Besides, Grandma definitely told me that her mother mentioned how much Opal's niece loved to hold Grandma when she was a newborn.* Even if the niece's nickname was Daisy, Molly had no question that Hazel was the same girl who'd spent the summer of 1943 at Hydrangea House.

Yet Hazel herself had introduced many reasons to doubt other parts of her story: as a child, she'd been prone to making up stories as a way of entertaining herself. She'd been traumatized by being separated from her father, as well as by her aunt's death, which undoubtedly had altered some of her memories. Plus, there were decades of time working against her recollection. More recently, Hazel had been on pain medication that she'd said made her feel "loopy," so that might have been affecting how well she remembered the past, too.

Although Molly didn't know quite what to believe, after hearing Hazel's story, she couldn't rid her mind of the niggling question: *I couldn't really be a descendant of Evelyn Frost, could I?*

Molly had always been proud of her family's history and of Beverly's occupation. When she visited Hydrangea House as a young girl, she could see how fond the guests were of her grandmother. Molly used to think of her as a kind of minor celebrity: Beverly Anderson, innkeeper. And she'd also been proud that her great-grandmother Dora had been so invaluable to her employer that Evelyn had entrusted her and her daughter with Hydrangea House—and Dora had accepted the responsibility. In Molly's mind, this spoke volumes about how highly both women esteemed each other.

However, she suspected Savannah would be appalled at the suggestion that her great-grandmother was a domestic servant. *Savannah already accused me of being gullible and there's no way she'll entertain the possibility that Hazel's account of our family histories might be accurate.* To be fair, Molly couldn't blame her for that. *The question is, will she think it's so absurd that she'll let me lift the floorboards, just to prove me wrong? Or will she flat out refuse on the basis that the notion Opal switched the babies is ludicrous?*

Molly tried to weigh whether asking permission to look beneath the closet floorboards was worth facing Savannah's scorn. She reminded herself, *Even if I found the bottle with the message in it, that would only prove Hazel was here as a young girl and that she believed Opal switched the babies. It wouldn't prove that's what actually happened.* Yet, knowing how much it would mean to Hazel if she looked for the bottle, Molly felt inclined to indulge her request.

*Maybe I could tell Savannah that Hazel hid something... it wouldn't be a lie if I called it a kind of diary... beneath the floorboard when she was young and she asked me to look for it,* she schemed.

No, that would never work. Savannah would ask too many questions, or else she'd speak to Hazel directly. And then Hazel would want to tell her everything because she'd tried to exercise full disclosure with Savannah from the very beginning, when she'd invited her to listen to her story. Molly intended to be honest with Savannah, too... eventually.

But right now, she wasn't ready—and not just because Molly dreaded Savannah mocking her. It was also because even though Savannah's recent text sounded friendly enough, they hadn't really resolved their disagreement yet about how guests at the inn should be treated. Molly was hesitant to introduce another potentially contentious topic before the last one was addressed.

Most importantly, she was concerned that Savannah would repeat Hazel's tale to her lawyer boyfriend. Even though Molly recognized that it was a gigantic leap to believe she might be Evelyn's rightful heir, she wouldn't put it past Austin to ensure she didn't inherit the inn. What if he urged Savannah to take legal action to block Molly from acquiring the estate? Or worse, what if he suggested barring Molly from the property? While she doubted very much it would come to that, Molly felt she had to anticipate every possibility now that Austin was in the picture.

After ruminating about the matter for hours, she called her mother for advice, but when she tried, she got voice mail. She left a message and turned her attention to searching for online tutorials about how to lift floorboards. *Maybe it'll be so easy I can do it by myself and then I'll replace them without anyone ever noticing, so I won't have to get Savannah's approval*, she hoped.

Indeed, the videos she watched made it *look* simple and she was confident Beverly had stored tools in the basement that Molly would have needed for the job. But if she accidentally cut into cables or pipes beneath the boards, she might create a major electrical or plumbing problem. Furthermore, she'd need to get Matt's permission to enter his room and that would require an explanation. She didn't want to tell him why she needed to raise the boards, but she didn't want to lie to him, either.

Around and around her thoughts continued to spin. Because Savannah didn't call as she said she would, Molly's indecision was prolonged for hours. By seven o'clock, she wasn't any closer to making up her mind about what to do next than she was right after she'd heard Hazel's story.

She kept picturing the elderly guest's disappointed expression when Molly had told her she needed more time to mull over the situation. *I can't postpone giving Hazel an answer. She came all this way, with two broken ribs, to find out if the bottle is still hidden beneath the closet floor—not to mention, she told me she doesn't think she has much longer to live. In good conscience, how can I not lift the floorboards while Hazel's still here to witness it? Regardless of whether her story checks out, it seems kind of mean not to indulge her in such a small request.*

Ultimately, she rationalized, *There's really no need to get Savannah's permission. After all, I don't call her every time I need to hire a carpenter or a plumber to make minor repairs around the house or at the cottage. Besides, I'll pay for this out of my own pocket, so she never has to know.*

When she told Hazel and Lauren her intention to call a carpenter in the morning, Hazel clapped her hands together and cried, "Oh, that's wonderful—thank you. I was so afraid Savannah wouldn't want you to disturb the flooring. It goes without saying that I'll pay for whatever it costs to hire a carpenter."

"Er, to be honest, Savannah never called me today, so I haven't had a chance to talk to her about this yet. I guess you could say I made an executive decision," Molly hedged, with a nervous laugh. "I should warn you, though, I *do* need to get permission from Matt to enter his room for non-housekeeping purposes while he's not there."

Hazel waved her hand. "He's such a kindhearted person, I'm sure it'll be no problem. Especially if you're the one asking. He has eyes for you, you know."

"Mom!" Lauren protested, as Molly felt her face flush.

"What?" Hazel asked innocently. "*You're* the one who told me his eyes lit up when he saw Molly the other day."

Lauren broke into a blush, too. She told Molly, "I only mentioned that in the context of him being relieved that he wasn't stuck sitting on the back lawn with *me*, that's all."

Trying to make light of the embarrassing situation, Molly put her hands on her hips and teased, "So you *don't* think he has eyes for me?"

"I-I-I didn't mean that, I just meant—" Lauren stammered.

"It's okay," Molly assured her, with a conspiratorial wink at Hazel. "I was just kidding."

"*I'm* not kidding," the elderly woman insisted. "I saw the way he looked at you at in the sunroom this morning—and don't try to tell me it was because you were carrying a tray of pastries, either, because he didn't even eat any."

Molly caught Lauren making a zipping motion across her lips, signaling her mother to be quiet. Hazel ignored her and kept right on talking.

"Believe me, with my mobility level, there's not a lot I can do, so people-watching has become my specialty. And I think Matt is enamored of you, Molly. If only you'd put down your dish cloth for a few minutes and—"

"Mom, shh!" Lauren sharply cut in, clearly mortified on Molly's behalf.

"I'm the mother here, so don't shush me. That's *my* job," Hazel shot back and after a brief, tense pause, all three women simultaneously broke into laughter.

*I'm really going to miss this mother-and-daughter duo,* Molly thought a few minutes later when she left their room. Admittedly, she felt a little self-conscious when Hazel had teased her about Matt being "enamored" of her. Self-conscious... and undeniably *pleased.*

It wasn't as if her self-esteem depended on a man's valuation of her, but Molly couldn't deny that after Jordan's infidelity and Austin's put-downs, it was flattering to believe Matt found her attractive. Especially since she felt the same way about him. Not that she could act on those feelings—it wouldn't be professional—but it was still a boost to think the attraction was mutual.

As she brushed her hair before going upstairs to speak to him, she reminded herself, *He's a* guest, *so no flirting!*

But it turned out that Matt wasn't in his room. Molly didn't want to wait until the morning to ask him, in case by chance she missed him. So she ended up texting. All she told him was that a guest thought something valuable of theirs was beneath the floorboards.

Hazel was right: he readily granted them permission to access the room, replying:

> Sure. I'll move my clothes out of the way. Just one problem.

Molly waited, but when he didn't send a second text, she asked:

> What is it?

A moment later came his answer:

> The closet is where I keep my running shoes. There may be a residual odor.

Molly cracked up at his geekiness. She dictated her response:

> I think we'll survive.

He wrote:

> Famous last words, but you've been warned. Good luck.

Molly giggled as she dictated back:

> Good luck surviving the smell or good luck finding what we're looking for?

But then she deleted the message because it was too silly. Instead, she typed a heartfelt, yet more professional text:

> Thanks, Matt. I appreciate it.

# TWELVE

Nick Armstrong, the local carpenter Beverly always hired for repairs, arrived at Hydrangea House shortly after 9:00 on Monday morning. His timing was perfect, since it was after the guests were awake and most of them had headed out to the beach, where his hammering wouldn't disturb their peace and quiet.

"Thanks for coming on such short notice," Molly said as she ushered him up the stairs.

"Glad I was available. I enjoy working in old houses like this. I'll miss chatting with your grandmother—and not just because she always served me coffee and a homemade muffin or a slice of pie," he said with a chuckle. "You mentioned in your message that you're looking for something valuable under the floor... Did a guest drop a ring or did an earring fall through the cracks or something?"

"No. We're looking for a hidden bottle." Molly felt compelled to explain, "When I said there was something valuable under the boards, I meant it had a lot of *sentimental* value—it's a long, private story. We're not even sure the bottle's under there, but since the guest made a special trip to

Dune Island to look for it, it feels like an urgent matter to her."

She thought he'd be annoyed that she'd exaggerated the urgency of the project, but Nick rubbed his chin and nodded. "My girlfriend inherited an old captain's house like this one. The walls—and attics and floors—hold decades of history. Sometimes if you want to reach back into the past, you've literally got to peel away the layers of the present."

Relieved, Molly tapped Matt's code onto the keypad and pushed open the door. He had lain the clothes from his closet flat across the bed and he'd neatly lined three pairs of footwear against the wall. His running shoes were conspicuously missing, although Molly smiled to herself when she noticed he'd left his windows open. "It's a really small space but it looks like the guest has completely cleared it out for you."

"Perfect." Nick crouched down and poked his head into the closet to run a hand across the boards. Then he turned toward Molly. He was tall like Matt, so he couldn't straighten up completely beneath the sloped ceiling. "I think I can raise most of these with minimal cutting. If it's important enough to your guest to make a trip to the island, then she's probably waiting with bated breath. Does she want to be present the moment I lift them?"

While Molly appreciated Nick's thoughtfulness, she was concerned that it might be too upsetting for Hazel to return to the bedroom where she'd slept during such a traumatic summer. To her relief, when she repeated what Nick had suggested, the elderly woman declined the offer.

"I'm in a bit of discomfort already. I don't think I should climb the stairs," Hazel said, and Molly noticed she did look peaked this morning. "Lauren, will you go in my place, while Molly stays here and keeps me company?"

"Sure," both Lauren and Molly agreed at the same time.

Before her daughter left the room, Hazel instructed her, "I

hid it beneath the third board from the back, but make sure the carpenter checks under all of them, just in case I'm remembering incorrectly."

"I will, Mom."

After Lauren closed the door behind her, Hazel invited Molly to take a seat. Instead of speaking, she closed her eyes for what felt like a long time. When she opened them again, she seemed to choose her words carefully. "I can see how much you love this house. This island. I see how much it means to your guests, too. But for me, staying here was like a bad dream."

"That's because you were here under extremely difficult circumstances as a little girl. You were separated from your father and from your best friend and your aunt was cruel to you. All the beautiful ocean sunrises and sunsets in the world can't make up for that kind of loneliness and heartache. Especially not to a child," sympathized Molly. "It took a lot of courage for you to come here as a little girl, and it took a lot of courage to return here now."

"Thank you for understanding." Hazel's eyes and nostrils were pink-rimmed and she dabbed at them with a tissue.

"Thank *you* for telling me what you remember about your summer at Hydrangea House the year my grandmother was born."

Hazel twisted her neck to look directly into Molly's eyes. "I've often tried to live up to my father's legacy by imitating what he would have done in my situation. I sense you know a thing or two about the desire to honor someone's memory in that way?"

"Yes, I do."

"I thought so. Then you understand I had no choice but to share what I experienced, no matter how outrageous it might seem. By telling you, I hoped that I could help your family claim your lineage—and your inheritance. But more than anything, I felt I owed it to my father's memory to be truthful."

Hazel put her hand on Molly's arm. "Regardless of what the carpenter finds or doesn't find, and regardless of what you choose to do with the information I've given you, I finally feel like my papa would be proud of me."

"I'm sure he would," Molly said, nodding thoughtfully, just as the door opened and Lauren came in. She was empty-handed.

"No bottle?" Hazel asked.

"No, it wasn't there. I'm sorry, Mom."

Initially, Molly had been concerned about how Hazel would respond if the bottle wasn't there; she hadn't expected *Lauren* to burst into tears.

"Oh, honey, it's okay, don't cry," her mother consoled her. "Like Molly said, that floor had been torn up once already. The bottle was probably discarded long ago. It doesn't change the facts. It just rules out one way of proving what happened."

"I-I-I know, but I'm just so disappointed," sobbed her daughter.

Molly rose to give Lauren her chair, and then she slipped from the room. She got the feeling that Lauren's meltdown had more to do with how overwhelmed she felt about other things happening in her life—like losing her job, and caring for an ailing parent—than about the bottle.

As she went upstairs to ask Nick to give her the invoice for his labor, instead of charging the inn, Molly felt a bit weepy, too. She reached the top landing and nearly bumped into a guest headed in the opposite direction, a suitcase in her hand.

"Oops, excuse me. I was lost in thought," Molly said warmly.

"It's amazing anyone could concentrate enough to *have* a thought around here," the woman snapped.

Molly was blindsided by her tone. "I'm sorry?"

"You *should* be. I came to Hydrangea House because supposedly it's quieter than any of the other inns in Port

Newcomb. What a joke! On Saturday there was a party on the patio right beneath my window—I could hear people gabbing and laughing for hours. Then this morning, I woke up to the sound of someone renovating the room next door. It's obvious you don't care about your guests' experience! I suppose now that you're shutting down and you don't have to worry about reviews, anything goes, is that it?"

"Really, I *am* so sorry about the noise." Molly had to raise her voice to be heard above Nick's hammering. "We want all our guests to have a pleasant, peaceful stay. I'm sorry yours wasn't, so please allow me to refund the charges for your visit."

"What good would that do? I have plenty of money, but this was the only week I got time off work. My vacation is ruined." As the guest rammed past her, her suitcase bumped into Molly's shin so hard, it made her gasp. Either the woman didn't realize what she had done or she didn't care, because she continued down the stairs.

Molly limped into the hall bathroom and lowered herself onto the edge of the tub. Allowing the cold water to flow over the red spot on her shin, she fought back tears. Partly because her leg hurt, but mostly because she'd felt as if she'd failed to live up to her grandmother's standards. *I doubt that Grandma ever had a guest storm off like that*, she thought. *Some innkeeper I'm turning out to be!*

But there was no time to wallow in her shortcomings; Hazel and Lauren were getting ready to leave. Patting her skin dry, Molly consoled herself, *It was partly* Savannah's *fault that the guest was so upset about the noise. I'm only responsible for Nick's hammering, not for Savannah's business meeting.*

Besides, checking beneath the closet floorboards for the bottle had meant so much to Hazel that Molly would do it again in a heartbeat—even if *all* the guests had left in a huff.

. . .

An hour later, Molly stood near Lauren's car as Lauren helped her mother ease into the passenger seat. Although Hazel's body appeared as fragile as when she'd arrived, there was something about her countenance that emanated an inner strength. An inner peace.

Once Lauren had stepped aside, Molly bent down and gently took her hand, "I've treasured meeting you, Hazel."

"And I've treasured meeting you, Molly *Frost*," she replied, a twinkle in her eye. "Just don't forget about plan B."

"Mom!" came Lauren's familiar protest. "Are you really going to keep pushing her, right up until the last second?"

"She wasn't pushing me, she was making a *suggestion*," Molly said with a chuckle. "If I do end up taking a DNA test, I'll contact you when I receive the results, if you want me to?"

"Thank you, Molly," Lauren replied emphatically. "We really appreciate it that you believe my mother's account enough to even *consider* taking a DNA test, don't we, Mom?"

"Yes, we do," her mother agreed. "But whether or not you take the test, will you do me one last favor, please?"

"If I'm able to, yes, I will."

"Will you keep an eye out for the bottle as you're going about your day in the house?" she asked and Molly nodded, but Hazel wasn't done yet. "If you find it, you may read the message to my father. But then, will you send it to me? I'd really like to see it, and one day, I want my daughter to have it as a keepsake of our family's history."

"Absolutely," promised Molly.

After Lauren and Hazel left, Molly changed the bedding in her room and put her personal belongings back in the dresser. Sydney and Lucy helped her carry the portable bed to the upstairs closet and then she assisted them with folding the laundry and tidying the sunroom.

Once their shift ended and Delores picked them up, Molly felt at a loss. Listless. She would have expected the woman's criticism this morning to motivate her to make sure conditions as Hydrangea House and Peace Place were even better than ever. Instead, she felt indifferent; a sure sign she needed to get away from the inn for a while.

Since the sky was overcast, Molly went for a drive around the island instead of a walk down the beach. It was a regrettable decision, because there was a family fun run in Lucinda's Hamlet, and traffic slowed to a crawl. By the time Molly returned to Hydrangea House, she felt even more listless than before she'd left.

Finally, after supper she went for a swim; as usual, it soothed her frayed nerves. For an unexpected bonus, right before it set, the sun peeked through the clouds, turning them into cottony pink and blue pastels.

*Baby colors.* The association made her think of newborns, Beverly and Harold. *Could it really be possible that Opal switched them at birth?* she wondered. Still not ready to go inside the inn, Molly wrapped her towel around her waist and sat down in one of the low beach chairs near the water's edge.

Her thoughts drifted to Hazel's comment about how different Beverly's life—as well as Molly and her father's lives— may have been as members of the Frost family. The closest Molly could come to imagining what that might have been like for herself was to picture trading places with Savannah.

*I definitely would have been wealthier growing up*, she thought. *I could have gone to a private high school and I wouldn't have had to take out student loans for college. I would have had a more expensive wardrobe and a brand new car every year, too.*

But she wouldn't have wanted to have a dad like Savannah's. Richard Frost had always seemed so driven by his pursuit of success that he rarely had time for his daughter. And

Savannah herself apparently had either learned or inherited the same unrelenting ambition to excel in her career, no matter the toll it took on her physical and emotional health. Frankly, the idea of trading places with Savannah wasn't very appealing.

However, the idea of inheriting control of Hydrangea House and Peace Place was a different story. *I wouldn't have to worry about convincing Savannah that I'd make a competent manager. I wouldn't even have to be the manager. I could hire someone to handle that part of the business. Sydney and Lucy wouldn't lose their seasonal positions and I'd return here every summer as the innkeeper.*

As enticing as her daydream was, Molly knew she couldn't get her hopes up. Because even if she could show she was related to Evelyn, that didn't mean she'd necessarily inherit the estate. At least, not without an enormous legal battle—and Molly didn't want to go through that. Still, she couldn't completely dismiss the possibility that Hazel's account was true and her curiosity was getting the best of her. *Maybe I should just take a DNA test to put the matter to rest once and for all,* she mused.

She was startled from her thoughts when someone suddenly plopped down in the sand beside her. "Hi, Molly, any luck?" Matt asked. Although he was dressed in his running clothes, he was holding on to a pair of binoculars. She assumed he was asking whether she'd seen any right whales this evening.

"No, but I did see a couple of seals."

"In my closet?" he asked incredulously.

"Oo-oh." The light dawned. "You were asking if I had any luck finding what we were searching for under the floorboards, weren't you?"

"Yeah."

"No. It wasn't there. Thanks for clearing out your closet for us, though."

"No problem. Too bad you didn't find whatever you were

looking for. Could it be somewhere else around the house? I can help you search for it." He stretched his arms above his head. "I'm tall, so I can reach the highest shelves and cabinets."

"I appreciate the offer, but for now, I'm just going to keep an eye out... kind of like a passive search." Molly didn't want to disclose more than that. "How about you, did you spot any whales?"

"Nope. I didn't even spot any seals." He pointed at the bruise on her shin. "That looks fresh. Did you kick a rock while you were swimming?"

Molly shifted her leg to look at the wound. "Nah. A disgruntled guest whacked me with her suitcase."

"You're kidding, right?"

"I wish I were. I don't think she did it on purpose, but yeah, a guest did this."

Before Molly knew it, she was telling Matt about the woman who'd complained that morning. Beverly never would have permitted Molly to speak poorly about a guest—or about anyone else, for that matter—in front of another guest. But Matt wasn't technically a guest; he was more like a short-term tenant. And Molly wasn't technically speaking ill; she was simply sharing the facts. Besides, Matt was such a sympathetic listener that the words just seemed to tumble out.

She finished her anecdote by clarifying, "I completely understand why she'd complain about the noise. But I don't get why she'd refuse a refund. It almost seemed as if she didn't want a satisfactory resolution—she just wanted to complain."

Matt shook his head. "I thought my students were imma-ture, but that lady almost makes them seem like reasonable adults."

"Why? What did your students do?"

Matt told her about several kids who decided to play volley-ball at the beach instead of participating in the field-work research the rest of the class was doing. When he gave them an

"F" on the assignment, they claimed he should have warned them they were being graded individually, since they thought they were being evaluated as a group.

Maybe it was a case of misery loving company, but by the time Molly and Matt headed inside Hydrangea House, she felt as though all her anxieties had been washed out to sea.

# THIRTEEN

In the days following Hazel and Lauren's departure, whenever a guest checked out of a room, Molly scoured the closets, shelves and cabinets to be sure they weren't harboring the bottle. She thoroughly scrutinized every nook and cranny downstairs, too, as well as the upstairs attic suite, but she didn't come up with anything except for a small amount of crumbs and candy wrappers, or a few yellowed newspapers.

On Wednesday, her mother happened to call during one of her searches. "Hi, Molly. I'm sorry I couldn't pick up last weekend. Do you have time to chat now or are you in the middle of something?"

"Now is good," she answered.

"You sound so far away. Where are you?"

"To be honest, I'm on my hands and knees in the living room, shining a flashlight into the heating vent."

"Did you drop something into it?"

"No. Just a sec, Mom." She shifted to her feet and went into the sitting room. Then Molly told her mother Hazel's story. She finished by asking, "What do you think? Is it possible that Grandma really was Evelyn Frost's daughter?"

"Anything's possible," her mother answered cautiously. "Although I have to admit, some of what you told me sounds awfully farfetched."

"I know. That's why I can't decide whether to get a DNA test done or not. On one hand, I feel like, 'what's the harm?' But on the other hand, I'm afraid to find out..."

When she didn't finish her sentence, Carol prompted, "You're afraid to find out what? That you're a Frost?"

"No. That I'm *naïve*." Molly's voice trembled. "It was so humiliating when I realized Jordan was seeing someone behind my back. I felt like a fool for trusting him even when some of his behavior and excuses weren't adding up. I liked Hazel a lot and I don't think she has anything to gain by deliberately deceiving me. But I still probably shouldn't accept her account at face value, especially since she's recalling things that happened during her childhood."

"I see. So, if you took the DNA test and discovered you're not related to Evelyn, you'd feel foolish all over again?"

"Yes."

"Yet you're crawling around on the floor looking for a bottle with a message in it?" Molly's mother gently kidded.

"I justify that by telling myself I'm doing a deep cleaning as I search," she explained with a chuckle. "But if I actually go through the process of taking a DNA test, I don't know, that seems more serious somehow. It's as if I'm officially buying into Hazel's story. I can almost hear Savannah mocking me already."

"Why would you tell Savannah that you took the test, unless the results indicated that you're related to the Frost family? In which case, you'd have science on your side," Carol pointed out.

"So you think I should do it?"

"Not necessarily. But I think you should feel *free* to do it, if you want to. You don't have to assign so much negative meaning to it. Instead of looking at it as a reflection of whether you're naive or too trusting, couldn't you just look at it as honoring a request from an elderly acquaintance? There's certainly no shame in that."

"Yeah, but..." Molly's volume dropped as she admitted, "I feel like if it turns out Grandma and Dad and I really are descendants of the Frost family, then that changes everything."

"It doesn't change who your grandmother or dad were, Molly, if that's what you're thinking. It doesn't change who you are, either. You're still the same person you ever were, regardless of your genetic makeup," Carol said emphatically. "The only thing that might change is you could possibly inherit the Frost estate."

"I doubt very much that would happen, no matter what the DNA results show. Because Evelyn's will goes back a couple generations, and even if Savannah and her father aren't biologically related to her, they were both raised as Frosts." Molly added longingly, "Although inheriting Hydrangea House *would* be a dream come true..."

"Careful what you wish for," her mother warned.

"What do you mean?"

"Owning an inn is a huge responsibility. It can be very stressful and time consuming."

"You sound like Savannah," Molly said with a laugh.

"She has a point," Carol acknowledged. "I just don't want you to end up feeling overwhelmed if—"

"I know you're looking out for my best interests, Mom," Molly interrupted. "But I haven't even decided whether to take a DNA test yet, so it's wayyy too early for me to start creating a business plan."

When her ring tone sounded at 10:45 on Thursday evening, Molly had just dozed off. She immediately reached for the phone before her eyes were open.

"Hello?" she answered in a groggy voice.

"Hi, Molly." It was Savannah. "You weren't asleep, were you?"

"Actually, yes, I was." Molly sat up in bed, rubbing her eyes.

"It's not even eleven yet. I'd give anything to get as much rest as you do."

Molly swallowed the retort on the tip of her tongue and asked, "What's up?"

"I told you I'd call to discuss your concerns, remember?"

"Yeah, I remember. That was days ago, so I thought *you'd* forgotten."

"No, I was just super busy, as usual. Anyway, I'll keep this short so you can get back to sleep." She began, "So, listen, I realize that you were bent out of shape because I had people over for appetizers at Hydrangea House."

"Your having people at the inn for appetizers wasn't really the issue," Molly clarified, because Savannah was obviously free to hold business meetings on her own property—even if it did make Hydrangea House feel like Savannah's personal conference center, instead of an inn. "And I wouldn't say I was bent out of shape—I'd say I was concerned about our guests' comfort."

"Right, that's what I meant." Savannah's voice had an exasperated edge to it. "My point is, you don't need to be *concerned* any more, because I won't be returning to the inn at all this summer. Neither will Austin, obviously."

"You won't? Not at all?" Molly's voice was a little too gleeful. "Why not?"

"Because I've nixed the renovation project." Savannah was practically singing. "Instead of converting the inn into my summer home, I've decided to sell it."

"You're *selling* Hydrangea House?"

"Yes, I am and I have you to thank for that, in a way."

"Me? What did I do?" *Whatever it was, I'm sorry.*

"Last spring when I told you I was shutting down the inn, you emphasized how satisfying it would be to give other people the opportunity to enjoy one of the most gorgeous locations on Dune Island."

"But I wasn't suggesting you *sell* the estate," Molly emphasized. "I was suggesting you consider keeping the inn and cottage open."

"Yes, but as you know, I'm way too busy—and too stressed—to take on a side business. Anyway, Austin had contacts who put him in touch with the execs at the Port Newcomb Yacht Club. That's why we met with them at the inn last Saturday. It turns out, they've been salivating over the property for decades."

"Why would the yacht club want to buy Hydrangea House? There isn't even a dock here."

"Not yet, there isn't. But I'm sure they'll build one. Even if they don't, the estate is so close to the marina that they can offer accommodations at the inn to their highest-level members." Savannah paused to laugh. "Although Austin was quick to tell them that *we* expect to have standing reservations."

*I'm sure he was,* thought Molly. "When will this sale take place?"

"Don't worry. I know how much it means to you—to both of us—to honor Grandma B.'s memory by hosting the final season of guests. So Austin suggested that we shouldn't start the sales process until September, which is why you don't have to worry about us coming back this summer."

"Oh." Molly was too dumbfounded to say anything else, but Savannah kept rambling.

"Like I said, the club is desperate to acquire the property, so they'll wait for as long as it takes. Austin expects that the delay will make them willing to increase their offer, because they'll question whether we're serious about selling or not. Clever, isn't he?"

"Yes, he is," acknowledged Molly. *Austin's one of the shrewdest people I've ever met.*

Molly was so upset by Savannah's news that she ended the call before telling her about Sydney's encounter with Austin in the parking lot. *I'll mention it another time, but at least I know it won't happen again since he's not coming back while Sydney's working here,* she realized.

Although she settled into bed again, she lay awake for a long time, staring at the ceiling, *I can't believe Savannah wants to sell the estate to the yacht club. It was difficult enough to try to come to terms with her decision to shut down the inn so she could have it all to herself. But this feels impossible to accept,* she brooded. *It's contradictory to everything our great-grandmothers envisioned for Hydrangea House.*

It wasn't that Molly bore any grudge against Port Newcomb Yacht Club. It was that, generally speaking, the people who were members of the most exclusive club on the island tended to be extremely wealthy. They either already owned summer homes in Hope Haven or they had the means to lodge at the finest resorts and inns.

By contrast, Dora and Evelyn's mission for Hydrangea House was that it would offer "luxurious accommodations at affordable prices." Not to mention, Peace Place had been established specifically to give low-income families the opportunity to enjoy one of the most beautiful vacation spots in the country. If the yacht club built a dock large enough for mooring yachts, it would disturb the ecosystem, as well as the aesthetics of the waterfront.

*Savannah was so adamant about keeping the house for herself. It seems fishy that she'd suddenly change her mind.* All Molly could imagine was that Austin must have had a very strong influence on her, since he seemed to be the driving force behind Savannah's change in plans. *I guess this was what he meant when he told Savannah that she wouldn't need money from the room rentals—it's because he'd already talked her into selling Hydrangea House and he knew she'd make a fortune.*

Molly couldn't figure out what was in it for *him* if Savannah sold the inn, since he neither owned a yacht nor was he a yacht club member. Was he really hoping to drop in at the inn whenever he wanted, and rub elbows with Dune Island's elite society? Maybe to network professionally and increase his clientele?

Regardless of why Austin had encouraged Savannah to sell the house and regardless of why Savannah had deferred to his advice, Molly felt she had to do whatever she could to stop this sale from proceeding. She owed it to the women in both families to preserve their mission for the house and cottage—and to protect it from being destroyed by a condescending man like Austin.

*If there's any chance I actually am a Frost family member, I need to find out ASAP,* she thought.

Molly's first item of business was to place an overnight order for a DNA test kit. She was keenly aware that even if the results indicated she was related to the Frosts, it didn't necessarily follow that she'd inherit the estate—there'd probably be years of legal hurdles to overcome. However, she also knew that *without* the test, she had no chance whatsoever of challenging Savannah's right to the inn and cottage.

*I want to gather all the evidence I can find, no matter how tenuous it is,* she realized. *So I need to intensify my search for Hazel's letter to her father.*

After the family checked out of Peace Place on Saturday, Molly would examine the carriage house for the bottle. And tomorrow she'd inspect the shed on the back lawn. It had only been constructed fifteen or twenty years ago, so there was no way that Hazel had ever stepped foot inside it. However, it was possible that the bottle may have gotten mixed up with other beach toys and it wound up being stored in the little hut.

If all those efforts proved unfruitful, Molly was going to have to descend into the basement. It was dark and dank and as Hazel had suggested, it might even contain rodents, but as Molly decided, *Better to encounter a rat in the basement than to allow a rat like Austin to destroy everything Hydrangea House represents.*

# FOURTEEN

On Friday afternoon, Molly removed every game, flotation device and beach chair from the shed, swept it out and then and replaced it all again. She even used a step ladder to look in the small loft. Unsurprisingly, she didn't find Hazel's bottle.

She didn't find it in any of the downstairs closets or cabinets or behind the dressers when she searched the cottage after the guests checked out on Saturday, either. Because the new guests arrived two hours early, Molly didn't have time to search the upstairs rooms. Technically, she would have been within her rights to refuse to allow the guests entry until official check-in time at three o'clock. If she, Sydney and Lucy had still been cleaning, Molly would have suggested the family go for a walk or lounge on the beach until they'd finished. However, she felt too guilty making the family wait to gain access to the cottage simply because she was on a wild goose chase for a bottle that probably no longer existed. Besides, she had other guests arriving at the inn soon, so she figured she'd just have to wait until the following Saturday to search the upstairs of the carriage house.

Now, here it was, almost seven o'clock on Saturday evening

and Molly stood on the eastern side of Hydrangea House, trying to work up the courage to go down into the basement, which could only be entered from outside the house. She couldn't seem to make herself descend the stairs, much less unlock the padlock on the door. Molly had only gone into the basement once when she was a child, and that was enough to satisfy her curiosity, until now. As far as she knew, the basement was relatively empty and clean, but it had a dirt floor and stone walls that made it a likely place for arachnids, if not rodents. Although Molly had a healthy appreciation for all living creatures, spiders and rats were two she preferred to see at a distance.

While she was dithering, flashlight in one hand, the padlock key in the other, Matt came striding up the back lawn from the beach. "Hi, Molly," he called as he approached. "Whatcha doing?"

"Oh, I was, uh, just going to go into the basement to, um, do some cleaning," she stammered.

"On Saturday night?" he wrinkled his forehead. "I guess that comes with the territory of being an innkeeper, huh?"

Realizing how pathetically boring she must have sounded, Molly confessed, "To be honest, I'm not really going to clean. I'm looking for something."

"That would explain why you're carrying a flashlight instead of a mop." Matt grinned at her. "You want some help?"

Chatting with another person while she was in the basement might help scare the vermin away. "That would be great, thanks."

Matt rubbed his hands together. "Okay, so what are we looking for?"

"Spiders, mostly. Possibly rats."

He did a doubletake. "Really?"

Molly laughed. "Well, that's what I *don't* want to find. But in general, I'm trying to get a sense of what's down there. I think there are a couple of shelves with tools on it, stuff like that."

"So in other words, you're looking for stuff that would fit beneath a floorboard?"

Chagrinned that her intention was so obvious, she nodded. "Yes. Specifically, we're looking for a bottle—but please don't ask me any more about it than that."

"I won't. I just needed to know what size object I'm searching for. I assume you want me to go first. I'll call you when the coast is clear." He held out his hand for the flashlight and she gave him the key, as well.

*My hero*, she thought, tongue-in-cheek as she watched him descend the stone steps, open the padlock and disappear through the cave-like entrance. A few moments later, he popped his head out and announced, "No spiders or rats. Other than the furnace and water heater and a few shelves, there's not much of anything down here. This is one of the cleanest basements I've ever seen."

Molly felt simultaneously relieved there were no critters, but disappointed because she'd hoped that somehow Matt was going to tell her he'd serendipitously discovered a trunk with a treasure trove of antique glassware inside it.

He shone a path of light for her as she crept down the stairs. Blinking, she surveyed the dim and musty area. As Matt had indicated, other than the furnace and water heater, the room was virtually empty, except for a few tall shelves lining the farthest wall. Molly pointed to them.

"If what I'm looking for is anywhere down here, I guess it's got to be on one of those."

Matt hunched over to avoid hitting his head on the beams as they crossed the room together. The first set of shelves contained very neatly arranged rows of paint cans and painting tools. Matt shone the flashlight in the cracks between them.

"We could probably lift each of these up and give them a

shake to make sure nothing rattles inside them," he suggested. "Or do you want to open them up to check if all they contain is paint?"

"I hadn't even considered being that thorough," Molly acknowledged. "Shaking them is fine—it might even be overkill. But you really don't have to stay here with me while I comb through all the shelves. It's going to take a while."

"I don't mind. Besides, you seem to be an amateur when it comes to searching for hidden treasures. Clearly you didn't have parents like mine who stashed your presents around the house so you wouldn't try to peek at them before your birthday."

Molly laughed. "Where's the oddest place they ever hid one of your gifts?" She figured it might help inspire their search.

"I found one in the trunk of our car once, which wasn't necessarily odd, but it was unfortunate because somehow it got mixed up with other stuff my father dropped off at the donation center." He lifted a can of paint, wiggled it, and then replaced it on the shelf. "Another time, I found my present in the attic. Once, I came into the kitchen the night before my birthday and I almost caught my mother in the process of wrapping my gift. She panicked and tossed it into the oven, which was turned off at the time. But then she had to chase me back upstairs and it was one distraction after the next so..."

Molly giggled. "I can see where this is going."

"Yep. You guessed it. The next day, she was preheating the oven to bake my birthday cake and she forgot my gift was still in there."

"Please don't tell me it was a chemistry set?"

"Fortunately, no. It was a baseball mitt. Amazing thing is, it didn't get ruined, although there were a couple of scorch marks from where it was resting on the rack." As Molly cracked up, Matt added, "Moral of the story is that the bottle you're searching for could be *any*where. So don't make any assumptions. You can't rule out any hiding place until you've thoroughly examined it."

"Got it," Molly agreed, lifting a can to her ear and jiggling it.

When they'd finished with the paint cans, they moved on to the two other stacks of shelves. After an hour of meticulously removing, examining and replacing every article, they only had one row of items left to inspect on the highest shelf. Molly's hopes surged when Matt pulled down two vintage, breadbox-sized wooden crates.

Carefully setting them on the floor, he said, "Sounds like there's a lot of loose ends in here. I hope nothing's broken."

While Matt held the flashlight for her, Molly wriggled the lid off the first of the wooden boxes. Inside were an assortment of antique cooking and baking tools and utensils, including a hand-held eggbeater, several rusting metal spatulas, a rolling pin and a set of tin measuring cups.

"Oh! I think these belonged to my great-grandmother," she exclaimed. Molly's grandmother had told her that Dora had been very particular about what kind of tools and utensils she used for cooking and baking. Beverly was constantly trying to persuade her mother to switch to using modern gadgets, as she called them, but Dora refused. She'd claimed that companies didn't make utensils like they used to, and that she was sure that the newer ones would alter the taste of her food. When Dora died, Beverly finally had the chance to get rid of her mother's cookware, but for sentimental reasons, she couldn't. So she must have been storing it in the basement all these years.

"Some of these things might be fairly valuable," commented Matt. "Or at least useable."

"Yeah, for someone who likes to bake or cook—and that isn't me," Molly said with a chuckle.

The kitchen items were the closest Molly had come to finding anything remotely resembling glassware and she dared to hope that somehow Hazel's bottle had gotten mixed in with the contents of the second crate. She eagerly lifted its lid to see several more utensils: a potato masher, a mortar and pestle and, ironically, a garlic press. Definitely not what she'd hoped to find.

However, her spirits soared as she removed an item that was cushioned in dingy yellow newspaper. *This feels like glass,* she thought as she unwrapped it—and she was right. But the item wasn't a bottle; it was an antique juice reamer.

"Oh, well," she said, trying not to let her disappointment show. "At least I found some of my great-grandmother's things, so this hasn't been a complete loss."

"Plus, you've ruled out the entire basement as a possible location," Matt pointed out. "In my gift-hunting experience, that's half the battle. At least, it always was until my mother started getting wise to my searches. That's when she started re-hiding my gifts and things really got interesting because I had to re-check places I'd already looked. I think she did that just to get back at me for ruining my birthday surprises so many times."

Molly had to laugh. Even if she hadn't found Hazel's message to her father, the searching process had been a lot more fun with Matt than it would have been if she had been alone. As he bent over to pick up one of the two crates she wanted to keep, she noticed something dark on his shirt.

"Matt," she exclaimed. "I think you've got a—you do! It's a *huge* wolf spider in the middle of your back."

He slowly straightened his posture and calmly asked, "Can you brush it off, please?"

Molly took a deep breath, held her arm out as far as she could in front of her and used a single finger to flick at it. But the spider must have sensed her hand coming forward because it scampered further up the fabric. "It's crawling toward your neck!" she shouted.

Matt either dropped or threw the flashlight, because the next thing she knew, it was rolling across the dirt floor. She couldn't see what happened next but he must have knocked into the shelf, because Molly noticed its shadow teetering. Just before it came crashing down, she shrieked, "Get out of the way!"

Other than the two crates of kitchen items that had already been removed from it, the shelf had contained fairly soft items, such as gardening hoses, tarps, extension cords and a stack of empty plastic pails. But the shelf itself was heavy and tall and when it fell on the dirty floor, it made a loud thump and raised a cloud of dust.

"Matt, are you okay?" Molly asked, coughing, her vision blurred.

"Yeah." He'd picked up the flashlight again and was directing it at the fallen shelf. "I jumped out of the way, so I'm fine, but I don't think the spider made it."

Only then did Molly realize he wasn't wearing a shirt; it was half-buried beneath the shelves.

"You took off your shirt?" she asked incredulously, trying not to laugh. "And I thought *I* was squeamish about creepy crawlies."

"I *had* to take it off. I'm allergic to wolf spiders—their venom makes me swell up even worse than cold water does. So when you said it was crawling toward my neck, I panicked and tore off my shirt." Matt chuckled at himself. "It would have been a smart move, if only I hadn't whacked my hand against the shelf and thrown it off balance."

"Oh, Matt, I'm so sorry. Is your hand all right?" Molly tried to step toward him, but the field of debris blocked her way.

Matt examined the outer edge of his palm. "It's fine."

"That's a relief, but now I think I know how your mother felt when you went kayaking without a wet suit," lectured Molly. "You really shouldn't have come down here knowing you could be bitten by a spider and suffer an allergic reaction."

"I wanted to help you," he said, shrugging his porcelain, sinewy shoulders.

*He's a guest*, Molly reminded herself. "C'mon, let's see if we can lift this up and salvage your shirt from the wreckage."

"I can lift it on my own, if you'll shine the flashlight for me." He tilted the shelf halfway to an upright position before he lowered it to the dirt floor again. He directed Molly to shine the light at the base of the wall where the shelf had been standing. The beam was waning but she held it steady while he reached down and pulled up a shoe box-sized package wrapped in brown paper. He brushed it off and handed it to her. "This must have slipped behind the shelf, because it wasn't with any of the other stuff the first time we checked. It's awfully dusty. It could've been back there for decades."

There was something scrawled across the outside of the box that appeared to be an address, but it was too faded to read beneath the dimming bulb of the flashlight. "This looks promising," Molly said, her heart suddenly racing. "Once we retrieve your shirt, let's take the box outside where the light's better."

After Matt propped the shelf against the wall, he shook off his shirt and put it on. "If you'd rather go look inside the box on your own, I can stay here and start cleaning up," he offered.

"No way. You've got to be with me when I open it." Molly figured if the package contained Hazel's bottle, she wouldn't read the message to Matt. But he at least deserved to know what was inside the box, since he was the one who found it.

When they climbed the stairs, they discovered the sun had already set and the light wasn't that much brighter outside. Molly was too antsy to learn what was inside the box to return to the basement and clean up the mess.

She suggested in a hushed voice, "I can put the rest of the stuff back on the shelves tomorrow. Let's go inside and look at this now."

They were almost around the corner of the house when

Molly heard guests' voices coming from the patio. She'd been so excited about finding the box that she hadn't considered what they might think if they saw her and Matt skulking through the yard in the dark. She stopped and whispered, "I don't want the guests to see me coming in with a package at this hour. They might ask questions. Let's go back around and use the front door."

As they doubled back past the basement, he asked, "You want me to run down to get those two old crates, too, just in case we missed something in them?"

"Good idea, thanks. I'll be waiting in the sitting room, which is at the end of the tiny hall on the eastern side of the house."

"I'll meet you there," he said softly.

There was something so deliciously conspiratorial about discovering the box with Matt that enhanced Molly's anticipation of looking inside it. It seemed to take forever before he finally rapped on the door of the sitting room and took a seat in the armchair beside her. By then, she'd pored over the handwriting several times and had analyzed the weight of the package, too.

"There aren't any stamps on it and the print is too faded to read. But I think this was a package that was meant to be mailed from here," she reported. "See? In the upper corner, the return address looks like it says Main Street, doesn't it?"

When Matt leaned closer, Molly noticed a minty smell. Was that what had taken him so long; had he gone upstairs to brush his teeth or get a mint? She knew she shouldn't read anything into it. "Yeah, that looks like the letter M, I guess," he said.

Molly had a theory that Hazel had decided to send the bottle through the mail instead of casting it into the sea, but as she'd mentioned, she didn't have any stamps. Molly figured by the time the box had been found in her closet, Hazel's father's name may have already faded. She could understand why someone would think the package was private and would hesitate to open it. Over the years, it was probably moved from one room to another, until no one could remember what it was or why they'd been keeping it.

She pushed the box into Matt's hands. "How much do you think it weighs? It feels kind of light to me, but it could be an empty bottle, couldn't it?"

Matt gently bounced the box in the air. "Yeah, it's possible. But there's only one sure way to find out." He handed it back to her. "Open it."

The tape was so yellowed that Molly was surprised the package was still fastened shut. With a swift tug, she ripped the entire piece of paper off at once. She lifted the lid. Beneath it were several wads of crumpled newspaper, which she pushed aside to reveal... a *doll*.

Dressed in a pink chiffon dress and white socks and shoes, the doll had a blonde curlicue painted on her forehead and two pinkish circles on her cheeks. When Molly pulled her from the box, its bristly-lashed eyes flew open.

"A doll?" she uttered. It wasn't really a question but an expression of disgust.

"Not at the top of your birthday wish list, huh?" Matt kidded, but Molly was too disappointed to laugh.

She remembered how Lauren had burst into tears when she'd told her mother that Nick hadn't found anything beneath the floorboards in the closet. Suddenly, Molly felt on the brink of tears, too. Matt must have noticed the change in her expression because he abruptly hopped to his feet.

"I'm sorry it's not the bottle," he said, shifting from foot to foot. "But if you want to keep searching, I'm happy to help. I'll pick up the stuff in the basement, too."

She managed a wan smile. "Thanks, but don't worry, I'll take care of it. You've done enough already." She'd meant it kindly, but when Matt nervously touched the corner of his glasses, she realized it didn't come across that way.

"Okay. Sure. Good night, then." He turned and ducked out the door before she could rephrase her comment.

*I'll have to talk to him tomorrow*, she thought, laying the doll back into the box. As she began stuffing the newsprint on top of it, she realized a piece of stationery was stuck to the bottom one of the crumpled wads. Unlike the outer covering, this sheet hadn't been exposed to the light and when she unfolded it, she saw the penmanship was perfectly legible.

The note read:

*Dear Mrs. Frost,*

*I hope this note finds you well. It was a privilege to serve you and your children at Hydrangea House last week.*

*I'm afraid there's been a tiny mix-up with the children's belongings. It appears that Ramona and Daisy must have accidentally switched dolls when they were playing together. I'm enclosing Ramona's doll here, as I'm sure she'll be very eager to have her "baby" home with her again.*

*If you'd kindly return Daisy's doll to us here on Dune Island, we would appreciate that, as well.*

*We apologize for the inconvenience and thank you in advance for your cooperation. We hope the rest of your summer is sunny and joyful.*

*Yours truly,*

*Dora Grant*

Molly had to reread the letter twice before she could fully make sense of it. *Hazel said that Jerome Frost's snotty niece took her doll, but she never mentioned that Ramona left her own doll behind.* Molly figured this omission must have been because Hazel either hadn't known or hadn't cared about Ramona's doll: all that mattered was that her own doll was missing and that Ramona had taken it.

Molly recalled Hazel telling her that Opal wouldn't ask for the doll back because she was too afraid of offending Evelyn. But Molly's great-grandmother Dora obviously didn't share that concern and she clearly knew how much the doll had meant to Hazel. Molly felt proud of Dora for penning such a diplomatic, yet no-nonsense letter.

*She probably forgot to mail the package after the babies were born because the household had become so chaotic. The box must have gotten misplaced in the shuffle and eventually, it was stored in the basement. Like Matt said, it could have fallen behind the shelf decades ago. Grandma might not have ever even known it was there.*

Molly's first impulse was to call Hazel right away and tell her she'd found Ramona's doll and the note from Dora. But it was almost nine o'clock and both Hazel and Lauren seemed to go to bed early when they were at the inn, so Molly didn't want to disturb them if they were already sleeping.

*I'll call her in the morning to share the good news,* she decided, feeling considerably heartened and hopeful. Even though she hadn't found the bottle, Molly figured that since Hazel had accurately recalled so many facts about Ramona taking her doll, it made her story about Opal seem more credible, too.

*When I receive my DNA test results in August, I won't be surprised if they show that Hazel's aunt really did switch Beverly and Harold at birth,* she thought.

It wasn't until hours later, after she'd tidied the kitchen, said goodnight to the guests lingering on the patio and went to bed that Molly recognized a less encouraging, but more likely scenario.

*What if Hazel's mind was playing tricks on her because she was feverish and imaginative and the babies' traumatic births coincided with Ramona taking her beloved doll?* she wondered. *What if all that really happened wasn't that* Opal *switched baby Harold and baby Beverly, but that* Ramona *switched her* doll *with Hazel's?*

The probability was so upsetting that Molly stayed up half the night fretting about it.

# FIFTEEN

If Matt came into the sunroom for breakfast the following morning, Molly missed him. Sundays were notoriously busy days, since it was Lucy and Sydney's day off. When guests happened to check out that day, Molly had to clean their rooms by herself. On this particular weekend, two couples were leaving, which meant she was doubly busy preparing rooms for the arriving guests.

Molly finally had a moment to slow down at half past one. She made a sandwich and took it to the sitting room. She told herself it was because she wanted privacy to call Hazel, but the truth was, she just wanted privacy, period. *I know it's my job as the innkeeper to chat with guests and make sure they're enjoying their stay, but sometimes, they seem needier than my middle school students,* she grumbled to herself.

After slowly finishing her meal, she entered Hazel's number into her phone. When the elderly woman picked up, her voice was so faint Molly hardly recognized it.

"Hello, Hazel. It's Molly Anderson, from the inn," she began. "Is this a good time to chat?"

"Depends on what you're going to tell me." Hazel's voice may have been weak, but her sense of humor was still intact.

"Well, I didn't find the bottle, but I found something else that might interest you."

"What's that?"

"It appears to be Ramona Frost's doll and a note from my great-grandmother." Molly explained about the package and then she read the letter aloud. When she'd finished, to her surprise she heard Hazel sniffling.

"Wasn't that a lovely thing for Dora to do? I always sensed she cared about me, but hearing that letter... Well, it feels like someone just reached back in time and gave the little girl I used to be a nice, warm hug," she said, her voice cracking.

"You weren't aware that my great-grandmother had written the letter?"

"No. She probably didn't tell me because she wasn't sure that Ramona's mother would return *my* doll. Dora wouldn't have wanted me to get my hopes up and then be disappointed."

*That makes sense*, Molly thought, relieved to know Hazel hadn't completely forgotten a major aspect of what had transpired with the dolls. "Would you like me to send you Ramona's doll now?"

"That old thing?" scoffed Hazel. "I thought it was spooky looking when we were children, with that horrid curl painted on its forehead and so much rouge she looked like a saloon girl instead of a baby. I didn't want it then and I don't want it now, thank you very much!"

Gleeful that Hazel remembered exactly what Ramona's doll looked like, Molly cracked up. "I don't especially want it, either."

"Where did you find it?"

Molly told her about how she and Matt came across it in the basement. She was glad she could make Hazel laugh at her anecdote about the spider and the shelf falling over. Molly concluded by saying, "But don't worry, all Matt knows is that I'm looking for a bottle. I haven't told him anything about your history at the inn as a little girl."

"I wouldn't mind if you did. I don't trust people easily, but I trust him," she said.

*I'm starting to trust him, too*, Molly realized. "Well, he's offered to help me keep searching for the bottle. I might take him up on it because I haven't exhausted all the options for where it might be hidden."

"In that case, I hope the two of you *don't* find it right away," teased Hazel. "It'll give you a reason to spend more time with him alone."

"*Mom*, stop," came her daughter's familiar, exasperated plea in the background. She must have come into the room and over-heard her mother's end of the conversation.

"Hi, Lauren," Molly called, laughing.

"Lauren says hi, too," Hazel reported. "But now she's telling me I need to get off the phone and rest. Anyone would think that *she's* the mother and I'm her child, instead of the other way around."

Molly's heart thudded. "Why do you need to rest—are you ill?"

"No, just old," replied Hazel with a chuckle.

"Oh, okay. I'll let you go, but I wanted to mention that I've gone ahead and taken a DNA test. I should get the results back sometime in August."

"That's wonderful," exclaimed Hazel. "Be sure to keep me posted, okay?"

"Yes, I definitely will."

"I appreciate it that you're still searching for the bottle," Hazel added. "I know the DNA test will show that genetically you're a Frost. But in every other way, you take after Dora Grant—you're probably a lot like Beverly was, too."

"Thank you," said Molly. "I consider that high praise."

. . .

Molly didn't realize she'd dozed off until she woke to her phone buzzing. "Hi, Savannah," she said in an extra perky voice to disguise the fact that she'd been napping. "What's up?"

"You tell me," Savannah demanded.

*She's been hanging around Austin so much she's starting to sound just like him,* Molly noticed. "What do you mean?"

"I mean why did we receive a one-star guest review that says—and this is a direct quote, 'Savannah Frost, the new owner of Hydrangea House, made a public pledge not to renovate until all the *paying* guests had vacated the inn at the end of the tourist season. Yet this morning I woke to the commotion of a carpenter installing a new floor in the room right next to mine. When I complained to the poor-excuse-for-an-innkeeper about it, she actually *screamed* at me.'"

"You've got to be kidding," groaned Molly.

"Do you hear me laughing?" Savannah jeered. "Not that it matters, since she's already defamed my character, but the next sentence out of your mouth better be that nothing this guest said is even remotely true."

"It *isn't* true. Or at least, it's not accurate. I mean—"

"Stop splitting hairs and answer the question," snapped Savannah.

"I *will* if you'll just calm down and listen," Molly snapped back. "Yes, Nick—the carpenter—was nailing down some boards the other morning. I thought all the guests were awake and at the beach, but apparently, I was mistaken. When that woman complained, we were standing in the hall and Nick was hammering so I may have had to raise my voice to respond to her. But I didn't *scream* or say anything rude. All I did was apologize and offer her a refund, which she refused to accept. For the record, she also complained about *your* guests talking and laughing beneath her window. And on her way out, she knocked into my leg with her luggage so hard that my shin is bruised. So if anyone should be filling out any kind of report or review, *I* should be filing a charge for assault and battery!"

Molly recognized as soon as she said the words that she was overreacting, but she was fed up with both the guest and with Savannah.

"*Don't* write that in your reply to her review!" Savannah warned.

*Duh, like I need you to tell me that,* Molly thought but she managed to keep her mouth shut. "I have no intention of replying to the guest at all. I regret that she didn't have a good experience here, but I apologized and I offered a refund, so my part is done. I'm not going to engage with someone who doesn't really want a solution. She just wants to try to make everyone else as miserable as she is."

"That's easy for you to say—she didn't criticize *you* by name. I have my reputation to protect, especially if I intend to continue socializing with people from the yacht club." Savannah let out a puff of air. "Oh, well, Austin says everyone has their price. I can make nice with her. Maybe a reply and an offer of a refund will mean more coming from me, since I'm the owner."

"The amount of the refund is still the same, no matter who gives it to her," Molly pointed out.

"Whatever. You know what I mean," Savannah responded dismissively. "Okay, I'm typing my reply now, so tell me how this sounds. 'I sincerely apologize for the misunderstanding. My innkeeper should have explained—should have *quietly* explained that the reason the carpenter was hammering was because...'"

*If I had* quietly *explained what Nick was doing, the guest would have complained she couldn't hear me. But thanks for the support,* Molly thought, peeved that Savannah was essentially berating her in a public forum.

"Some floorboards had come loose. Because our guests' safety and comfort is paramount at Hydrangea House, the carpenter had to repair the flooring as early in the morning as possible.' How does that sound?" Savannah asked.

Even though she didn't want to correct her assumption, Molly's conscience wouldn't allow Savannah to submit the reply. What if Nick read the review? He'd been so kind to Molly and Hazel; she couldn't allow him to be involved in a half-truth.

"It's wrong," Molly replied to herself, as much as to Savannah. "I never told you that Nick was hammering the floorboards because of a safety issue. He was nailing them back down because he'd just lifted them." She squeezed her eyes shut, anticipating Savannah's reaction.

Her tone overflowing with sarcasm, Savannah asked, "And why, exactly, would you hire a carpenter to raise floorboards only to hammer them back into place again?"

"So he could check beneath them for something that belonged to a guest."

"You mean Matt, the science geek? What could he have lost beneath the boards? He's not married, so he couldn't have dropped a wedding ring down there."

"No. I didn't mean Matt." Molly couldn't prolong the inevitable, so she admitted, "I'm referring to Hazel Walsh, the woman you met who stayed here the summer our grandparents were born. She thought she might have left behind a... a glass container of letters when she was a child."

Savannah snorted. "Why am I not surprised that she's the one to send you on a wild goose chase? I overheard the two of you talking while I was in the kitchen that day. Half the stuff she told you was ridiculous."

*I knew she was eavesdropping, even though she pretended she wasn't interested in what Hazel had to say,* Molly thought.

"What part of Hazel's story seemed so ridiculous?"

"For starters, I'm not entirely convinced that she actually stayed here the summer our great-grandparents were born. And even if she did, I don't believe her sob story about how my great-grandfather was supposedly such a horrible person just because he didn't want Hazel spreading germs to his pregnant wife. I didn't buy her accusation that some other little girl in the family stole her doll, either." Savannah snickered. "For someone who was so eager to return to the inn, Hazel sure seemed to enjoy casting the Frost family in a bad light. Either that, or she has memory issues... Do I even need to ask if she found her letters beneath the floorboards?"

"No, she didn't," Molly meekly admitted. She could have defended Hazel's powers of recollection by telling Savannah about the box and enclosed note she'd found in the basement, but she knew that this wasn't the right time to set Savannah straight. So instead she reassured her, "I didn't charge the cost of Nick's labor to the inn—I paid it myself. And if the guest who complained about the noise ends up accepting a refund, I'll personally reimburse her, too."

"That's right, you will. But how do you expect to make up for the damage that was done to *my* reputation by her review?"

"I-I don't know." Molly was at a loss. Even though the woman had complained to her personally about Savannah's guests, she hadn't written anything about them online. So it wasn't as if Molly could emphasize that Savannah was partially responsible for the negative review, too. "I'm genuinely sorry."

"So am I—I'm sorry I let you talk me into keeping the inn open for the summer," Savannah sniped. "You were supposed to be honoring Grandma B.'s reputation, not trashing *mine*."

Then she disconnected, leaving Molly to feel like she really *was* a "poor-excuse-for-an-innkeeper."

. . .

"Hey, Molly. Is it okay if I come in?" Matt asked, poking his head into the kitchen, where she was standing at the sink, washing the vintage tools and utensils they'd found the previous evening.

"Sure." She turned off the faucet, dried her hands and turned to smile at him.

He pointed at the sink. "Does this mean you've decided to take up cooking after all?"

"Ha. No way. I thought I might give some of these to Savannah." It was only a token gesture, but Molly hoped it would help make amends. "She loves to cook and bake—she's really good at it. When we were girls, she'd hang out in the kitchen with my grandmother while I went to the beach. It was great. I'd come back starving because of all the swimming I'd done, and there would be some fantastic lunch or dessert in the oven."

Molly recalled that her grandmother usually would be washing the pots and pans, while Savannah perched on a stool at the kitchen island, chatting away. Molly's mother once said she'd felt bad for Beverly, because Savannah was so clingy as a teenager, but Beverly never seemed to mind. "I don't know if she'll be able to use them, but she might want them as keepsakes."

Matt adjusted his glasses. "That's awfully nice of you."

"Yeah, well, it's sort of a peace offering. And speaking of peace offerings... I'm sorry if anything I said yesterday evening came across as unappreciative, because I've been really grateful for your assistance." That sounded too stiff, so she added, "Searching the basement with you was the most fun I've had on a Saturday evening all summer."

"I had fun, too," he agreed. "But after you opened the package, it seemed like you needed to be alone with your thoughts, which is why I left so quickly."

"By 'needing to be alone with my thoughts,' you mean you

were afraid I was going to start bawling," She was chuckling, but Matt tilted his head at her.

"Well, did you?" His expression was so concerned that it caught Molly off guard and she answered honestly.

"Yeah, I did."

"Because you were disappointed about finding a doll instead of the bottle?"

She nodded. "Mostly, yes. But beneath it all, I was upset about other stuff, too."

"Like about Savannah selling the inn?"

"What?" Molly yelped, clasping her head in surprise. "How did *you* know about that?"

"Sorry—I thought you knew I knew." Matt nervously inched backward.

"No, I didn't." She repeated in a quieter voice, "How did you find out?"

"Austin was schmoozing with people about it at the yacht club that day I went to lunch with him and Savannah and Gina." He reiterated, "I really am sorry for not mentioning I knew sooner. I figured it wasn't any of my business one way or the other, so I kept my mouth shut about it... until now, which was stupid."

"No, it's fine. I understand why you wouldn't have wanted to bring it up sooner, and I'm glad you're telling me now. I'm just surprised, that's all," Molly said. "What else do you know about the inn being sold?"

"Only that Austin wants to broker the sale."

"But he's a corporate attorney, not a realtor. He can't do that, can he?" Molly asked and Matt shrugged. "I guess that explains why he's so invested in the process—he's going to get a big fat commission out of it. Unless *I* can stop him—and I think I can," she declared.

"Is your plan somehow related to your search for Hazel's bottle?" guessed Matt, impressing Molly.

"Wow, you're *good*. How did you know it's Hazel's bottle I'm looking for?"

"Call it a hunch—or my analytical background as a biologist." He grinned. "Does the bottle contain a long-lost deed or something?"

Molly put a finger to her lips and pretended to covertly scan the area. "I'll tell you all about it, but let's take a walk down the beach where no one can hear us talking."

"We got it! We got it! We got the grant!" Jenny was shouting so loudly that Molly had to hold the phone an arm's length from her body.

"Oh, Jen, I'm so happy for you. I was starting to get nervous that I'd botched the application."

"Nope—they *loved* the case statement you wrote. They mentioned it in the award letter," gushed Jenny. "I owe you big-time. This money is going to make a huge difference for the center. I wish you were here so I could take you out to celebrate."

"I wish I were there, too, but we'll go out when I get back after Labor Day."

"Great. I'll take you to The Loft," said Jenny. "But I have to warn you, it might be challenging to find a free night. By then I'll be up to my eyeballs in work—I'll be getting ready for our autumnal gala. You're going to help me host it this year, aren't you?"

"Mm," Molly hedged. "Public events aren't really my thing."

"Don't be modest. If you can host an inn full of guests for an entire summer, co-hosting a one-time party will be a breeze. The attendees will love you and we'll raise millions and millions of dollars."

"You might not be saying that if you read my recent guest

reviews." Molly told her friend about the person who'd given her a one-star rating, as well as about Savannah's reaction to it. Because she didn't feel right sharing Hazel's story without her permission, Molly omitted certain details but Jenny got the gist of the situation.

"It's hard to say whose behavior is worse—the guest or Savannah's," she remarked, disgusted. "But if I had to choose, I'd say it's Savannah's. You're providing her a valuable service and she is *so* fortunate to have you there, Molly. You should tell her off."

"If I did, she'd probably fire me."

"She can't *fire* someone who's working for free," Jenny reminded her.

"You know what I mean—she'd send me home early. And then what would happen to all the guests who are looking forward to coming here for vacation?"

"Again, you're free labor. Savannah recognizes a good thing when she has it—trust me, I feel the same way. You saved the women's center about 30K by writing that grant for us, so I intend to roll out the red carpet for you when you get back—"

"That's not necessary, Jen. I did it because it's a good cause and you're a good friend and I wanted to help."

"I understand and appreciate that. My point is, Savannah knows how valuable your services are to her, too. She might not treat you like you're valuable, but she *knows* you are. And she's not going to risk losing you."

"You don't know Savannah like I know Savannah," Molly said. "Next topic. Do you want to hear about the oceanographer in Room Six?"

"Is he devastatingly handsome and irresistibly charming?"

"Mm... in his own way, yes."

"Which way is that?"

"Well, he's very tall and he has soulful brown eyes. He's

super smart and thoughtful and he loves the ocean as much as I do, even though he doesn't go in it..."

"He doesn't go in the ocean?" Jenny sounded dismayed. "Why not?"

"He's allergic to the cold—it literally makes him break out in hives."

"Okay, that's not a dealbreaker then. Tell me more."

After Molly finished describing Matt, Jenny said, "He sounds like the perfect guy for you. Are you going to go out with him?"

"No, I can't. He's—"

"A guest, and you don't date guests." Jenny completed the sentence for her. "It's unprofessional, blah, blah, blah. I can't believe you're still following your grandmother's archaic rule."

"I wasn't going to say he's a guest. I was going to say he's getting over a breakup with his fiancée. They worked together and after they broke up, things got really intense in the office, That's why he came to the east coast for the summer," explained Molly.

"So, what's the problem? His fiancée's loss is your gain."

"The problem is that he came to Dune Island to get away from a relationship, not to find one. Besides, what if we started seeing each other but it didn't work out? It's not like he's leaving next weekend. We'd be stuck living in the same house until Labor Day. It would be awkward for me—and it would be a repeat of his work situation all over again."

"That excuse is even flimsier than the one you gave me about why you don't tell Savannah off!" Jenny protested.

"Maybe, but I'm sticking to it." Molly sighed, wishing she'd met Matt under different circumstances. "Sometimes it feels like meeting the right guy at the right time is as rare as... as spotting a right *whale*."

"A what?"

"Never mind," Molly replied with a giggle. "Sorry, I hear a

car pulling in. I've got to go greet the guests. Big congrats on the grant!"

"I couldn't have done it without you—and I *know* it," said Jenny emphatically.

"You want me to check the closets, since I can reach the higher shelves easier than you can?" Matt asked.

For the past several evenings, he and Molly had been strolling down the beach together, under the guise of discussing possible locations for Hazel's bottle. Or else they'd brainstorm what steps Molly should take next if the DNA tests indicated she was biologically a member of the Frost family. Eventually, their conversations would drift from matters concerning the estate to more personal subjects. But since tomorrow was Saturday and the Peace Place family would be leaving, they stayed on topic, discussing Molly's plan to thoroughly search the rest of the rooms in the cottage before the new guests checked in.

She smiled. "I appreciate the offer, but I don't think it's a good idea for you to come with me to Peace Place."

"What?" Matt stopped short and clutched his heart. "You're eliminating me from the mission?"

Molly smiled; he was such a goofball. "Sorry, but Lucy and Sydney are very territorial about any areas they're clean-ing. *I* can hardly get their permission to enter the cottage when they're in it—even when I'm supposed to be helping them!"

"All right." Feigning disgust, Matt kicked at the sand. "But remember what I told you—don't make any assumptions. You have to check *every*where."

"Oh, I see how it is now." Molly playfully pushed his arm. "You think you're smarter than I am."

"Not smarter, just a better searcher," he said with a smirk.

Continuing toward the inn, he called over his shoulder, "I'm a faster walker, too."

Molly had to jog to catch up to him. "Okay, wise guy, tell me this. If you're such a good searcher, why haven't you spotted a right whale yet?" She gestured toward the water.

"Like I've said, it's harder to locate a moving object than a stationary one," he smugly replied. "Any other questions?"

"Yes." She stopped walking again and so did he. Trying to think of a topic that would stall him long enough to allow her to catch her breath, she asked, "Why is the ocean blue? Is it really because it reflects the sky?"

His face lit up. "Partly, yes. At least, the *surface* of the water reflects the sky. So that's why it appears blue on a clear day—or pinkish during a sunset, like it is now. But deeper down, the water in a sense is creating its blue color. That's because sunlight contains the entire spectrum of colors, and when it shines into the ocean, the colors with the longest wavelengths are absorbed first. The color blue has one of the shortest wave-lengths, so it's still visible deeper down..." Matt continued to list in detail the other variables that affected the ocean's color. When he finished, he asked, "Did that explanation make sense?"

"Yes—and it allowed me time to catch my breath, so thanks on both counts." She gave him a saucy grin to show that she was teasing but he groaned and held his forehead.

"I was being too longwinded again, wasn't I?"

"No, I was kidding. I like hearing you talk about the ocean."

"I wish my students felt the same way. The most common complaint on their mid-semester faculty evals of me was that I talk on and on and on. And on, apparently." He chuckled self-consciously. "Which is a rambling way of saying I ramble."

"Pfff." Molly waved her hand. "Reviews and evals have their purpose, but you've got to keep them in perspective. I'm sure there are just as many—if not more—students in your class who gave you high ratings for being so thorough and excited about your subject matter."

"Yeah, I guess you're right." He touched his glasses. "It's just that a permanent, year-round research position has opened up here, but it involves teaching one seminar per quarter. So I've got to make a good impression if I want to apply for it."

Molly hadn't seen that coming. "You like the Institute here so much you'd consider relocating to the east coast?"

"Yeah, but it's not just the Institute. I like a *lot* of things about Port Newcomb enough to consider relocating to the east coast. I'm really falling for this place." When Matt met her eyes without blinking, Molly had the distinct feeling he wasn't referring to the town's dramatic ocean views or its historic harbor.

She licked her lips, reminding herself for the millionth time, *He's a guest and he just broke up with his fiancée.* But that didn't stop her from responding with just a hint of innuendo, "I'm very glad you feel that way, Matt."

The words were barely out of her mouth when Molly's phone buzzed with a text notification. She slipped it from the back pocket of her shorts. "Oh, no—it's the guests from Room Two," she said, even as she typed her reply. "The keypad on their door isn't working and they can't get into their room. I think they must be entering the wrong code, but I'd better hurry back to the house."

When she arrived, Molly discovered the problem was that the guests, who were more than a little tipsy, had the right code, but the wrong door; they'd been attempting to get into Room 3. Molly tried not to feel resentful that her evening walk with Matt had been cut short for such a silly reason. *I guess it's better this way,* she thought. *Who knows what might have happened if our conversation hadn't been interrupted...*

Later that night, as she lay in bed, listening to the rhythmic advance and retreat of the waves on shore, Molly replayed Matt's comments in her mind. *I wonder if he really will relocate* here. *Not that it would make any difference to me, since I won't be back next summer—unless it turns out I really am Evelyn's oldest surviving descendant.*

In her drowsiness, Molly allowed her thoughts to wander even further. *If I could find a teaching position, I could move here year-round. Maybe during the off-season, I'd find a way to host even more families for no charge at Peace Place...*

Picturing how furious Austin would be, Molly dozed off with a smile on her lips.

## SIXTEEN

"What are you looking for?" Sydney asked the following afternoon when she came into the upstairs bedroom and discovered that Molly had pulled an antique desk away from the wall.

Because the carriage house had been thoroughly renovated decades after Hazel had visited Dune Island, Molly really didn't expect to find the bottle hidden in a cabinet or a drawer. Especially not since Beverly had insisted on keeping the dressers and shelves almost completely empty, so that the guests would have plenty of space to store their belongings. However, as Matt suggested, Molly was trying to keep an open mind and not make any assumptions about where the bottle might be hidden. It occurred to her that the antique desk might have had a "dummy drawer" that opened from the back.

Since she couldn't tell Sydney the truth, she fudged, "I'm just checking for dust bunnies. I wouldn't want them to make our guests sneeze."

"Are they allergic to bunnies?" Sydney asked innocently.

"No. I was making a joke. Dust bunnies aren't really rabbits. They're clumps of dust that *look* like bunnies because they're fluffy," Molly explained.

Sydney gave her a strange look and left without saying anything else. Molly resumed her examination of the desk, but there wasn't anything unusual about the drawers. She slid the desk back into place against the wall and continued inspecting in and around the other furniture, before examining the bookshelves and closets. Then she moved on to the second upstairs bedroom.

Until she stepped into the walk-in closet, Molly had forgotten all about the overhead hatch to the scuttle attic. The attic hadn't been part of the original carriage house; it was added when the carriage house had been converted into a cottage. For the same reasons she didn't like going into the basement, the idea of climbing into the attic made Molly shudder. *Maybe I should have included Matt in my search today after all,* she thought.

Since she wasn't tall enough to remove the panel—much less, to hoist herself through the hatch—without a stepladder, she headed downstairs to get one. She'd been so absorbed in hunting for Hazel's bottle that Molly wasn't aware that she hadn't heard any vacuuming sounds until she noticed the dusting of sand near the entryway door.

*Why hasn't Sydney vacuumed yet?* she wondered as she headed into the living room.

Lucy was sitting on the couch, literally twiddling her thumbs—a sign she was anxious about something. When Molly asked her what was wrong, she replied, "Sydney's in the bathroom. She's crying."

Molly rushed to the bathroom door and gently tapped it with her knuckle. "Sydney? Are you ill?" she asked. No answer. "Sydney? Can you answer me, please?"

"Sydney's crying," Lucy repeated. "You made her sad."

Molly spun around. "I did? How?"

"You said the rooms are dusty." Lucy spun her thumbs around each other faster. "I can't clean the bathroom. Sydney locked the door. The guests will sneeze and you'll be mad at me, too."

"No, I won't, I promise. I'm not mad at Sydney and I won't be mad at you," Molly said in a rush, feeling like she herself was on the brink of tears to realize how much her offhanded remark about dust bunnies had upset both Sydney and Lucy. She tapped the door again. "Sydney? I'm sorry I hurt your feelings. You and Lucy and the two best housekeepers I ever met. I didn't mean it about looking for dust bunnies. You caught me being nosy and poking around, so I fibbed about what I was doing, which was very wrong of me. Sydney? Sydney, I'm sorry."

Molly paused, not wanting to pressure her. Then she repeated, "I'm not mad at you. I think you're a terrific house-keeper and when you're ready, I'd love it if you'd come out and help us finish cleaning."

Since she knew she'd further insult Sydney by beginning to vacuum, Molly took a seat on the far end of the couch, careful not to crowd Lucy.

She'd just sat down when someone pushed open the main door to the cottage, calling, "Hellooo. Anyone home?" A woman stood in the entryway, shaking her wet umbrella. Three bare-foot children pushed in behind her.

"The guests are here. I didn't clean the bathroom. Sydney locked the door," recited Lucy, as Molly jumped to her feet, rushed across the room and plastered a smile across her face.

"Hello. I'm Molly, the innkeeper, and I'm very glad you're here. Unfortunately, we're not quite ready for you to come in. We want Peace Place to be sparkling for you, but we haven't quite finished cleaning yet." The check-in time was at three, so they still had half an hour to get everything ready.

"I can see that," the woman said, huffing. "But we're here now. You can just mop around us while we're bringing in our stuff."

Molly groaned inwardly. Lucy and Sydney were already

upset and having to work around these guests would only make things worse. "I'm sorry, but it'll be a lot more efficient for us to finish if we're the only ones in here. It will only take half an hour and then you'll have the entire place to yourselves," she said, still forcing a smile. "There's a public library on the other end of Main Street—they put on free puppet shows on rainy afternoons. Or there's a children's education center at the cranberry farm in Rockfield. I can give you directions. It's not too far from here."

"*A puppet show?*" the boy repeated derisively. "That's for babies."

"I don't want to go to an education center on summer vacation," his sister whined.

Molly could hear Lucy repeating her concern that Sydney had locked the door; she sounded more agitated by the second. Molly said to the guest, "If you'd like, I can take you to up to Hydrangea House. I think we still might have some dirt bomb muffins left from breakfast. They taste fantastic if you dip them in a cup of coffee or a glass of milk."

"Is it chocolate?" asked the boy. "I don't like white milk."

"No, it isn't," Molly answered sharply before softening her tone. "But I'll check to see if we have juice, instead."

"Muffins dipped in juice? You don't have children, do you?" the woman scoffed. "I really don't want to traipse from one place to another."

Molly had almost completely lost her patience. "You're very welcome to wait in your car in the driveway," she said, trying her best not to bark.

The woman's eyebrows shot up and she opened her mouth to say something but before she could, her daughter whined, "I don't *want* to get back into the car again."

"*Fine*, we'll go have a muffin at the other house," the woman said with a sniff, as if she were doing Molly a favor. "But check-in time is at 3:00, so I hope you've finished cleaning by then, because that's when we're supposed to be allowed to come in."

"I'm sure we'll be all set," Molly said sweetly, even though she was seething and even though she wasn't at all sure they would finish by then.

She may not have ever heard Beverly speak poorly of guests, but Molly suddenly had an inkling why one of her grandmother's oft-repeated truisms was, "Good manners are free, so there's no excuse for anyone, poor or rich, not to use them."

By the time she returned from serving the woman and her children in the sunroom at Hydrangea House, Molly's temper had cooled down a few degrees. She figured the woman was probably stressed from the trip and her children were either overly tired or overly excited. To her delight, Sydney had emerged from the bathroom and was vacuuming and Lucy was scrubbing out the tub.

The three of them finished cleaning at 2:58, on the dot. Before Sydney and Lucy dashed out to where Delores was waiting for them in the parking lot, Molly reiterated how much she valued their work. Neither of them met her eyes and Lucy didn't say anything, but Sydney mumbled, "Beverly never looked for dust bunnies."

"I know she didn't. That's because she knew there weren't any." Molly understood that Sydney's remark wasn't intended to be accusatory; it was meant as an explanation for why *she* hadn't moved all the furniture to check behind it for dust. But it still upset Molly to be reminded once again that she'd fallen short of Beverly's standards—primarily because her failure had hurt Sydney and Lucy's feelings. Her eyes blurred with tears as she apologized, "I made a mistake and I'm very sorry."

Sydney abruptly threw her arms around her in such a tight squeeze it made Molly gasp, as much from surprise as from the force of the embrace. "I forgive you," she said. Just as abruptly as she'd hugged her, she released her and shot out the door.

Lucy followed in her footsteps, but she stopped at the threshold. "Nobody's perfect," she stated, still not looking at Molly. "Beverly burned a cake once and said a bad word. Everybody in the sunroom heard her. Nobody's perfect."

Then she took off, too, leaving Molly astonished. Later, she'd have to call Delores to tell her about the incident, as she was required to do whenever something significant happened to upset Sydney or Lucy during their shift. She just hoped their home's manager would be half as understanding as they were.

Molly turned off the handheld vacuum cleaner and scanned the floor beneath the end table for any crumbs she may have missed. It was apparent that the new Peace Place guests had made the mess in the living room; Molly recognized the children's plastic drinking glasses they'd left behind.

*I wish the kids would have stayed in the sunroom to enjoy their refreshments,* she brooded. *And I wish the adults would wipe their feet better before coming into the house. Sydney and Lucy just cleaned but there's already more sand on this floor than there is on the beach!*

Molly recognized she was hyperbolizing and that she wasn't truly cranky about the crumbs or about sand in particular. She was peevish about *everything* in general. The guest's rudeness. The fact that it was pouring outside, which meant she wouldn't be able to take an evening beach walk with Matt. Her awkward phone conversation with Delores, who'd reminded her that this was the second time in a matter of weeks that Lucy or Sydney had been upset enough to cry. She'd also made a point of reminding Molly it had been four years since either of them had shed any tears over a workplace issue.

*That's partly because they're already on edge trying to adjust to Beverly's absence—just like I am,* Molly had thought. She didn't say it though, because she knew if she hadn't been trying to disguise the fact that she was searching for Hazel's bottle, she never would have made the upsetting comment about dust bunnies to Sydney. In turn, Molly felt guilty for being so distracted by what happened in the past that she wasn't concentrating enough on the present. *Maybe I should scale back my search—and scale back how much time I'm spending with Matt, too.*

Both thoughts depressed her. Molly reminded herself that she wasn't focusing on finding the bottle for her own sake; the DNA tests would provide the information she really needed. But she'd continued searching for the handwritten message so Hazel could have a keepsake of her family's history to hand down to Lauren. Furthermore, Molly wasn't ready to sacrifice her time with Matt. *Our walks are the highlight of my day. After serving everyone else, I deserve to have a little fun, don't I?*

Besides, even though several things had gone wrong today, most of them had turned out all right in the end. Yes, Sydney and Lucy had been upset, but they seemed to have recovered already. Despite her rocky start with the Peace Place guests, Molly had smoothed things over with the mother. And even if the children left crumbs on the living room floor, at least they hadn't spilled their grape juice on the white couch.

As she circled a damp cloth over a sticky spot on the end table, Molly mumbled aloud, "I guess it could've been a whole lot worse."

"What could have been worse?" asked Matt, suddenly towering over her.

"My day." Molly straightened her spine and smiled at him.

"That doesn't sound good. You want to talk about it?"

"No, thanks. Everything turned out fine."

Matt's eyes went wide and he dropped his voice to a whisper. "Does that mean you found the... you-know-what in the cottage?"

"I said it turned out *fine*, not fantastic." Molly chuckled.

"Believe me, if I had found the bottle, I wouldn't be vacuuming —I'd be dancing around."

"That's sort of what I figured, but I was afraid to ask." Matt still hadn't cracked a smile. He fidgeted with his glasses and hedged, "Er, your, uh, your day might not turn out so fine after all, which is probably my fault."

"Why, what happened?" Molly couldn't imagine Matt doing anything to ruin her day. "Does this have something to do with the bottle?"

"Not *the* bottle. *That* bottle." He pointed to the ship-in-the-bottle on the highest level of the built-in bookshelf. "This afternoon I happened to walk through this room when a woman was having a snack in here with her children. She asked if I could take the SIB—the ship in the bottle, I mean—down from the shelf because her son wanted to see it and she wasn't tall enough to get it for him. I told her I thought it was an antique, not a toy, but she was pretty persistent." He grimaced.

Molly could anticipate what had happened. From where she stood, the ship appeared intact but she asked, "Don't tell me, the boy shook it and a mast broke?"

"No, nothing like that—I didn't even give it to him. That was the problem. But the woman kept bugging me to take it down and I finally said I wasn't comfortable moving the home-owner's possessions without permission."

"Good for you!" cheered Molly. She cupped her hand over her mouth and added quietly. "I'm sorry if your interaction with the guest negatively affected *your* day, but I don't see why you'd think it would have a negative effect on mine?"

"Because when I was leaving, I heard her gripe, 'The guests here are as rude as the innkeeper.' I assumed that meant you'd already had an issue with her. I feel like I added fuel to the fire and I know you don't want to get any more bad reviews..."

"Aw, that's really sweet of you to be concerned, but please don't worry about it. You did the right thing. Even if she leaves a bad review, it's better than if you'd given the boy the bottle and somehow the ship had gotten damaged."

"That's what I thought, too, but from what you've told me, Savannah might not agree."

"I think she would. She's always loved that ship." Molly hoped she sounded more confident than she felt. Glancing up at the SIB, she casually remarked. "I wonder when putting messages and ships in bottles became so popular, anyway."

Matt held a finger in the air, a spark of enthusiasm illuminating his features. "I know the answer to that. Do you want the condensed or the expanded version?"

"The expanded version—if you have time for it." Molly eagerly plonked herself down on the couch, but Matt suggested they talk while walking on the beach, instead. She protested, "It's pouring out there."

"So?" He gently tugged her fingers, his big brown eyes pleading with her. "You won't melt, will you?"

"No, I won't," she said, their fingers still linked until she rose to her feet. *I'm already melting.*

# SEVENTEEN

On Monday morning, the sound of the rain against the window was louder than the surf against the shore. *Not again*, thought Molly. It had been showering steadily since Saturday, which meant the guests had been hanging around the inn more often than usual. It seemed she hadn't had a moment to herself on Sunday, which was when she'd intended to call Hazel. Although Molly regretted that she'd have to report she hadn't found the bottle in Peace Place, she'd been looking forward to chatting with Hazel and Lauren. Their warm, humorous mother-and-daughter bantering always brightened her mood and she regretted not being able to speak with the pair.

So on Monday after Molly had completed her morning chores, she retreated to the sitting room and called them—but Hazel didn't answer her phone. Molly had to think quickly about how much information to leave in her message, since she wasn't sure if staff members from the assisted living facility had access to Hazel's voice mail.

"Hello, Hazel. It's me, Molly. I didn't find that item I've been searching for." She had learned to preface her remarks with a disclaimer so she wouldn't get Hazel's hopes up. "But I wanted to check in. I'd love it if you'd call me when you get a chance. Meanwhile, I hope you and Lauren are both well. We're all fine here at the inn, just a little soggy. Talk to you soon!"

By the end of the day, when Hazel hadn't returned Molly's call, she began to worry. The last time Hazel hadn't called as often as Molly expected she would, it was because she'd broken her ribs.

"I hope she's all right," she fretted aloud to Matt as they tromped down the beach that evening, wearing hooded jackets, their heads bent against the rain. "I know I only called her this morning, but I thought I would have heard back from her by now. It's not like she goes out a lot—she lives in an assisted living facility."

"She may have had a doctor's appointment today and it wore her out," he said. "Maybe she wants to wait until tomorrow to talk to you, when she feels more rested."

"Yeah, maybe that's it." Molly lifted her head to scan the water for breaching whales in the distance. She didn't really expect to see one, but since whale watching was supposedly one of the reasons she and Matt had ventured out in the crummy weather, she figured she should at least pretend to be hopeful. "You know, when a guest asked me why we were going for a walk in the rain, I almost slipped and told her about the right whale sightings."

At first, Molly thought Matt's silence indicated he was annoyed by her confession. But when she twisted her neck, she realized he wasn't beside her. The lenses of his glasses were steamy and he had stopped to unzip his jacket, wipe them on his dry T-shirt, rezip his jacket and then put his glasses on again. Every thirty seconds, it was the same process.

"Wouldn't it be easier to leave those off entirely?" she asked.

"Sure, but if I take them off, I won't be able to see a thing. You'd have to lead me down the beach by hand." He stopped wiping his lenses against his shirt and squinted at her. Molly couldn't tell if he was making a serious proposal or not.

She half-joked, "You'd better put them back on then. If the guests see us holding hands, they might think there's something going on between us."

"They probably think that already," Matt mumbled, as he lifted his glasses to his face again.

"Oh, no—I hope not!" Molly exclaimed.

He jerked his head back in surprise. "Shudder at the thought, huh?"

"No. I-I didn't mean it like that," Molly quickly objected. "It's just, you know, I wouldn't want someone to post a review that said, 'The innkeeper couldn't bring me fresh towels because she was taking a romantic walk on the beach with another guest,' or something like that."

"I see. Well, then, for the sake of your reviews, maybe I should keep my distance." Matt grinned to show he was teasing before he strode off, at twice Molly's pace. But within half a minute, he had to stop and wipe his glasses again, so she caught up with him and they finished the rest of their walk side by side.

On Tuesday morning, it was Lauren, not Hazel, who returned Molly's call.

"I know it's early, but I figured you'd be awake to go buy goodies for the guests," she said.

"You're right. In fact, I'm heading back from the bakery in Rockfield, now. Just give me a second to pull over—it's pouring so hard that I'd better not drive and talk at the same time."

"You want to call me back when you're at the inn?"

"No, really, I've been eager to hear from you and your mother and this is a perfect time to talk." Molly turned into the sandy parking lot in front of Rockfield's conservation land. To be honest, she was glad for the excuse not to return to

Hydrangea House just yet. Molly felt bad that the guests were experiencing a stretch of bad weather on their vacation and she understood why they had cabin fever. But being cooped up inside with a houseful of grouchy people was wearing on her nerves, too. "When I didn't hear from your mother, I was worried. Is she okay?"

"She's better now, but the night before last I had to take her to the hospital."

Molly inhaled sharply. "What was wrong?"

"She was having difficulty breathing, which is always a concern with broken ribs. Because of the pain, sometimes a person doesn't inhale deeply enough. In turn, fluid collects in their lungs and they develop pneumonia, which is what happened to my mother, unfortunately."

"That's awful, especially after all of the pain she has already endured because of the injury itself." Molly was so distraught her eyes filled with tears. Her elderly friend's current situation reminded her of when Hazel was a little girl and she had survived a grueling summer of her aunt's cruelty and death, followed by her own long illness and recovery—only to lose her father a few months later.

"Yes, she's had a rough time of it," Lauren agreed. "They're keeping her in the hospital one more day, which is making her spitting mad, but she's definitely doing much better now."

"What a relief. I'm so glad to hear that." Molly imagined how stressful the situation must have been for Lauren to handle on her own. "How are *you* doing?"

"I'm doing better, too, now that I know my mother's going to be okay." Lauren chuckled. "Can you believe that last night, she asked the pulmonologist if he's married. It was so obvious she was trying to set me up—I could have died of embarrassment. When he left, I was like, 'Mom, knock it off.' And do you know what she said? She told me I had to let her do whatever she wanted because she was on her deathbed."

Molly laughed because she could picture Hazel and Lauren's interaction. "Sounds like she's *definitely* feeling like her old self again."

"Yup, she sure is."

"I'm so glad," Molly repeated the sentiment before telling Lauren about searching Peace Place for the bottle. "I'm disappointed I didn't find it, but I'm still on the lookout—Matt is helping me, too."

"My mom will be *very* happy to hear that," Lauren said wryly and they both laughed.

After chatting a few more minutes, Molly ended the call by telling Lauren, "Please give your mother my best wishes for a speedy recovery. I don't expect to receive my DNA results for a while, but if it's okay with you, I might call again in a few days anyway, just to see how both of you are doing."

"I'd welcome a call from you any time—we both would," said Lauren. "I hope the sun comes out soon, so your guests can get outside to enjoy Hydrangea House's beautiful location again. Although in my opinion, it's so gorgeous there that even one day of looking out the windows in the rain is worth a week of sunshine anywhere else."

Molly had always felt the same way. As she turned on her windshield wipers and pulled into traffic, she thought, *It's too bad Hazel had such a disturbing experience at Hydrangea House, because if it ends up that I really am Evelyn's beneficiary, I'd love to invite her and Lauren to return to the inn as my personal guests...*

On Wednesday afternoon, Molly dictated a text to Matt:

Sorry to interrupt your work. When you get a sec can you please call me? It's important. Thanks.

She expected a *Yes* or *No* reply text, but instead her phone immediately buzzed.

"Hi, Molly. What's up?" He sounded breathless. "Did you get your results?"

"No, nothing that exciting, but this is still pretty good—"

He interrupted with another guess. "You found the bottle?"

"No." Molly laughed. "I appreciate your enthusiasm, but now what I have to tell you is going to seem kind of anti-climactic."

"That's okay. What is it?"

"I was wondering if you could do a favor for me tonight after work."

"Sure, no problem."

His answer made her laugh again. "Don't you want to know what it is, first?"

"Yeah, what is it?"

"The woman who's staying at Peace Place just informed me that her son told his little sister there were rats in the attic—"

"That's the same thing you said about the basement, but I didn't see any evidence of rats."

"That's because there *aren't* any. But if you don't stop inter-rupting, I'll never get to the part of the story where I ask you a favor," Molly facetiously scolded him and he agreed to be quiet.

So she explained that the little girl claimed she could hear the rats scratching at night. She was so upset about it that she slept in her mother's bed, which meant the mother had hardly gotten any sleep. She subsequently insisted that Molly inspect the attic before the end of the day.

"That seems kind of demanding," Matt suggested.

"I thought so, too—but then it dawned on me..." She paused for theatrical effect. "The scuttle attic in the cottage is the only place I haven't searched for the bottle yet."

"Ahh, and you want me to help you," he guessed, and Molly

could tell by his voice that he was grinning. "Sure, no problem. What time do you need me there?"

"Probably about six o'clock, which I know is kind of early, since you don't usually get back to the inn until six-thirty or seven. That's why I called you to check. I don't want the kids around while we're conducting our search. I figured I'd give the family a gift certificate so they can go to the arcade and pizza place in Lucy's Ham while we're up in the attic." She added, "I could pick you up from the Institute if you want me to?"

"No, that's okay. I'm usually done at five or five-thirty. The only reason it takes me a while to return to the inn is because I stop on the way and get something to eat."

"I don't want you to miss your supper. I could make something for you here at Hydrangea House?"

"Thanks, but no thanks," he objected a little too vehemently. "You said you don't like to cook."

"Not usually, but I wouldn't mind making a simple meal. Really."

"You might not mind making it, but *I* might mind eating it ..."

"Who told you that? Savannah?" Molly asked, more amused than annoyed.

"Uh-oh, I gotta go now." Matt was clearly dodging the question. "I'll meet you at Peace Place at six o'clock. I'll be the one wearing the wetsuit."

"The wetsuit? We're going into the attic, not into the ocean."

"Yeah, but it provides as much protection against spiders as it does against cold water."

Molly couldn't be sure whether Matt was serious or if his comment was another example of his dorky sense of humor. Either way, for the rest of the afternoon whenever she pictured him in a wetsuit, appearing like a self-described "string of licorice wearing glasses," she laughed out loud.

. . .

When Matt showed up on the doorstep to Peace Place, he was wearing his usual clothes. Or almost his usual clothes, anyway. Despite the humidity, he was dressed in a long-sleeved cotton shirt and sweatpants, which he said would reduce the chance of being bitten by spiders.

Molly used the code to enter the cottage. A trail of flip flops and wet towels led to the living room, where a raspberry-colored jam handprint decorated one of the sliders. The coffee table in front of the couch was nowhere in sight; it had been replaced with what appeared to be every cushion and pillow in the cottage.

"Looks like they've been using the sofa as a trampoline," Matt observed. "The question is, are those pillows there to break their fall, or are they deliberately landing on them?"

Although Molly personally thought their mother should have demonstrated more care for the belongings in the cottage, she also understood how the children's behavior might have been difficult to manage after nearly five straight days of rain. The carriage house was undeniably a mess, but no furniture appeared to be broken. More importantly, the guest hadn't mentioned that any of her little ones had gotten hurt.

"Yeah, the place is a wreck. I can't wait to hear what Sydney and Lucy have to say about it," she acknowledged. "The family left at four o'clock, so they might be back any minute. We've got to hurry if we're going to search the attic before they return."

Matt carried the stepladder as he followed her upstairs and into the walk-in closet in the bedroom. Since the two young girls hadn't hung up any clothes, they had easy access to the hatch. Matt suggested he go up first, just as he had done in the basement. Molly turned on the light switch on the wall that illuminated the attic and Matt pushed aside the board to the hatch. He only had to climb two steps of the ladder before the upper half of his body disappeared through the opening.

He immediately exclaimed. "Oh, yeah, I see something!"

"Rats?"

"Nope. Boxes."

Molly held the ladder steady so he could climb to the top step, and then he boosted himself into the attic. When he reached down to help her up, too, the ladder wobbled beneath her. She was too nervous to allow him to pull her the rest of the way. So Matt said he'd do a thorough search and tell her what he'd found. She could hear him tromping around for what seemed like a long time before he peered down through the hatch at her again.

"There are several boxes up here," he reported. "Most of them contain tiles."

"Tiles?" Molly's heart sank. "Oh. Those must have been left over from when all the bathrooms were remodeled."

"That would explain the other things I found—a green sink and a matching toilet." Matt grinned, but Molly was too disappointed to see any humor in the situation.

"Green? That means they came from the bathroom at Hydrangea House. The contractors were carting stuff all over the place, so I guess I shouldn't be surprised a sink and toilet ended up being stored here, instead of being hauled away." Molly sighed. "Are you sure there's nothing except tiles in the boxes?"

"In most of them, yes. I can tell by the way they're stacked, there's no room for anything else in the boxes. I could bring them down so you can double check, but they're heavy, so it might be a chore putting them back again."

"No, that's okay. If you say they only have tiles in them, I believe you."

"I said *most* of them have tiles in them. One looks like a box of clothes and shoes and another seems to have glass items in it

—the stuff in that box is wrapped in paper though. We'll have to go through it piece by piece."

"Matt!" Molly was utterly exasperated. "Why didn't you lead with that? I'd almost lost all hope."

"There still aren't any guarantees," he reminded her, handing down the lighter box, the one with the clothes in it.

He descended the ladder halfway before pulling the second, heavier box down after him. They started going through that one and as soon as Molly unwrapped the first item, she recognized it was an old light fixture from the formal dining room.

"We're getting closer," she exclaimed. "This stuff is from when the new lighting was installed downstairs in Hydrangea House. The contractors had to lift the upstairs floors to gain access to the ceilings in the downstairs rooms, so it's possible if they found the bottle, they threw it in here with the rest of the odds and ends."

As she and Matt quickly worked their way through the box, Molly's optimism deflated a little more with each item they opened. After unwrapping the last one, she tearfully announced, "That's it. There aren't any more. It's not in here."

"We've still got one more box to check." Matt pulled a bathrobe from the second box, and then a long, belted raincoat. "These clothes might have been hanging in the closet in my room. I bet the contractors put them in here—look at how they're not even folded. If your grandmother had stored them, they'd be neater."

He was clearly trying to sound upbeat, but Molly couldn't allow herself to feel hopeful. She rewrapped the light fixtures in newspaper and put them back while he emptied the box of clothing, piece by piece. As she expected, all he found was an assortment of outdated wardrobe pieces she didn't recognize and a pair of winter boots.

Trying to keep her sense of humor, she remarked, "Those look like something someone would wear to walk on the moon."

"Yeah, but they're nice and stiff and the perfect place to cushion something breakable." Matt let his sentence hang in the air while he slid his hand into one of the boots and pulled out a wool sock.

"You're really grasping at straws now," Molly told him, just as he reached into the second boot and fished out something that was square and amber and made of glass.

"This doesn't look like a straw to me. It looks like a *bottle*."

"No way!" she shouted. "That can't be Hazel's, can it?"

Matt held the object up to the light. "It *can* be and it *is*. Look, there's a little scroll inside it!"

Beaming, he handed it to her. Unable to quite believe it was real, Molly lifted it to the light again, and fingered the raised lettering across the bottom: MILLER & CO. BOSTON, MA. A decaying chunk of cork kept the note from slipping out, but Molly didn't need to read it to know it was a letter to Hazel's papa.

"I can't believe it," she uttered, unsure whether she was going to burst into tears or break out in a dance. Instead, she flung her arms around Matt's torso. "Thank you, Matt. Thank you so much."

"Glad to help." He leaned down and enveloped her, too.

The next thing Molly knew, she was on her tiptoes, with her lips pressed against his. Their first kiss was quick and firm, like a declarative *yes*. Both Matt and Molly pulled back in surprise, but only for a moment. Their mouths immediately found each other's again and then again, softer and slower *yeses* each time.

Molly forgot about the bottle she was still gripping behind his neck. She forgot about her grandmother's code of conduct and the fact that Matt was a guest. And she definitely forgot about her ex-boyfriend, whatever his name was...

"There's a light on in the closet," a little boy's voice announced out of the blue.

Molly and Matt untangled their arms and leaped apart just as the boy popped his head through the door. Matt made an irascible growling sound and began stuffing the clothes back into the box. But Molly felt too indebted to the child to be angry he'd interrupted her make-out session with Matt.

"We didn't find any rats or mice in the attic," she told the boy and his sisters, who'd come up behind him. Their mother was apparently still downstairs. "No bats or raccoons, either. So everyone can sleep in their own bedrooms tonight. But thanks for letting us know you thought you heard something—it's always good to check. Did you have fun at the arcade?"

"Yeah, it was awesome," the boy admitted, which made Molly happy.

"I liked the educational center at the cranberry farm better," said his sister, who'd claimed she didn't want to go there on her school vacation. "But the arcade was fun, too. And finding starfish on the beach—that was my most favorite thing we did."

The littlest sibling held up a stuffed toy lobster. "Look what Mason won for me."

"What a nice brother," gushed Molly. She was so elated about finding the bottle and kissing Matt that she probably would have complimented *Austin*, if he'd been there.

As they were crossing the lawn to Hydrangea House a few minutes later, carrying the boxes of old light fixtures and clothing, Molly was a loss about whether to acknowledge what had transpired between her and Matt in the closet. So instead she remarked, "They might not be the best-behaved children on the planet, but I'm really glad to know they're having a good time here, after all."

"Yeah, but I feel sorry for Lucy and Sydney having to clean

up after them," he said. "So, you're going to open the note tonight, aren't you?"

"Yes, if I can reach Hazel. She gave me permission to read it and the suspense is killing me, but I feel like she should know what it says the same time I do. If she's feeling up to it, I'll read it to her over the phone. Otherwise, I'll wait until tomorrow."

"Makes sense." Matt didn't ask if he could hear what the letter said, too, which Molly appreciated. "After you call her, do you want to take a walk? The sun isn't down yet and we may have found the bottle, but we still haven't spotted a right whale."

Molly didn't need any convincing to spend more time alone with him this evening. "Sure," she said, nodding.

However, when they reached the patio, they were greeted by almost the entire household of guests. "There you two are," one of them exclaimed, as if he were addressing a couple. "Come, join us for champagne."

Her cheeks burning, Molly asked, "What are we toasting?"

"The sun came out today!" several people on the patio chorused.

Molly laughed. "Just let me put away these boxes, first. Matt's so tall that I asked him to help me check the attic next door for critters—there *weren't* any, I promise—but we found some stuff that I'm going to take to the donation center." She awkwardly emphasized, "That's why we weren't here to join your celebration earlier. Right, Matt?"

Matt was looking askance at her, but he nodded and followed her inside to the sitting room, where he set the box on the floor inside the threshold. "I guess this means we're not going on a walk alone?"

"I-I can't," she stammered. "I have to be hospitable to the guests."

"*I'm* a guest." He stepped closer and touched her hair.

*If we start kissing again, we'll never go back outside this evening*, Molly thought. She gently pushed his hand away. "Matt, I'm sorry. It's nothing personal—it's part of my role as the innkeeper. Believe me, I'd rather not hang out on the patio with the same people I've been cooped up indoors with all week, especially since it means I'm probably not going to be able to call Hazel until tomorrow morning." She started toward her bedroom, so she could lock the bottle in her desk. "You're coming out to watch the sunset, too, aren't you?"

"No, thanks. I need to take a shower. I'll see you tomorrow." His voice sounded flat with disappointment but when Molly turned to see his expression, he was already halfway down the hall.

As spectacular as the sunset was, Molly kept glancing toward the house, instead of the horizon. Even after the last sliver of the orange arc disappeared and everyone applauded, she'd hoped Matt would change his mind. She lingered on the patio until most of the guests had gone in and most of the stars had come out.

The woman seated beside her leaned over and remarked in a slurry voice, "Lovers' quarrel?"

"Excuse me?"

She pointed to the sky, apparently to indicate the second floor of the inn. "With the guy in Room Six next to mine?"

"No, we didn't' have a quarrel," she protested. "And he's not my—I'm not his—I mean, he's a *guest*, that's all."

The woman tried to tap the side of her nose in a conspiratorial gesture, but she missed and poked her eye instead. "Don't worry. Your secret's safe with me." She leaned back in her chair. "If I were single and twenty years younger, I'd give anything to be the innkeeper here. What a life... You only have to deal with guests at check-in and check-out. You meet new men every week. Someone does all your housekeeping for you. And, you get to work on your tan and live near all this beauty."

She threw her hands in a wide arc, knocking a champagne flute onto the patio stone and shattering it. Molly was glad for the excuse to cut their conversation short. She suggested it was time for everyone to go into the house so they wouldn't cut their feet on the broken glass.

*Is that how the guests see me—as someone who's lazy and unavailable and is only doing this because I want to meet men and work on my tan?* Molly worried while she was sweeping the shards into a dustpan. Even though the woman had clearly had too much to drink and her characterization of Molly was completely skewed, she felt utterly dejected. *I can't imagine anyone ever implying things like that about Grandma.*

Then again, her grandmother wouldn't have ever spent so much time alone with a male guest—and she certainly never would have *kissed* one. Molly couldn't control what guests thought of her, but she *could* control how she acted. And she knew that no matter how much she didn't want to, tomorrow she was going to have to tell Matt she'd made a mistake by kissing him and it couldn't happen again.

# EIGHTEEN

When Molly woke up coughing in the middle of the night, she figured she was having a reaction to the dust on the boxes Matt had removed from the attic. She rose and took an antihistamine, but two hours later, she was still hacking away. She took a second pill but she decided it was useless to try to sleep, so she got up and unlocked the desk that held Hazel's bottle.

Until then, she hadn't allowed herself to remove the paper scrolled inside it—she was afraid once she had the note in hand, she wouldn't be able to resist the temptation to read it. Now, she told herself, *I should take it out so I don't have to fiddle with it while I'm on the phone with Hazel.*

As she wiggled the cork, it crumbled beneath her fingertips. Molly gently picked at the little chunks until the mouth of the bottle was clear of debris. She closed one eye and peered into the bottle at an angle. Although the letter appeared to be tied with a string, the knot must have loosened over time because the scroll had opened slightly, and it was too wide to shake from the bottle.

Molly retrieved a pair of tweezers from the medicine cabinet in the bathroom. When she first attempted to remove the note, a little triangle of the brittle paper broke off, but the rest of it remained inside the bottle. *I'd better be careful so I don't damage it worse,* Molly thought, just as she was gripped with another coughing spasm and had to set everything down.

It was painstaking work, but by pushing the letter against the glass, she was able to use the tweezers to re-tighten the scroll. She eventually pulled the paper all the way through the mouth. In the process, the string slid off; when Molly shook it out of the bottle, she realized it wasn't a string, but a strip of faded ribbon. *Hazel must have sacrificed wearing this in her hair,* she thought, smiling as she examined the two treasures lying side by side.

By then, the extra dose of medication had finally made her drowsy. She carefully tucked the bottle, ribbon and scroll into the desk drawer, relocked it and went to back to bed, feeling proud of herself for not even peeking at the signature line.

Molly woke to the sound of a woodpecker tapping on a tree outside her window. In her dazed state, she thought she heard the bird say, "Molly, wake up. There's work to do and people to serve."

She sat up with a start when she realized it wasn't a bird, but Lucy talking. *What's she doing here so early?* she wondered, reaching for her phone to look at the time.

"It's nine-thirty!" she exclaimed aloud. Then, "I'll be right out, Lucy."

Scrambling to put on her clothes, Molly figured most of the guests were already awake and waiting for breakfast. *I was supposed to pick up fruit yesterday,* she thought. *I don't even have yogurt to tide them over until I return from the store and bakery.*

The only person she found in the sunroom was the same woman who'd broken the glass on the patio the night before.

She lowered her sunglasses and remarked, "Someone looks like they had as much to drink as I did last night."

*No one had as much to drink last night as you did*, Molly thought, but she ignored the comment. "Good morning. I'm sorry I'm late serving breakfast, but I took allergy medication last night and it knocked me out."

The woman took a sip of coffee before replying, "A likely story."

"No, it's true. I heard her hacking all night," another guest said as he entered the room. "Does this mean you're not serving anything to eat this morning at all?"

"Yes, but it'll be more like a brunch than a breakfast. Sorry about that—and sorry my coughing disturbed your rest." As Molly twirled to go into the kitchen, she felt dizzy; antihistamines sometimes had that effect on her.

*I can't drive like this*, she thought. *I'll have to call the bakery and ask them to deliver something. I'd better call the market, too.*

By the time the food had arrived, and she'd set it out, it was almost eleven o'clock and all the guests, including the two who were in the sunroom, had left the inn. Molly coughed so much while she was re-wrapping the goodies that she didn't feel comfortable serving them later as a snack.

*Considering how high the delivery charge was, this was super-expensive. I can't let it go to waste*, she thought. So she labeled it: MOLLY'S FOOD – DO NOT EAT!!! In smaller letters she wrote, "health hazard," just in case any guests trespassed in the kitchen and decided to help themselves.

Feeling crummy, Molly checked with Sydney and Lucy to be sure they didn't need her help, and then she returned to her room to shower. On the nightstand, her phone buzzed with a text message from Matt.

> Are you okay? I missed seeing you this morning but there's always tonight? I hope you're able to connect with Hazel soon.

Until then, Molly had completely forgotten about calling Hazel, which showed how discombobulated she was. Because she didn't want to encourage Matt's hope that they would get together tonight, she dictated a brief reply text:

> I'm fine, but I overslept so I haven't had a chance to call Hazel yet. Will do soon. Thanks for asking.

After hitting send, she sat down on her bed—she was *really* woozy—and pressed the phone icon next to Hazel's name. Molly figured that Lauren would be screening her calls and if it wasn't a good time for her mother to talk, she'd pick up instead. However, she didn't recognize the voice of the woman who answered.

"Oh, hello. Is Hazel available, please?"

"No, she's not. This is Felicia, her nursing assistant. May I ask who's calling?"

"My name is Molly Anderson. I'm, well, I'm sort of friends with Hazel and her daughter Lauren. I'm the innkeeper at Hydrangea House on Dune Island." Molly paused. She didn't want to disclose too much information to this stranger, but she wanted to be sure Felicia understood it was imperative that she passed along her message. "Hazel left something important here that I just found. I'd really like to speak to her about it when she's able to return my call."

There was a long pause and Molly wondered if the nursing assistant was writing down her message. But then Felicia gently said, "Hazel was recently hospitalized for pneumonia. I'm very sorry to have to tell you this, but... she died last evening."

"What? No!" Molly cried and fell back the rest of the way onto the mattress, pressing the phone to her ear. She couldn't have heard correctly. "Lauren told me her mother was getting better—she was supposed to be coming home from the hospital."

"I know, it's very upsetting," Felicia said in a soothing voice. "Hazel took an unexpected turn for the worse. She had a reaction to the IV antibiotics she was receiving, and her body just shut down. Lauren said her passing was very peaceful though, and she was right there beside her, holding her hand."

Although Molly could imagine it was comforting for Hazel to have Lauren with her, she still felt unspeakably sad for both of them. She began to shiver and her teeth knocked together as she asked, "H-how is L-Lauren?"

"She's sleeping now. If you'd like, I can ask her to return your call. Does she have your number?"

"Yes, she does. But there's no pressure for her to call me back right now." Molly pressed her palm against her cheek to stop the tears that were trickling toward her hairline. "Please be sure to tell her how sorry I am to hear about her mother's passing and that I'm thinking of her... And please don't mention that I found anything of Hazel's. I'll tell her another time but she has too much on her mind for that right now."

*This can't be happening*, Molly told herself, after disconnecting the call. *I must have a fever and my mind is playing tricks on me, just like Hazel's did when she lived here. This is a nightmare, but I'm going to wake up any moment now, and when I do, there will still be time to read Hazel's letter aloud to her...*

Molly's phone startled her from sleep. Groggy, she glanced around at her surroundings as reality slowly started sinking in. "Mom?" she asked when she picked up the phone, without checking the screen. It was more like a wish than a question: her mother would know just what to say to console her about Hazel's death.

"No, it's *Savannah*. Where are you, anyway?"

"I'm in the inn, of course. Where are *you*?"

Savannah ignored her question. "I've received two complaints this morning that you didn't serve breakfast and I want to know why not."

"The guests *called* you?"

"No, they completed the daily survey."

"What *survey*?"

"If you ever checked the website, you'd know I added a guest experience tab that includes a survey," Savannah said. "After that woman from Room Five dragged my name through the mud in her one-star review, Austin suggested I should give guests a chance to voice their complaints to me directly, so I can address their issues before they escalate."

"In other words, you're micromanaging me. That's just plain fantastic."

"If I were micromanaging you, I would have called you on Monday, the moment after the Peace Place guest reported that you treated her and her kids like they were inferior to the guests at Hydrangea House."

Molly was aghast. "She didn't really say that!"

"Yes, she did. On the survey she wrote that you were unwelcoming to her and her kids when they arrived early on Saturday. She said you offered them leftover food and suggested they stay outside in the rain until you'd finished cleaning. But I couldn't imagine you ever being condescending toward a guest and she kind of seemed like a whiner. So I explained our check-in policy and informed her that anyone who showed up early at Hydrangea House also would have had to wait to enter their room until it had been thoroughly cleaned, too. I said you probably offered the same treats the other guests had been served that morning because that was all you had on hand and you didn't want her children to become too hungry while they were waiting." She ended by crowing, "See? I gave you the benefit of the doubt."

*That was big of you*, thought Molly. Just because Savannah

had defended her in front of one guest didn't make up for her secretly posting an online survey. "If you wanted updates about what's going on at the inn, I wish you would have spoken to me directly instead of fishing for reports from guests."

"That's why I'm calling you now. You're off the hook about the woman who's staying in Peace Place. But I still want to know why you didn't serve the Hydrangea House guests breakfast this morning."

Even though Molly didn't appreciate Savannah's tone or her approach, she figured the sooner she answered her, the sooner their call would end. "To be honest, I overslept because I—"

Savannah interrupted to scoff, "I should have guessed you were sleeping! Is that all you ever do?"

"For your information, I'm awake every day by five-thirty and if you could kindly refrain from making another snide remark for two seconds, then I'll tell you this morning was an exception," retorted Molly. "I was utterly wiped out from taking antihistamines last night because I couldn't stop coughing. I must have been having an allergic reaction to all the dust—"

This time, it was Molly who interrupted herself. She was so vexed by Savannah's attitude that she'd almost blurted out what she'd been doing the previous evening. She hoped her comment would escape Savannah's notice, but she jumped all over it.

"The *dust*? You claimed everything at the inn is always immaculate. Now you're telling me there's enough dust to trigger you to have an allergic reaction? You can't have it both ways, so knock it off and tell me the truth about what happened."

"You really want to know? Okay. *Fine.*" Energized by anger, Molly flung her legs over the bed and rose to her feet. She swayed at first but then she steadied herself and began to pace, gesticulating as she spoke. "The dust was on boxes from the attic at Peace Place. Matt went up there to look for a bottle that

Hazel said she'd hidden when she was a little girl—it's what I've been looking for ever since she left—and he *found* it. The bottle contains a letter that she wrote to her father that proves Opal, the maid, switched your grandfather and my grandmother at birth. Which means *you're* the descendant of a domestic servant and *I'm* the beneficiary of Hydrangea House!"

Molly almost immediately regretted her outburst. For one thing, she hadn't even read the letter, so she didn't know for sure what it said. Secondly, even if it recorded Hazel's version of events, it didn't actually *prove* anything. But mostly, she regretted her emotional tirade because it caused her to dissolve into a coughing spasm. She sat back down on the bed, bracing herself for Savannah's disparaging response.

Surprisingly, Savannah waited for her to catch her breath. Even more surprising, when she spoke, her tone was strangely calm, almost pacifying. "I don't know why you're so eager to engage in a child's fantasy, Molly. Maybe it's because you're jealous that I've inherited Hydrangea House. Or it might be a strange manifestation of bereavement, in which case, I feel for you, I really do. But if you don't get your act together, I'm going to have to ask you to resign your position as innkeeper."

That was the final straw. "Don't bother," rasped Molly. "I quit."

"You can't *quit*," Savannah immediately argued, her voice rising. Apparently, Jenny had been right; she'd been bluffing. "You *begged me* to let you do this in honor of Grandma B.'s memory."

"What do *you* know about honoring her memory, Savannah? All you care about is your*self*!" Molly's hands were shaking so violently she could hardly press the button to end their call. She collapsed sideways onto the mattress. Shivering but too fatigued to pull the summer blanket over her body, she closed her eyes and fell asleep again.

. . .

"Molly? It's three o'clock. Time to go," Lucy called in a sing-song voice from outside the door. "Delores is waiting."

She opened one eye and called back, "Okay. Thanks, Lucy. See you tomorrow."

It wasn't until Molly had slowly shifted into a sitting position that she realized she might *not* see Lucy tomorrow. *Do I have to give two weeks' notice for quitting a voluntary position?* she wondered. *How long will it take Savannah to cancel the rest of the guests' reservations, anyway?*

Then a more hopeful thought occurred to her: Savannah had been so obsessed about her reputation being maligned that maybe she'd hire a replacement innkeeper for the last few weeks of summer instead of shutting down the inn and ruining everyone's vacation after Molly left.

Given how miserable she felt at the moment, Molly couldn't imagine driving back to Delaware. Even the thought of walking across the room seemed overwhelming, but she knew she had to do it; there were two new guests checking in at any moment. She put her feet on the floor and stood up, but she was gripped by a coughing spasm and doubled over.

*I'll have to welcome the newcomers by text instead of in person. It'll be better than exposing them to whatever virus or cold I've got,* she thought, since it had become clear that she wasn't simply having reaction to dust. Besides, now that she'd had some rest, Molly couldn't deny the reality that Hazel had truly died, and she didn't trust herself not to break down in tears in front of the guests.

*Hazel.* There was one thing she still had to do for Hazel. Inching to the desk, she plunked herself into the chair, opened the locked drawer and pulled out the little scroll. She gingerly unfurled the yellowed paper and held it flat against the desk's surface. In penmanship that was surprisingly neat for a child, the letter read:

*Dearest Papa,*

*I hope you are well and that your knees aren't sore from scrubbing the deck. Aunt Opal's knees hurt if she kneels to scrub the floors, so that is one of my chores now. I also help wash the windows, make the beds and dust the ~~furnicher~~ tables and bookshelves.*

Molly smiled at the young girl's familiar sense of humor and her attempt to spell the word "furniture."

*Is the food good on the ship? There is a cook here named Dora. She makes ~~delishous~~ yummy muffins and she saves me the best one. She wraps it in a dish cloth to keep it warm. But don't tell anyone. It's a <u>secret</u>.*

Touched that her great-grandmother's small act of kindness had such an effect on the little girl, Molly reread the paragraph. On second glance, she noticed Hazel had underlined the word, "secret." Was that significant?

She continued reading:

*I am trying to be brave and good. There aren't many books here but I read the big Bible on the bookshelf every night. I finished reading Genesis and now I am reading Exodus chapter 2. Sometimes the words are very hard.*

*I liked the stories you read to me at bedtime better. I wish you were here to read me one again, even if they are for little children.*

*I miss you, Papa. I hope you will write back soon. I check the beach every day for a message from you. Sometimes I find bits of glass, but I never find a whole bottle.*

*Your loving daughter,*

*Daisy*

Molly ached at the thought of the little girl waiting daily for a message that never came. She paused to wipe away a tear before turning the page over and holding it taut, looking for a postscript about the babies. There wasn't one.

She flipped the paper over again and reread the letter in its entirety. *That's all?* she thought. *There isn't even any mention about Beverly and Harold being born!* Molly considered whether Hazel might have hidden *two* separate messages to her father, and that this one predated the second letter. But that didn't seem likely, since Hazel had specifically referred to hiding only one note in one bottle beneath the closet floorboards.

As poignant as the letter was, and as precious as it would have been to Hazel for sentimental reasons, the note didn't contain any evidence at all that what Hazel remembered as a little girl had really happened.

If there was any consolation in not finding the bottle until after her elderly friend had died, it was that Molly didn't have to tell Hazel that she'd been mistaken about what she'd written in the note to her father. Molly herself could hardly stand to face the likelihood that if Hazel hadn't recalled her message correctly, she probably hadn't recalled the past correctly, either. Molly locked the letter and bottle in the desk again and then she crept back into bed for the third time that day, feeling utterly deflated.

It wasn't that she believed Hazel had deliberately intended to deceive her. And no matter what, Molly was glad that she'd met Hazel and that she'd learned about how her life had inter-sected with Evelyn's, Dora's and Beverly's. She was also glad she'd searched so hard for the bottle. Even if it was too late to give it to Hazel, Molly knew Lauren would treasure her mother's note forever. So Molly had no misgivings in relation to Hazel.

What she regretted was that she'd been so desperate to somehow keep Hydrangea House and Peace Place that in the process she'd completely failed to do the two things she'd meant to do that summer: honor her grandmother's memory and provide the guests a lovely, memorable vacation. Despite all of Molly's hard work, the guests didn't feel she'd served them well and she'd quit her role as innkeeper, which was a disgrace to Beverly's memory, not a tribute. Her resignation would also cause unnecessary disruption and distress for Sydney and Lucy, not to mention for all the guests. Plus, she'd blurted out to Savannah why she'd been looking for Hazel's bottle, which would undoubtedly result in endless humiliating comments from her in the future.

*With any luck, maybe Savannah will be so angry I quit that she won't speak to me again,* Molly thought, laughing to herself. Her laughter made her cough and her coughing turned to sobs and then, mercifully, her sobbing gave way to sleep.

# NINETEEN

When Molly woke at first light on Friday morning, every muscle and joint in her body ached and her head felt as heavy as a bowling bowl. Parched, she dragged herself to the bathroom. She cupped her hands together beneath the sink faucet to drink from them, but she couldn't get her fill, so she staggered down the hallway to the kitchen.

As she balanced precariously on a stool, sipping juice, she had the presence of mind to think, *I should call the bakery to place an order for breakfast delivery.* But her phone was in her bedroom and she didn't have the energy to shuffle back there yet. After she'd drained the glass, she laid down her head on the kitchen island. The ceramic tile was cool against her cheek and she stayed like that for at least half an hour.

"Molly?" a man asked, his hand on her shoulder. "What are you doing?"

She opened her eyes but didn't lift her head. Matt's face was sideways next to hers, his eyebrows knitted. "Cooling off," she mumbled, wishing he'd go away. She didn't want to talk; she wanted to sleep.

"Yeah, I heard you were ill. Can I bring you anything?"

"No." She closed her eyes again.

"Wouldn't you be more comfortable in bed?"

"It's too far away."

"How about if I help you get there?"

"The guests will talk," she said, sort of chuckling. Then she covered her head with her arm and began to weep. "Hazel died. I didn't get to read the note to her in time. It wasn't about the babies anyway. The only secret was that my great-grandmother saved her a muffin in a dish cloth."

"Aw, Molly, I'm so sorry," Matt replied, giving her a side-hug. Or was he trying to budge her from the stool?

"Back *off*." She pulled away and almost toppled sideways, but he caught her. Half delirious, she babbled, "My grandmother's going to be so disappointed in me. I don't date guests. We never should have kissed and it can't happen again."

"No problem." Matt released her and turned to leave. Over his shoulder, he said, "For the record, you were the one who kissed me."

Molly dreamed her mother was sitting on the edge of the bed, offering her a mug of tea. Except then it wasn't her mother, and it wasn't tea. It was Savannah and she was urging Molly to swallow spoonsful of soup that she had poisoned. Molly knew if she did, she'd die and then Savannah would inherit Hydrangea House. So she kept resisting, no matter how delicious it smelled or how persistently Savannah tried to coax her to eat it.

Another time, she dreamed it was her grandmother sitting in the armchair at the foot of the bed. Molly couldn't see her, but she could smell her perfume—although that might have been the ocean scent, wafting through the windows.

"I'm sorry, Grandma," she mumbled tearfully. "I tried my best."

"Shh, shh, shh," Beverly replied, her voice washing over Molly like gentle waves.

The third dream was her favorite. Hazel and her papa were strolling down the beach, hand in hand, toward the west. Hazel was a little girl wearing braids tied with blue ribbon and her father was dressed in a crisp white sailor's uniform. Every now and then, one of them would pause and bend to lift something from the sand. They'd press their heads together, examining it, and then they'd place it in the pail Hazel's papa carried.

When they reached the horizon, he tossed the pail's contents toward the sky, which suddenly became a stained-glass window that shone with all the colors of a sunset. It was so vivid and brilliant, Molly kept blinking and blinking at it, trying to focus...

And then, Hazel and her papa were gone, and Molly was in her bedroom at the inn, with the sun shining directly into her eyes.

"It's about time you woke up," said Savannah, adjusting the window shade. "You've got to get up and out of here today."

Molly remembered that Savannah was angry and she knew she only had herself to blame, but she couldn't believe she was kicking her out in her condition. "I..." Her mouth was cottony. She licked her lips and started again. "I've been sick."

Savannah snickered. "No kidding. Who do you think has been taking care of you the last five days?"

"*Five* days? It's not Saturday?"

"No, it's Wednesday." Savannah handed Molly a glass of water from a tray on the dresser. "The nurse practitioner said you need to get out of bed and walk around today."

*Savannah's not kicking me out after all?* thought Molly, both relieved and confused. "I went to see a nurse practitioner?"

"No, the nurse practitioner came to see you. She's a guest in Room One and she said you have acute bronchitis. Don't you remember her telling you that?"

Some of this was starting to come back to her. "I do, but I thought I was dreaming." Molly took a long draw of water. "If you've been here for five days, that means you're missing work."

Savannah shrugged before plonking down into the armchair at the end of the bed. "So what? I've accrued tons of vacation time."

"Still, I appreciate it that you took time off to take care of me."

"I didn't. I took time off to take care of the *inn*," Savannah clarified. Molly noticed she had dark circles under her eyes, but she didn't know whether this was because she was unusually tired or if it was because for once she wasn't wearing makeup. "In case you don't recall or you thought you were dreaming, you resigned your role as the innkeeper. I don't know anyone else I'd trust to manage this place, so I've had to do it myself. When I got here on Saturday, you were out cold, so I didn't really have a choice in that matter, either."

"Well, I still appreciate it." Molly pulled a tissue from the box Savannah must have placed on her nightstand. Bits and pieces of the last few days started coming back to her. Regardless of whether she had a choice about taking care of her or not, Molly recalled how comforting Savannah had been to her when she was at her weakest. Her unexpected kindness made Molly feel twice as embarrassed by her impetuous decision to quit her role as innkeeper. "I shouldn't have resigned the other day, Savannah. I was exhausted and stressed and I had just found out that Hazel—you know, the guest who'd stayed here as a child—I had just found out that she'd died."

"Yes, Matt told me," Savannah replied. "I was sorry to hear

that. I know you really liked her. We arranged to have flowers sent to her daughter."

Once again, Molly was taken aback by Savannah's kindness. "Thank you. That was thoughtful. You're right, I liked Hazel a lot. She was a very special person and it was a privilege to meet her, especially because she stayed here the summer our grandparents were born." Swallowing her pride, Molly admitted, "But I found out she was wrong about, you know, Opal switching them at birth."

She waited for Savannah to laugh or say, "I could have told you that." Instead, Savannah just cocked her head and softly asked, "How did you find out?"

"I read the note Hazel had written as a little girl that she thought would prove what she remembered was accurate. I hadn't looked at it yet when I talked to you on the phone the other day," Molly explained. "Anyway, as upset as I was about Hazel's death, it was unfair of me to quit on the spot like that and I'm sorry."

Savannah narrowed her eyes. "Does this mean once you're feeling better, you'll finish out the summer as the innkeeper?"

"You'd really let me do that?" Molly quizzically tilted her head—and quickly realized she was still a bit dizzy.

"Yeah. The guests have been driving me nuts. Kind of needy, aren't they?" Savannah was being completely earnest; she'd obviously never truly realized how much work was involved in innkeeping. "But they do love my cooking. I've gotten lots of compliments."

"You *should* get lots of compliments. You're very talented."

"I enjoy it, too. It's so much more relaxing than being at work... which is why I've decided to take a few weeks off and cook breakfasts for the guests."

Molly *knew* there had to be a reason she was being so friendly. She figured Savannah had an ulterior motive for taking an extended vacation on Dune Island—and it probably had something to do with preparing to sell the estate to the yacht club. "So, are you and Austin staying at his friend's house again?"

"Who said anything about Austin?" Savannah's mouth flattened into a frown. "*I'm* staying here at the inn. I'll let you have this room a couple more nights, but then I need it—my back is killing me from sleeping on the portable bed. You can stay in Room Six."

"That's Matt's room," Molly protested, wondering if this was Savannah's idea of a joke or if she was making another dig.

"Not any more. A room opened up at the Institute and he moved out this morning."

"He did?" Molly sounded whinier than she'd intended. "Did he say why he didn't want to stay here any more?"

"Don't worry, it's not like he filled out a negative survey. He told me it was easier to bunk right there on campus, since he doesn't have a car." Savannah grinned, "Which works out great for me, since his room was pre-paid, and you'll need a place to sleep."

"Yeah, you're right. It's perfect," Molly agreed even though she couldn't have been more disappointed.

When Savannah left her alone in the room to get dressed, Molly brooded about Matt's decision to move out of the inn. She doubted very much it had anything to do with his wanting to be right on campus. He'd enjoyed his daily walk along the harbor to and from the inn so much that he never caught the free shuttle that ran every fifteen minutes during the summer months.

*The commute wasn't the reason he left. I was,* she fretted. Molly didn't remember exactly how she'd phrased it, but she hazily recalled that the morning he'd found her in the kitchen, she'd told him she regretted kissing him.

*I can understand why he'd feel angry or hurt, or why he might want to avoid awkward interactions with me in the future.*

*But it seems kind of childish for him to move out altogether—
although I guess he has a habit of this kind of behavior*, Molly
thought. *Even if we can't be romantically involved, I kind of
thought we'd developed a special connection. But I guess it's not
the first time this summer that I've been wrong...*

"I was afraid you'd wear yourself to a frazzle," Carol said,
clucking sympathetically after Molly had told her how sick
she'd been. "Do you want me to come there and help you at the
inn while you recover? I don't have a training session until next
month, so I could take the time off work. Ted wouldn't mind
making the trip, either, now that he's feeling stronger."

"Thanks, but I'm doing a lot better and Savannah's keeping
the inn while I recover. She also took care of me while I was at
my sickest. I mean, I was mostly sleeping, but she brought me
soup and medication and stuff like that."

"I'm surprised—but I'm grateful that she was so supportive.
You still sound hoarse, though, so remember to stay well
hydrated."

"I will." Molly chuckled to herself because her mother's
comments reminded her of the way Hazel had sometimes
treated Lauren as if she were still a young child.

She told Carol about finding the bottle and taking a DNA
test after all, as well as about Hazel's death, and Savannah's
plan to stay at the inn for several more weeks this summer.
Again, her mother sympathized, especially about Hazel's passing. Then she asked, "Were you terribly disappointed to learn
you're not the beneficiary of Hydrangea House?"

"Well, I'm still very sad that Savannah's going to sell it to
the yacht club, but to be honest, it's kind of a relief that I didn't
inherit the inn," Molly admitted in a tremulous voice. "I'm a
*terrible* innkeeper, Mom. I messed up everything and the worst
thing is I resented the guests at least fifty percent of the time. I

don't know how Grandma did it—or why she *loved* it. In fact, when I realized I'd been sleeping for almost five days, one of my first thoughts was, 'Good, that means five less days of waiting on guests before the end of the summer.' This experience has shown me how selfish I am. Or at least it taught me it's a bad idea to work full-time at the same place I usually go on vacation."

"I'm sure you aren't a terrible innkeeper, Molly. You just aren't *Beverly*," her mother pointed out. "Your grandmother was an extrovert. She loved hosting people. It was her gift. Your strengths lie in other areas. I admire you for giving this your best effort and I know you provided the guests with a vacation they'll always remember."

"Even if they try to forget it," Molly quipped.

"Stop that," her mother scolded. "Your grandma would have been deeply moved to know you dedicated your summer to serving the guests in her honor. But she would have wanted *you* to enjoy being at Hydrangea House, too. I think it's time to let go a little."

"Let go of what?"

"Of your expectations of yourself." Her mother suggested, "The guests will survive without you for a few hours, especially now that Savannah's there to help you. For the rest of the season, no matter what's happening at the inn, you should make it a daily practice to get away for a while—and I don't just mean going swimming or for a walk, although that's important, too. I mean maybe you should go into town and browse the shops. Or go out for a nice meal and to an evening concert at the pavilion. You always love doing that."

"Good idea," Molly agreed, even though she doubted she'd go out alone in the evenings. The only person she would have wanted to accompany her was Matt.

*Unfortunately, that ship has sailed*, she thought ruefully.

. . .

Because it was humid that night, Molly and Savannah left the door between their rooms open, to circulate the air. Maybe it was because she'd had so much rest over the past several days, but Molly couldn't sleep. Savannah apparently was still awake, too; Molly could hear her sniffling in the next room.

*I hope she didn't catch bronchitis from me.* She got up to bring her the box of tissues. There was enough moonlight for her to see that Savannah was curled up on her side, and if Molly wasn't mistaken, she was crying.

With the portable bed expanded, there wasn't any extra space in the tiny room for her to sit, so after handing Savannah the box, she hovered over her. "Do you want to talk?"

"No, I don't," she answered sharply, so Molly started to turn toward her own room. But Savannah blurted out, "I broke up with Austin."

"Oh, Savannah, I'm sorry."

"No, you aren't—you didn't like him. I could tell."

Molly couldn't deny it. "What I meant is that I'm sorry that you're sad."

"I'm not sad. I'm *furious.*"

That was the same way Molly had felt about Jordan and it made her wonder if Austin had been unfaithful, too. Tentatively perching on the end of the portable bed, Molly repeated, "Furious?"

"Yeah, because he's such a snob. The other day I asked him what he'd advise me to do if I found out that what you said about Opal switching our grandparents at birth was true..."

Molly braced herself for what she anticipated would be Austin's boorish response.

"I thought he was going to give me his legal opinion, but he said, 'I'd tell you to find another boyfriend because I don't date people related to domestic workers—I employ them.'"

Molly groaned; his answer was even more disdainful than she'd expected. "Was that his warped sense of a joke?"

"He laughed like it was supposed to be funny, but I know he was dead serious. I mean, I don't think he'd actually break up with me just because it turned out that my great-grandmother was a cook. But I *do* think he'd break up with me if it turned out that Hydrangea House wasn't mine."

Molly was angered, but not surprised by Austin's remark, which confirmed what she suspected about him. But because Savannah was already livid, she kept her thoughts to herself and simply asked, "How did you respond?"

"I said, 'Great advice, but why wait? I'm going to find another boyfriend *now*.'"

"Good for you!" exclaimed Molly in a hushed tone.

"Yeah, well, you're the one who gave me the idea—I spoke to him the day after you told me I couldn't fire you because you were already resigning."

Molly giggled. "I'm glad I inspired you to dump him. He was a real jerk. Did you know the last time he was here he nearly drove into Lucy in the parking area and then he had the nerve to call *her* an idiot?"

"He *didn't*?"

"Unfortunately, he did. I was going to tell you about it but then you said he wasn't coming back here, so, problem solved."

"What a loser. Now I'm twice as glad that I broke up with him." She half-sobbed, half-snorted in disgust. "At first, I believed he truly loved *me* for who I was. But now I see he loved how much money I earn. Or how many summer homes I own—especially because he was going to get a commission from selling one of them. How could I have been so blind? What is *wrong* with me?"

Molly had never seen Savannah this upset and she'd never heard her this vulnerable, either. "Nothing's wrong with you. Sometimes people just sort of fly beneath our radar and we don't see them for who they are," she consoled her. "That's what happened with Jordan and me. I thought he was such a great guy, so bighearted—especially when he suggested we sign up to volunteer at a kids' camp together. But it turned out that he'd been seeing the director romantically, which was how he heard about the camp in the first place. I had absolutely no clue. None at all. I was blithely looking forward to spending the summer volunteering with him."

"Oh, no." Savannah moaned. "You haven't learned, have you? When it comes to guys, you're still too trusting for your own good."

Molly didn't have a problem admitting she'd been taken in too easily by Jordan; that was exactly the shortcoming she'd just pointed out about herself. But she objected to the way Savannah made it sound as if Molly had a long history of dating two-timers. "What do you mean by saying I'm *still* too trusting for my own good?"

"What happened with Jordan is just like what happened with Adam Garfield when we were teenagers."

"Adam didn't go out with anyone behind my back," protested Molly. "He went out with *you*, right in front of my face. But that was after I'd already broken up with him."

"I'm not talking about him going out with *me*. I'm talking about him going out with Britney Ferguson."

"Britney Ferguson?" The name was vaguely familiar but it took a moment for Molly to remember who she was. Once or twice she'd shown up with a few friends on the beach where Molly and Adam were working. She recalled that he'd been annoyed because Britney seemed to expect him to socialize with her and the other girls. He'd ended up telling her that his sole focus was supposed to be on conducting swimming lessons. She got the hint and she didn't come back again. "Do you mean his coworker at the yacht club?"

"She wasn't just his coworker—she was his girlfriend. His *other* girlfriend," Savannah claimed, sitting up. "I saw them

together on the boardwalk one weekend. They were wearing
their uniforms, so it was easy to recognize them."

Molly was unconvinced. Adam may have been an immature
lout for choosing Savannah over her, but that didn't necessarily
qualify him as the kind of creep who'd go out with someone
behind Molly's back. "They were probably hanging out after
their shift ended or before it began, no big deal. They were
friends."

"Friends who shared the same ice cream cone—at the *same
time?*" challenged Savannah. "Trust me, I know what I saw.
Besides, I told Adam the only way I'd ever go out with him was
if he dropped Britney for good. He didn't even deny he'd been
seeing her. He called her right away and told her it was over
between them."

Molly's mind was reeling and she spoke her thoughts aloud.
"I get it that Adam was a loser. But I didn't know that at the
time and you did. Why would you want to go out with a boy
like that?"

"I *didn't* want to go out with him," Savannah said. "But I
didn't want *you* going out with him, either. I resented it that he
was cheating on you."

"So you're saying you deliberately broke us up because you
were trying to keep me from being humiliated by him?" Even if
Savannah's plan to spare her feelings was inherently flawed,
Molly was touched. She didn't think Savannah was that protec-
tive or that thoughtful. Maybe she had misjudged her.

"Partly. But mostly I was trying to keep *myself* from being
humiliated," she unabashedly admitted. "We were only sixteen.
Some of the summer people at the yacht club were friends with
my family and their kids gossiped a lot. It would have been
embarrassing for me if word got around about how Adam and
Britney were making a fool of you."

Molly should have known that Savannah hadn't wanted her
own reputation tainted by association. "Why didn't you just tell

me that Adam was seeing Britney at the same time he was dating me?"

"You wouldn't have believed me. You hardly believed me just now. You thought Adam was *soo* great just because he had good rapport with the little kids he taught. See what I mean? That's almost what you said verbatim about Jordan twenty years later."

Molly couldn't deny it. As she reflected on the past, it occurred to her that her grandmother may have known more about the situation with Molly, Adam and Savannah than she'd let on. Maybe that was also why, instead of taking sides, she'd encouraged the two girls to work it out by themselves. She asked, "Did my grandmother know why you went out with Adam? Did she know he was a cheat?"

"Probably, although she didn't hear it from me," Savannah said. "She always seemed to know what was going on. And she always wanted us to be better friends than we were. Like, when she faked that headache to force us to work together so we'd finally make up."

"What? Grandma was *faking* that headache?"

Savannah laughed. "Like I said, you were too trusting for your own good and sometimes, you still are."

"Giving people the benefit of the doubt isn't always such a bad thing," Molly said.

"No, it's not. Unless someone takes advantage of your trusting nature and cheats on you... or convinces you it's in your best interest to sell the inn where you spent some of the happiest times of your life." Savannah sighed and returned to the topic they'd been discussing before they started talking about Adam. "I kept envisioning spending the summers here with my own family someday. I could picture myself teaching my daughter how to cook in the same kitchen where Grandma B. taught me..."

Did Savannah really have almost as strong of an emotional

attachment to the house as Molly did? She gently suggested, "You can still pursue that dream. You don't have to sell the estate, just because you said you would."

"Actually, I'm not sure I *can* sell it, even if I wanted to." Savannah leaned forward and emphasized, "That's because I don't think it's mine to sell—I think it's *yours*."

It was late and dark and Molly's brain was starting to feel fuzzy again. She pinched the skin on her wrist to be sure she wasn't dreaming. "What makes you say that?"

"I think Hazel's story was true. I'm not a hundred percent positive, but I bet if you took a DNA test, it will show that you're related to the Frosts."

"Yeah, sure. You suddenly believe Hazel's story. I might be gullible, but I'm not *that* gullible." Molly rose to her feet and started back toward her room. "I've got to hit the hay. Have a good sleep."

"My father took a DNA test around eight years ago, when he was tracing his ancestry. He suspected something was fishy because the results didn't indicate a match with Evelyn's younger brother's descendants, and he knew they were in the database. My dad realized he might lose the estate and access to the family's trust fund if it turned out he wasn't a Frost," Savannah said in a rush. Molly stopped in the doorway, listening. "So he dropped the project and he never mentioned it again until shortly before he died and he was under hospice care. When he told my stepmother the story, she chalked it up to the painkillers."

Molly slowly turned to face Savannah. Even in the moonlight, she could see the guilt written across her features. "So... you knew your father wasn't related to the Frosts? That means you knew the estate probably shouldn't have passed to you in the first place..."

"I *didn't* know—" Savannah began to say but Molly cut her off.

"Okay, so you didn't *know* for certain. But even if you attributed your father's story to drug-induced delirium or whatever, you still had an *inkling* that the estate might not belong to you. It's been *four years* since he died. You've had all that time to get a DNA test or at least to explore his concerns. Instead, when Hazel came here and tried to share what she remembered about the past, you discredited her. And you treated *me* like I was having, what was it you called it... a 'weird manifestation of grief' because I believed her! How could you do that to me?"

"I *didn't* do that, I swear. I didn't find out about what my father said until Thursday evening. It was after our phone call when you told me you found a bottle with a message from Hazel in it. I-I-I was so angry at you for quitting that I called my stepmother to vent about it." Savannah crawled to the end of the bed. Kneeling on the mattress so they were eye-to-eye, she placed a hand over her heart and pleaded, "You have to believe me. I admit I was poking fun at you for being so gullible. My stepmother was like, 'Well, Molly might not be so naive after all.' Then she told me what my dad had said when he was dying. Why do you think I asked Austin for legal advice?"

Tears filled Savannah's eyes, but Molly answered without blinking. "Because you were afraid your deception would be exposed and then you'd get in trouble."

"No!" shrieked Savannah, wheeling her arms in protest. "It was because I wanted to make the transition of the estate to you go as smoothly as possible."

"As if you'd ever just hand over Hydrangea House to me like that." Molly snapped her fingers to illustrate her point. "But whether you want to or not, you might be *required* to relinquish the deed, because for your information, I've already taken a DNA test."

"Good, I'm glad. I'll take one, too, if that helps. Don't you see? It's not about the *house*—it's about Grandma B. I'd never knowingly steal something that belonged to her, especially not after all the time and care *she* gave to me..." Savannah became choked up and she had to pause to clear her throat. "I'm telling you the truth, Molly. Please believe me."

Molly's legs felt weak; this was the longest she'd stood upright in five days and she was tired. She sighed. She'd been mistaken about so many things this summer, but she trusted herself on this one.

"I do believe you," she uttered, turning to go back to bed. "Goodnight, Savannah."

# TWENTY

On Thursday morning, Savannah served the guests seven-layer breakfast tacos in the formal dining room. She said they were too messy to eat on the love seat and armchairs in the sunroom and besides. everyone had seemed to enjoy sitting down together the previous morning when she'd served eggs Florentine. Even though serving a full meal in the dining room was more work, Savannah preferred it to offering a continental breakfast.

Molly was still fatigued, so she hadn't been able to help set the table or prepare the meal. However, she slowly brought the dirty dishes into the kitchen after everyone had left. Then she sat on the stool at the island to eat the tacos Savannah had kept warm in the oven for her.

"These are fantastic. No wonder the guests were raving about them."

"I'm glad your appetite is returning." Savannah rinsed a plate and set it in the dishwasher rack. "For the first few days while you were sick, you'd hardly even eat a spoonful of soup, no matter what kind I made for you."

"I sort of remember that." Molly giggled. "The medication I

was taking must have really messed with my mind because I dreamed you were trying to poison me. So I had to refuse to eat the soup even though it smelled really good."

"Ha." Savannah seemed genuinely amused. "Speaking of poison, why are there boxes in the fridge with your name on them labeled, 'health hazard'?"

Molly had to think hard before she could remember. "I handled that food when I was first getting sick. As a precaution, I didn't want to serve it, but I didn't want to throw it out, either."

"Oh. I thought maybe the health hazard label meant it was something *you* had *cooked*." Even though it was sort of a dig, a friendly smile played at Savannah's lips.

"Very funny. For your informa—" Molly's sentence was interrupted by the sound of glass breaking and then a woman's scream.

She and Savannah both bolted into the living room, where Sydney was standing on the second step of a stepladder, holding her head in her hands, weeping. Shards of glass and wood were scattered on the floor in front of her.

"Sydney, are you hurt?" Savannah asked.

"I broke the bottle and the boat. I didn't mean to. I was checking for dust bunnies on the top shelf," she explained. "I'm really, really sorry."

"That's okay," Savannah assured her. "As long as you're not hurt."

Sydney shook her head, still buried in her hands.

"I'll go get a broom," Molly volunteered. When she returned, Sydney was gone and Savannah was cautiously collecting the larger glass fragments and dropping them into a wastebasket. Molly apologized. "I'm sorry about the bottle getting broken. It's sort of my fault."

In a quiet voice, she told Savannah about her search of Peace Place and the previous "dust bunny incident." She ended by offering to pay to have the ship restored to its original condition, adding, "I know how valuable it was to your family."

Savannah looked incredulously at her. "You *still* don't know, do you?"

"Don't know what?"

"My father and grandfather built that ship from a kit. Look, here's the manufacturer's imprint." Savannah handed Molly a splintered piece of the hull and she examined it, her mind blown.

"But I thought it was made by one of the whalers who originally lodged in the house when the captain owned it," she objected.

"Ha!" Savannah chortled. "That's the story all the adults told you, but it was only a family myth. Like Santa Claus or something."

"But you believed them, too, didn't you? I always thought you treasured that bottle."

"I figured out it was a fake when I was nine or ten and I saw a similar kit online." Savannah took the whisk broom and dustpan from Molly to sweep up the slivers of glass. "But I wasn't allowed to let on. Everyone thought you were so imaginative and they didn't want me ruining the fantasy for you."

*I guess I really am a lot more gullible than I thought I was,* reflected Molly. At least she wasn't the only one; Matt thought the SIB was authentic, too.

"I can't believe everyone let me believe a lie for all these years," she said with an exaggerated sigh. "Oh well. I'm glad it was just my illusions—and not a family heirloom—that have been completely shattered."

"Hi, Matt." Molly's casual tone belied how surprised she was when he phoned her on Friday at lunchtime.

"Hi, Molly. I've, uh, wanted to call you but I thought I

should wait until you had some time to recover." He sounded nervous. "How are you feeling now?"

"Much better, thanks. How have you been?"

"Okay." He paused and Molly could picture him adjusting his glasses. "I assume Savannah told you I moved to the Institute?"

"Yes, she said you were tired of walking to work."

"That's what I told her, but, uh, that wasn't the reason."

"Then why did you leave?" She had a feeling she already knew, but she wanted to give him a chance to express himself.

"Because I wanted to ask you out."

*Not* the answer Molly was expecting. "That doesn't make sense."

"Actually, it's perfectly logical," Matt argued. "You told me you don't date guests. So now I'm not a guest. Will you go out with me?"

Molly laughed in response; she had really missed him.

"Is that a no?"

"That's a yes! I'd love to go out with you." *The sooner, the better*, she thought. She added quickly, "I've got to stick close to the inn this evening in case the guests need me—Savannah and I are taking turns—but I can get away tomorrow."

"Could we at least watch the sunset together tonight?"

"Sure. Do you want me to pick you up from the Institute?"

"No, that's okay. I know you've got to be available to the guests."

"The campus is only a few minutes away. I'd like to see how your new place compares to your little room at Hydrangea House," Molly said.

"Well, it's about the same size, although it feels smaller because the bunk bed takes up a lot of space," he replied.

*He's over six feet tall and he's sleeping on a bunk bed just so he can go out with me?* Molly was completely charmed. "Sounds cozy." She repeated, "I'd love to see it."

"Sorry, but you can't," Matt said. "Girls—and women—aren't allowed in the boys' wing. I'm a 'dorm dad' now, so I have to follow the rules and set a good example."

"Enough said—I understand completely." Molly's smile was so broad her face muscles were beginning to ache. "I'll see you this evening. The front door will be unlocked, so come on in. I'll be around downstairs somewhere."

But she was so eager to see Matt that she waited on the front steps beneath the portico. The breeze was just strong enough to make the hydrangea blooms bounce up and down against the fence, like heads nodding in approval. When Matt strolled up the walkway, Molly dashed forward to greet him.

"Welcome to Hydrangea House," she announced with a flourish.

"I'm glad to be back." He grinned at her. "You look great."

She was wearing a button-down olive shirt dress that Savannah had remarked looked like a park ranger's uniform, but somehow, Molly knew Matt would like it. "Thanks. Let's go inside for a minute. All the guests are outside or away from the inn and I want to show you something."

They sat beside each other on the sofa in the living room and she explained, "I've tried a few times to get in touch with Lauren, but I haven't heard back from her yet. If she doesn't call me soon, I think I'll send her the letter that her mother wrote. Before I do, I wanted you to read it—I'm sure Hazel wouldn't mind. She told me she trusted you." She produced the paper from her breast pocket and handed it to him.

"I'm honored." Matt carefully unrolled the little scroll and Molly leaned toward him to look at it, too, their shoulders touching. It was a good thing she'd read the note half a dozen times already, because she was too distracted by memories of their last kisses to absorb what the message said.

When he finished reading, Matt leaned back against the cushion and blew the air from his cheeks. "Wow. That's really touching." He somberly shook his head. "But I thought you told me there wasn't anything in here about Hazel's secret."

"There isn't—not unless you count the part about Dora saving the best muffin for her."

"I don't think that's *the* secret," Matt clarified. "But look, she underlined the word. I think that she's signaling there's a secret somewhere in the letter. You have to consider that Hazel was a very observant little girl. This was written during the War, so she probably overheard a lot about what was happening in the world. Maybe she wrote about the secret in code because she was afraid that her letter would fall into the wrong hands."

"You mean she was afraid the Nazis would intercept it?" Molly teased. She and Matt had been wrong about the SIB, so she didn't want to let their imaginations get carried away with them again.

"No. But maybe she heard about the military using codes to communicate and she decided to do that, too, because she was afraid that Opal might discover her note and read it before she had a chance to cast it into the sea."

"Then what's the code? Did 'the best muffin' really stand for 'the best baby'?" asked Molly, still not taking him seriously.

"Nooo," he said slowly. He lifted the letter closer to his nose and squinted at it, as if the secret were literally hidden between the lines. "Listen to this. 'I am trying to be brave and good. There aren't many books here but I read the big Bible on the bookshelf every night. I finished reading Genesis and now I am reading Exodus chapter 2. Sometimes the words are very hard.'"

"What about it?"

"Doesn't that sound like a child who is torn about making a major moral decision? Or like she's trying to do the right thing but it's too difficult?"

"I suppose, but it could just be a literal account of what she's reading and how she feels about it," Molly said, taking the letter from him. "In the next paragraph, she writes, 'I liked the stories you read to me at bedtime better. I wish you were here to read me one again, even if they are for little children.' To me, it's clear that she misses her father and she wishes things could go back to the way they used to be when she was younger. That's all there is to it."

Matt gently nudged her leg with his. "When did you become such a skeptic?"

"I just want to be careful not to get my hopes up too high." Molly had intended to wait until they were walking on the beach to tell him about her conversation with Savannah, as well as about the SIB, but since no one was around, she decided to tell him now.

She ended by saying, "My DNA results will be back in a couple weeks and Savannah has taken a test and expedited her results, too, so they'll provide far more conclusive evidence than our guesses about whatever Hazel's note meant. I only showed it to you because we'd searched so hard for it and, well, it seemed like a good way to mark her passing with someone else who knew her, at least a little."

Matt met her eyes and nodded slowly. "Thanks for letting me read it, Molly. Even though I only met Hazel briefly, I really liked her." He pushed the corner of his glasses. "If you don't want to explore the meaning of her note any further after this, I won't push. But I wouldn't feel right if we didn't at least read the chapter of the Bible she referenced in her letter."

He looked so earnest that Molly couldn't refuse. She hopped up and pulled the Frost family's old King James version of the Bible from the bookshelf. "It was in Exodus, right?"

"Yes. Chapter two."

She flipped to the second chapter and began to read aloud. She barely made it three verses before she recognized the account: it was about how after the Egyptian Pharoah ordered all Hebrew male newborns to be cast into the river, Moses's mother hid her son for three months, eventually placing him in a basket in the reeds. When the Pharoah's daughter came to the river to bathe, she discovered the baby. Filled with compassion, she wanted to keep him, so Moses' sister, who was watching the scene unfold, tricked the Pharoah's daughter into allowing Moses' mother to breastfeed the baby. After he was weaned, as the tenth verse said, "she brought him unto Pharoah's daughter, and he became her son."

Molly didn't have to read any further to agree that Matt was probably right: Hazel had deliberately obscured the truth in code. "What a smart little girl she was," she marveled, closing the Bible and placing it on the coffee table. "And what a smart man *you* are! How did you know her hidden message contained a hidden message?"

"Lucky guess." A blush broke out across his face. "Like you said, the note isn't conclusive evidence. But given what Hazel wrote and what Savannah told you, I'd bet anything the DNA tests are going to indicate you and Evelyn Frost are related. Have you thought about what you'll do with the inn if you are?"

"I don't want to get too ahead of myself, but it's safe to say I *won't* be selling it to the yacht club," joked Molly. "Enough about me and the inn. I want to hear what's been happening with *you* ever since you jumped ship here and went to become a dorm dad for the high schoolers."

His expression clouded. "Well, I found out I didn't get the permanent research position I applied for. They said it was a tough decision but their other top candidate had more teaching experience, so that was the tie-breaker."

"Aw, that's too bad, Matt. I'm so disappointed for you." Molly touched his arm in sympathy, but somehow, the gesture turned into an embrace—which was perfectly appropriate, since he was no longer a guest.

# TWENTY-ONE

Molly heard Savannah open the door between their rooms to allow the ocean breeze to circulate. It was only a little after 10:00 p.m., but Molly still got fatigued quickly, so she'd gone to bed shortly after Matt left at 8:30. However, she quickly discovered that although her body was tired, her mind was wide awake.

"Did you have a nice evening out?" she asked.

"Yeah. Sorry if I woke you." From the sound of it, Savannah was easing onto the portable bed. Tomorrow, Molly would move into Room 6.

"You didn't wake me. I was lying here in the dark, listening to the waves breaking." Still not tired enough to sleep, Molly made small talk, asking if Savannah and her acquaintances went to a club after dinner.

"Everyone else did, but I stayed at Captain Clark's restaurant, because I ended up in the kitchen, questioning the chef about where he went to culinary school."

"Why? Was the food that bad?" Molly asked, picturing Savannah giving the chef an earful.

She snorted. "No, it was delicious, as usual. That's why I wanted to learn more about him."

"I guess you really meant it when you told Austin you were going to start looking for a new boyfriend immediately, huh?" Molly kidded.

"Nah, the chef is married. I was interested in hearing about his background because... I'm thinking of changing careers."

"You want to own a restaurant?"

"No—not at first, anyway. I want to become a professional chef."

Molly was floored. "I know you love to cook and obviously, you're great at it. But being a chef is... it's so different from being a VP in the payments industry."

"Exactly. That's why I really want to try it." Savannah flopped over in bed with a sigh. "All my life I've done what my father has wanted me to do. I've felt driven to live up to the 'Frost family's legacy of success.' But now that I've discovered my great-grandmother was probably a cook, I feel like the pressure's off."

Molly couldn't put a finger on why Savannah's sentiment bothered her. "Somehow, that sounds kind of condescending... it almost seems like you're saying that you're relieved Dora was *only* a cook because now there's no pressure for you to be successful."

"I didn't mean there's no pressure for me to be successful— I'd still feel driven to succeed as a chef. I meant there's no pressure for me to continue working in a career that would satisfy the expectations the men in the Frost family have always had, instead of doing what *I* really want to do," Savannah clarified.

"Oh. I get it." Molly was quiet a moment before she reminded Savannah, "Whether or not it turns out that you're related to Dora, you can still become a chef, you know."

"I know. But discovering I might be related to her feels... it feels empowering, if you know what I mean."

"Yes, I do," answered Molly. *Because that's how I've always felt about having her as my great-grandmother, too...*

Although the following morning was a Saturday, Molly checked email on her phone before she got out of bed. To her delight, the DNA results had been sent overnight and it was clear from the report that she was a Frost descendant. Evelyn Frost's younger brother's children were even listed in the shared match category.

She could hear a commotion coming from down the hall; it was probably Savannah in the kitchen, preparing breakfast. Although Molly knew she should go help her, she laid back against the pillow again, thinking about Evelyn and Harold, and Dora and Beverly, as she'd done so many times after hearing Hazel's story. Now that the truth was confirmed, she was gripped by a mix of emotions.

She felt both sadness and anger that her and Savannah's great-grandmothers, Evelyn and Dora, had been so severely deceived by Opal. That they hadn't ever known who their true children were, and vice versa. Yet in a way, Molly also wondered whether it was a blessing in disguise that as more time passed, not one of them had discovered the truth. She could only imagine how devastating it would have been for either mother to give up the child she'd loved from the start—or for Harold and Beverly to be separated from the only mother they'd ever known.

Although Molly briefly pictured how her grandmother might have led a more privileged life if she'd known she was a Frost, the thought was fleeting. It was as she'd told Hazel: her grandmother loved being an innkeeper. She wouldn't have traded her vocation for anything.

*But I don't love being an innkeeper,* Molly thought. *And I don't love serving guests.* Her experience this summer had taught her that she preferred to work behind the scenes. In fact, she'd already told Jenny she'd be glad to complete another grant application or work on a marketing campaign for the women's center, but she wasn't going to help host the autumnal fundraising gala. Molly didn't intend to personally host guests at Hydrangea House next summer, either.

*I should be able to find a qualified innkeeper before then, shouldn't I?* she wondered. Her plans for Hydrangea House and Peace Place had seemed much more appealing when they were merely dreams. Now that she was facing the reality of actually being the estate owner, Molly had a better appreciation of why Savannah hadn't wanted to keep the inn running. Just the idea of hiring a third-party to manage the inn was an overwhelming prospect.

*How am I ever going to balance teaching* and *running a business remotely?* she wondered. As she was pondering her dilemma and trying to decide whether the first person she shared her DNA results with should be Matt, Savannah or her mother, Molly's phone rang. It was Lauren, and suddenly, she knew exactly what she was meant to do.


Molly and Matt went to Captain Clark's for supper. The food was great—Matt abided by his own rule and didn't make any professional comments about the fish Molly ordered—but the place was buzzing with people. So after they'd finished eating, they returned to Hydrangea House for a leisurely walk on the beach. Within half a mile, Molly's stamina began flagging. They stopped and sat down in the cool, soft sand, just in time to watch the sun ignite the horizon and the water with color.

Over their meal, Molly had told Matt about the DNA test results and now he asked, "How did Savannah react when you told her you're related to the Frosts?"

"She's actually really happy about it. She's going to do

everything she can to facilitate the transfer of ownership of the estate." Molly chuckled. "You might not believe it, but she's like a different woman. She said discovering the change in her family history has been very liberating. Now that she knows she's not a descendant of the Frosts, she doesn't feel the pressure to live up to the standards of success the men in her family set for her. So get this—she's quitting her job to become a chef."

"She'll be really good at that—she made crepes for breakfast one day while you were sick and they were awesome. I think I ate about forty of them," he said, making Molly laugh. "What comes next for the inn?"

"That's my other big piece of news. Hazel's daughter, Lauren, is going to live in Hydrangea House during the off-season when we don't host guests anyway, along with a couple of visiting medical professionals."

"Wow, that's a huge development. How did that come about?"

"Very naturally," Molly said. "Lauren's been going through such a rough patch, first with losing her job and then with losing her mother. It seems like she'd benefit from a little R and R near the oceanside. And since it was her mother who saved Evelyn's life and helped Dora during labor, providing that opportunity for Lauren seems like the least I can do. She used to work in HR, so in the spring, she's going to recruit a new innkeeper and a manager for the business, which will be a huge help to me."

"It's great that everything is coming together." Matt smiled but his voice sounded forlorn. After a pause, he added, "I have to admit, I kind of wished…"

When he didn't finish his sentence, Molly guessed, "You wished we'd spotted a right whale?"

"Yeah, that, too." Matt nodded, gazing at the water instead of at her. "But I also wished I would have gotten the permanent research position and you would have moved here to run a year-round nonprofit at Peace Place or something and we'd, you know, see where our relationship went…"

"We can still see where our relationship goes. There are almost four weeks of summer left—and there's always next year. Even though I won't be innkeeping, I intend to come back for the entire summer." Molly leaned over to kiss Matt on the cheek before whispering into his ear, "I hope you'll come back, too?"

As he turned toward her, their faces were so close his whiskers grazed her chin. "Absolutely." He sealed his promise with a long, intense kiss. "Will you keep in touch throughout the year?"

"Yes." She kissed him twice as ardently, if that was possible. "I'll write you a letter and put it in a bottle. Then I'll toss it into the ocean from the end of the jetty."

Matt pulled back, his brow furrowed. "But I live in California. The current would never carry it—"

Molly interrupted his oceanographic lecture by placing her finger to his lips. "Don't worry. It will find its way from my heart to yours."

# A LETTER FROM KRISTIN

I want to say a huge thank-you for choosing to read *My Grandmother's Inn*. If you enjoyed it and want to keep up to date with all my latest releases, just sign up at the following link. Your email address will never be shared and you can unsubscribe at any time.

*www.bookouture.com/kristin-harper*

In this story, Hydrangea House reminds me of a residence I stayed at during a writer's retreat on Martha's Vineyard. The large, luxurious house was owned by a very generous woman who had an affinity for the arts. She didn't occupy her summer home during the off-season, so she made it available to writers for a nominal fee. At the time, I was working on my first novel, which, incidentally, was never published. Regardless, I always look back on that retreat as being a marvelous experience. The extravagant accommodations and glorious seascape were inspiring—and so was the homeowner's willingness to share them with people she didn't even know. What a gift!

If reading *My Grandmother's Inn* was a fantastic experience for you, I'd really appreciate it if you'd share what you loved about it in a review. Your perspective means a lot to me and your enthusiasm makes a big difference in helping new readers discover one of my books for the first time.

Keeping in touch means a lot to me, too, so please don't hesitate to reach out through Twitter, Goodreads or my website.

Thanks,

Kristin

kristinharperauthor.com

 twitter.com/KHarperauthor

# ACKNOWLEDGMENTS

Huge heaps of thanks to my enormously gifted and encouraging editor, Ellen, and to each and every single member of the Bookouture team who works on my books with me *and* behind the scenes.

Thank you also to my daily, steadfast supporters—you know who you are, and I do, too!

Made in the USA
Las Vegas, NV
05 August 2023